PRISONERS OF A DARK NIGHT

By

Timothy Bryan

"Right or wrong, it's very pleasant to break something from time to time."

-Fyodor Dostoevsky's
Notes from the Underground

Table of Contents

Chapter One

Visingsborg Castle, Sweden's Vising Island. 1715 AD

"I thought it was a matter of common knowledge," said Jacob Aminoff, and standing near the heavy oak-door entrance, he shifted his weight impatiently from one leg to the other. Glaring ahead with predatory eyes, his spoken Swedish contained a mild accent, with just a hint of a Slavic upbringing evident in his otherwise flawless pronunciation. "It has been a matter of rigid importance to my interests for several decades. How could such a transgression occur under your…careful watch?"

In his forties, Jacob maintained a clean-shaven face, and dressed in a fine tunic and expensive robe, his appearance was of a man who indulged and expected the best in life. Such was the value of his imported clothing that a peasant could work a lifetime and still fall short of the wages necessary to own them.

But though Jacob's expression and features were those of a polished and wealthy aristocrat, with clean and groomed hair worn long and handsome, something else lay under his steely expression. Even though cultured and accustomed to comfort, Jacob's invasive gaze was fierce and assured, revealing the attitude of one accustomed to hardship and physical trauma; indeed, Jacob exuded the confidence of a man who was neither soft nor unworldly, despite the trappings of his elevated social status.

The castle's main communal area was a place of refinement, and several flags of various noble houses ran along the sides of the extended hall. Gentle fires burned from plentiful candles and torches scattered throughout the open room, and expensive tapestries of lively colors hung at assorted points to serve as decorations for the keep's reception area. Lining the exterior were stained glass windows that ran at intervals on the finely hewn rock wall.

The area in front of the duke's table was for audiences who would petition the resident lord in charge of various government functions for the local community. Currently, Duke Maximilian Von Essen sat behind the thick table, and his unhappy features suggested he wasn't enthusiastic about his current visitor.

Sitting up straight, the duke ran a soft and manicured hand over his graying beard. In a bid to give himself the upper hand in the ongoing discussion, he cast a judgmental gaze at Jacob.

Though the effect was meant to be intimidating, there was some discomfort under Von Essen's stern expression, as if he wasn't sure he was the one with the power in the room, despite this place being his personal stronghold. Worse, his eight guards standing near him, burly and armed men with firm gazes and imposing statures, also appeared uncomfortable in the flickering light.

"I would suggest you watch your tone, Lord…Aminoff," Von Essen said, showing some contempt for his visitor by pronouncing Jacob's non-Swedish surname with unhidden annoyance. "How the prisoners are treated from our majesty's latest campaign is entirely at my direction. It is not, nor will it ever be, your prerogative to judge my methods."

Jacob's intense face did not waver as he engaged the duke's eyes, and after a moment he stepped forward, moving closer to Von Essen's table. The chainmail shirt underneath his silken top jingled as he crossed his arms in a challenging gesture. "How the prisoners are treated is entirely my business, my Lord. It is, in fact, one of my most important duties to fulfill for the king."

Leaning back in his chair, Von Essen affected an ironic smile, using his sarcastic demeanor to try to assert some control over the disagreeable situation. "His Majesty, King Charles, asked that I house the prisoners until the peace negotiations are completed. I have fulfilled that request and will continue to do so, as is my duty."

Fixating on his host, Jacob took two more steps, bringing himself uncomfortably close to the duke. Von Essen's men placed their hands on their thick swords, even though Jacob appeared out of their lord's reach—at least for the moment.

"You have starved and tortured at will, without regard for rank, stature, or noble lineage. Your actions are those of a rogue and a murderer," said Jacob, his voice calm and icy cold. "It is as if you enjoy hurting those who have done you no harm personally…and are completely helpless to your depredations. You are a scoundrel and not fit to clean stables, much less represent the king's interests."

Using such terms of open disrespect, even amongst fellow nobility, did not sit well with Von Essen. His features grew enraged, and he quickly stood from his creaking chair. Even if he was a soft man, he arrogantly drew himself up to his imposing height of 6 feet 5 inches, which made him half a head taller than Jacob.

"Such brazen behavior is too much, even for you, Lord Aminoff," Von Essen said, his tone dripping with undisguised hatred. "I will have your tongue cut from—."

The war dirk, a short dagger that was broad at the hilt, was made to be used in melee combat. If wielded with enough force behind it, it could pierce even the thickest armor. Consequently, it was the perfect weapon to settle matters of violence at close distance. Moving impossibly fast, Jacob produced such a shiny blade and took three strides, bringing the sharp weapon up with practiced skill.

But now there was no need to penetrate armor. Ramming the tip of the blade into Von Essen's cheek, its sharp edge tore a gash in the shocked man's face, flaying a flap of skin open and revealing his off-color and bloody cheekbone underneath. Reversing the knife's cut, Jacob rended through the duke's facial tissue, severing the lip from the inside and leaving a jagged slit across half his astonished features.

Stunned, the duke's hand shot up to his wound, and blood poured through his fingers from the gaping cut. Trying to control the flow, his eyes went wide in terror. Unable to comprehend the assault, he gasped and gurgled on his own blood, his hand quivering as he vainly sought to stem the flow. Overwhelmed, his eyes shot to the sides, back and forth, as he vainly awaited help from his guards.

Grasping hold of Von Essen's noble vestments, Jacob drew him close. Staring into his eyes, he nodded at the duke, as if to reinforce the horrified royal's sudden realization that the rules governing their interaction had changed dramatically. *Yes, my Lord, this is really happening to you. How does it feel to be the victim now? It is not so pleasant, no?*

Holding up his bloody blade so Von Essen could see the source of his agony, Jacob smiled at the man, flashing a grin that would have looked positively friendly under different circumstances. From Jacob's calm demeanor, it was instantly apparent that such a merciless assault caused him no misgivings whatsoever. Violence was a means to an end that Jacob was familiar with and truly enjoyed.

Jacob now reached down and slipped his knife back into a jewel-encrusted scabbard inside his shirt, returning it to the place he secretly removed it from when his arms were crossed moments before. Proceeding with the unhurried detachment of a professional, he pulled Von Essen even closer, all while his victim mewled in fear and shock.

Moving crisply, Jacob withdrew the duke's own knife from the man's loose shirt. The long blade was ceremonial and unwieldy, but its pointy edge was sharp enough for Jacob's purpose. "And now, Lord Von Essen, make no sudden movements. My work requires the utmost precision, and I will not have you cause more harm to my personal business."

Acting almost bored, Jacob inserted the blade below Von Essen's chin and slowly pressed upward into the soft flesh. As he drove the blade deeper, inch by inch, more spurts of blood streamed from the grievous puncture wound, and the duke's eyes went wider, becoming ever more bewildered, until they locked open entirely.

Using freakish strength, Jacob pressed the tip upward, and its point only came to a stop when it met the interior top of his opponent's skull. For a moment, he held him up with his sheer strength, and Von Essen's spasming feet gyrated on the floor as Jacob extended his thrust, almost lifting the heavy man entirely off the ground. With his arm muscles corded and taut, Jacob kept the aristocrat for several seconds in that position, treating him like a mortally impaled marionette.

Yanking back the weapon, the duke's corpse collapsed with slopping finality to the floor. With legs and arms inclined at strange angles, the expiring man's nerves continued firing randomly, causing his feet and arms to flinch and recoil uselessly while he bled out on the formerly clean stone.

Dropping Von Essen's knife onto his body, Jacob stepped back and breathed slowly. As he peered at the destroyed noble, his demeanor was calm and unperturbed, like he was curiously examining a dead field mouse that had been run over by a wayward wagon.

Slowly, Jacob raised his head to stare at the men-at-arms, those who had been billeted to protect the unfortunate duke. As one, the wretchedly afraid soldiers avoided Jacob's gaze. None of them currently held their hands on their weapons, nor did they appear eager to avenge their master.

This dangerous and wicked noble was known by all of them, and they were aware that any who were believed to oppose Jacob faced short and violent ends. Such was Jacob's reputation and reach that to cross him, even from within the upper rungs of society, was equal to a death wish.

"You may tell the family that he was distraught and decided to end his own life due to some unknown personal matter," said Jacob, and by his tone, it was clear this was far more than a suggestion. "I will pass the word around that I came soon afterwards and witnessed this unfortunate aftermath…it will provide the cover you need to ensure you are believed concerning his…tragic death."

Stepping in between the group of men—there were four on each side—Jacob moved his eyes between each guard, waiting to see that they agreed with this new situation in a castle they were sworn to protect. One by one, each of the protective sentries dropped their gazes to the ground, acquiescing silently to Jacob's demands. It was clearly more honorable for them to live to serve another master than to face the wrath of the vicious person standing before them.

After nodding with satisfaction, Jacob spun and left the room, leaving the duke's underlings to deal with his now-unmoving body in any way they saw fit.

#

Light from flickering torches barely lit the walls of dank and shadowed pathways in the deep interior of the castle. Moans and wails of suffering men reverberated along the rough-cut stone corridors of the maze-like tunnels, creating an ambiance of wanton misery amongst a series of neglected cells in the scattered confines of the dungeon.

A large and plump rat stood still in the faint light of a central corridor in this morbidly destitute area. Perched on its filthy claws, the diminutive creature stared toward the shifting light, its eyes shining and alive in expectation for a meal, either from the fetid remains of a prisoner's discarded food or, in a more hopeful and satisfying primal consideration, the recently deceased flesh of a nearby captive.

Scurrying out of the way, the animal just avoided the kick of a foot clad in a clean leather boot, one that was shiny, expensive, and out-of-place on the weathered rocks of the filthy area.

Jacob strode fitfully along the keep's dusty pathway, offering the rodent a disgusted stare as he made his way determinedly through the stronghold's twisting passages.

Facing ahead, Jacob kept his eyes on the periodic sconces of firelight that lit the way forward through the shadowy interiors of underground tunnels. Twisting through barely illuminated corridors, he made rights and lefts without stopping to consider his direction, and after a time, his puzzling maneuvers would have made lesser men lost and confused.

But move ahead Jacob did, banking his way through a host of tunnels and moist rocks on his considered way towards an important goal. After a few last turns, he stopped and collected himself, looking to the left at a large and thick wooden door. To its side stood a servile guard, and the weathered and leathery man nodded to Jacob, gulping deferentially at his sudden appearance.

After a flick of Jacob's impatient head, the dungeon guard nodded and heaved the door aside with the creaking of worn hinges. Stepping back, the silent man quickly reassumed his position next to the entryway.

The room beyond was brighter, but the horrible waft of air from the inside area was overpowering. Something of a mix between smoke, human waste, rotten food, and death assaulted Jacob's nostrils, and for a moment he blanched at moving into the foul interior.

Shaking away the odor and associated thoughts of what lay beyond, Jacob hardened his senses and stepped inside. Looking around, he took in the horrid scene of confinement.

The walls of the room housed a long and rectangular space, and on an exposed length on one side were held torches and lamps burning quietly at intervals along the shiny stone surface. Between the light sources were a host of sturdy chains that were affixed to the wall. These chains were now empty, but the stains of old blood that decorated the iron cuffs on their end told the story of men who must have been in bondage for some time in the recent past. This was a place accustomed to torture and suffering.

The rest of the room was contained by two borders of bars that served as a barrier to a host of dirty men inside the cell area. Kept separate, the people held there sat and stood near makeshift mattresses and patches of dirty straw. They wore tattered, dark military uniforms, but their condition was such that after a long period of captivity, their uniforms and ranks had now been covered by grime.

In captivity, in an area that should have held only a few prisoners, there were now twenty disheveled and filthy individuals, and as Jacob stepped near the bars, several looked up to see this new visitor to their horrific home.

Taking in the atrocious state of the men, Jacob scowled at their treatment and plight. With barely enough room for them to stand or sit, their situation was made worse by the fact that some of the crowded captives were already dead and had yet to be extricated from the mass of their friends. The effect and condition of these people was one of chaotic and indifferent torture, like they were less important than the swine that might live within fenced pits on a typical hog farm.

Pushing away the urge to cover his nose to avoid the stench, Jacob spoke amicably in Russian to the prisoners. "I realize you have been here for an excessive time."

Setting his hands on his hips, Jacob scanned through the group, taking some time to fix each of the men and evaluate their expressions. The eyes of each answered him with a range of emotions, from fear to open defiance and even indifference. The air around them was expectant and full of curiosity at Jacob's appearance in this sad domain.

"And I realize that you have suffered," said Jacob, and he nodded knowingly to their silent inquiries at his sudden presence. "You have suffered more than any men ever should."

From the back of the cell, one of the prisoners suddenly pushed his way forward. Moving from where he had been tending to a sickly friend, Stanislav Volkov slid his way close to the bars and their visitor. Tall and gaunt, he was nonetheless a strapping man of thirty-five, and even if his current predicament meant his health and pallor were weakened, he was sturdy and controlled in his movements.

Leaning two hands through the bars, Stanislav rested his arms on the crossbar and set his gaze on Jacob with some degree of contempt for the well-dressed newcomer. "How do you speak our language? What have the Swedes paid you to betray Russia?"

Jacob arched an eyebrow, surprised at the forcefulness and candor of the man. Holding up his hands, he made a mollifying gesture to appease the prisoner. "Nothing like that, I assure you. I am, in fact, one of you."

Stanislav cocked his head with unconcealed doubt at the oddness of such an admission. Looking at Jacob's fine clothing and pampered appearance, he shook his head in open cynicism. "One of us? Looking at you, I see a fancy pig speaking our language without an accent, and…I'm not impressed."

There was silence for a time as Jacob took in Stanislav's skepticism. As the moments passed, they held each other's glare, and though Stanislav's gaze was fierce and intimidating, it was the aggressive captive that looked away first. Turning around and having nothing more to say, Stanislav leaned his back against the bars and ignored Jacob.

Jacob smiled mildly, then sighed. Moving to the side to address the whole group, his voice became magnanimous, almost as if they were all longtime friends. "I've come here to tell you the truth…and to also give you something else. First, truth: I want you to know you will never return to Russia. Sweden will be your final place of rest, the last location you will call home in this world."

Heads around the crowded cell dipped in response. They must have expected such a result, but the scattered and bedraggled men were still heartbroken by Jacob's honest evaluation of their prospects to survive their captivity in this foreign land.

Jacob continued with a reserved and compassionate flash of a humorless grin, his voice rising perceptibly. "Your families will find a way to move on from your loss. Such is the way of the world with grief…we all must persevere, even when losing those most dear to us. Then, they will eventually be gone themselves, lost to time and history."

As one, the prisoners raised their heads, their quizzical stares focusing on Jacob. *Who was this man who visited them, only to torture them with thoughts of home and family, and what in hell was he now referring to?*

Taking a step closer to the group, Jacob came within easy reach of the men, moving within inches of the bars. If he was worried about being assaulted from this gaggle of desperate humanity, his face showed no fear of it. His features remained confident and even pleasant as he ran a hand over his whiskerless jaw.

Motioning to the few corpses on the cell floor, Jacob kept his tone steady. "Yes, you can never go home. But, if you come with me, you can choose how you will live from THIS moment on."

Reaching forward, Jacob grasped the bars in his firm grip, and his eyes shined with the reflection of the firelight. As he flexed his fingers around the cold metal, the bars creaked under his strength, and the stares of many prisoners looked surprised, as if Jacob might break through the heavy bonds with his own raw physical power. For the briefest of time, it appeared the cage might serve to protect those inside, instead of merely keeping them in custody.

Jacob drew a long breath and exhaled slowly as he released his hold on the barrier. Assuming a self-assured demeanor, Jacob's striking tone grew clear and convincing, as if his was the voice of truth in a wilderness of lies. "You will have a new family, and we will take care of each other—whatever the cost."

Turning back around, Stanislav tilted his head and peered inquisitively at their wealthy visitor. Squeezing through his friends, he now struggled to get closer to Jacob. When he came near Jacob's face, Stanislav's probing eyes locked on his, and he stared for several moments before speaking. "Of what do you speak? What are you about, and what is the cost for such an offer?"

Jacob thought for a moment, absorbing the doubts of Stanislav and the rest of the extended party with his thoughtful gaze. Jacob's vague smile grew wider, and he rapped the bars with his knuckles before shouting, "Guard!"

From outside, the footfalls of the guard and several more jailors approached. Coming into the room, the reserved men in dirty uniforms began to unlock the cell and let the prisoners out. After the clanging lock was disengaged, each of the guards seemed unwilling to look at Jacob, as if they were scared to do so. It was like each man knew that acknowledging Jacob could bring some horrible result for the effort, and that was something none were willing to risk.

With the cell door now open, the constricted captives staggered free, their eyes glancing about cautiously. The strong amongst them helped the weak emerge on injured legs, as many of them, stooped and feeble, could barely hold themselves erect. Panning their heads, the baffled and dirty prisoners shuffled free from captivity and inspected the area around them.

After some hesitation, each of the captured soldiers, downtrodden and filthy, peered at Jacob with unrestrained appreciation. Their faces and teeth were broken and ghastly, their bodies stinking and sick, but their eyes had come alive, showing a hesitant enthusiasm for the world beyond.

Wasting no time, Jacob nodded and left the horrible place, pacing away from their heinous prison cell with a disgusted shake of his head. Moving out of the foul dungeon, the suddenly-free captives followed him, tepidly making their way to a new and very different future.

Chapter Two

Arlanda Airport, Stockholm. Present Day

Dreary light from the morning's overcast sky leaked through an open partition of the economy class window. Outside, the surface of the glass and large wings of the parked 787 Dreamliner were covered with droplets of moisture from the day's intermittent bad weather, and the extended gate area was filled with airport workers dressed in bright rain gear as they moved about the bustling ramp.

Seated and appearing entranced with this activity, Liam Stone stared out into the scene of controlled chaos surrounding his recently arrived flight. In his mid-thirties, he was of average build, with brownish hair cut close over a mildly receding hairline and a reddish complexion. Neither ugly nor handsome, his was a face that would not inspire others, but at the same time, it didn't exactly cause fits of derision or negativity. As with his entire life, his looks allowed him to move under the radar, to remain anonymous in an existence that always seemed to just pass him by.

Around Liam, the rest of the passengers were collecting their bags and getting ready to deplane as they chatted quietly. It was something of an art form in the flying world for people to strategically place and collect their personal belongings to exit quickly, but with Liam that wasn't an important consideration. Instead, his eyes were misty as he considered the external airport grounds, and he ground his jaw as he fought off a wave of sadness that perfectly matched the depressing weather outside.

In a fit of curiosity, Liam wondered how many of those people out there marshaling planes, collecting luggage, and servicing the aircraft were happy. Whatever their place in life, whether a professional manager or a beefy front-line hauler, had these working strangers found their place in the world? Did they go home to a partner that made their lives a bit more tolerable? Maybe someone in their lives made them a tasty dinner and offered a welcoming smile when they arrived home?

Liam noticed a woman talking into a radio alongside a private plane in the distance, and he found himself wondering about her life specifically as she went through a set of flight checks on the expensive-looking aircraft. She appeared relatively young and attractive, and dressed in a flight suit from some contracting company or another, her professional movements made her seem part of the wider environment of happy people he found himself thinking about so much lately.

But…despite her carefree bearing, Liam couldn't help but think, maybe this lady had just broken some other poor lad's heart, just like his own? What was the power that certain women had over guys like Liam, men who were happy to prostrate themselves and get walked on by pretty ladies? It was like it was part of Liam's DNA and perhaps other nice guys to accept the abuse of indifference and ridicule such women routinely provided.

In fact, it seemed that being boring was kind of a prerequisite for dudes to find themselves alone in a world of single people—even or especially when they didn't want to be.

He had heard this explained to him by a single friend of his, Marie was her name (also not interested in Liam, but at least she was a friend and a nice person), that the worst thing a guy could be was boring or needy. Even if a man had a job, money, and great prospects for a career, to be boring and clingy was the kiss of death for mating opportunities. Scowling, Liam realized it wasn't fucking fair, and the more he bitched about it inside, the more he wanted to scream about his inability to deal with the simple reality of life's love lessons.

Sitting up straight, Liam sighed and tried to control himself. He knew that acting like a pussy wasn't going to make this trip any better, so he better get ahead of this foul mood and grow some balls. It wasn't like he had a horrible life, all things considered…*I mean, how many people got to make their livings writing about and making sports bets? Millions of dollars were on the line daily according to my thoughts and prognostications, so cheer the fuck up, dude!*

Looking up, he saw the last of the people around him had exited the area, and because Liam always flew in cheap-ass basic economy, he was now in the back of the plane, slouching around and acting like a love-lost teenager. Shaking his head, he stood and yanked his dark leather backpack, the one his grandmother had given him in high school, from the overhead bin. Checking to see that nothing had fallen out of its poorly tied pockets, he slung it over his shoulder and started up the aisle.

As he moved towards the front of the aircraft, he saw a cute flight attendant, youthful and pert, waiting for him to exit. Standing next to the connected jet bridge, she waited expectantly to move on to whatever job she had next to do when this last lazy American passenger finally deemed it appropriate to exit the aircraft.

When he came close to the young lady, Liam saw in her eyes the universal unattraction that women seemed to feel for men that were emotionally distraught. There was just something about their feminine radar that allowed them to see weakness in a guy, and as Liam got close to her, her sixth sense grabbed onto his pathetic self-pity, making her pleasant smile difficult to hold as he went past.

Nodding politely, the attendant restrained her inner desire to frown at this meek and dejected man, not quite knowing what was compelling her to not show a bit of genuine kindness to Liam on his way off the plane. Liam felt her inner war for civility as he passed by, and he shrugged at her as if to say, *"What can you do? Losers are gonna lose.*

As Liam disappeared from her sight down the interior bridge, Liam felt shame crawl up his neck, and both he and the airline employee worked to put one another from their minds as they mentally prepared for their altogether separate days ahead.

#

The baggage collection area was a large one and full of multiple carousels meant to bring luggage to people making the Stockholm Region the final destination of their journey. On either side of the long hallway were four huge circular machines, and above each of them was an enormous LCD screen announcing the incoming flights' luggage to be hosted on each apparatus.

In this area, three of the separate conveyors normally shuttling bags from incoming flights were closed down, but currently, there was one making that odd squeaky sound as it coughed up the personal items of passengers. Near machine number 8, a large group of recently arrived travelers collected their things, and crowds of travelers from several ethnic groups chatted in a barrage of languages as they wound down their journeys from various originating cities.

The harangue of large crowds continued for some time, and the pile of luggage to be claimed dwindled to a few cardboard boxes. Unfortunately, the boxes weren't Liam's, and he found himself lucky enough to be the last person to fetch his personal things.

In the background, the sound of an announcement being played echoed through the area, reminding people to not leave their belongings alone, as it could lead to their items being seized. The message played over and over in both English and Swedish, and because Liam had a hard time understanding the latter, he decided that his command of the former was good enough for life in this country. Just as always, English was spoken fluently here, far and wide.

Liam had come to Sweden fifteen years before to study in college, which most people here referred to as "University" in the decidedly British way of describing post-high school academic endeavors. Living in the medieval town of Uppsala, he had ended up staying for a total of six years, mostly because he was enjoying his life, much as young people often liked to do while exploring the world.

Liam had spent those early years of adulthood discovering that he really liked this country, and in turn, had found a gig teaching English at one of the local "gymnasiums" after his bachelor's degree was completed. Taking the step from student to teacher took some getting used to, but the strangest part was that most Swedes spoke, or at least understood in a technical way, English as well as he did. *In fact, probably better.*

Grinning, Liam remembered the one time he had a student ask him a question after school, at a time when the upper-level English specialist needed information about a term paper that was soon due. Struggling to perfect his project, the diligent guy needed to know what tense he should use to describe an academic discussion.

The teen had spent some time describing in English his preference for tense, only for Liam to not really understand what he was talking about. It wasn't that his accent made it hard, it was because he himself had never taken the time to understand how tenses were described in other languages—or even in English itself. The reality of languages to Liam meant that you had to "feel" what was needed to use at any time, and this in turn meant people needing the right answers were stuck without a proper understanding of the correct answer.

Playing dumb, Liam had managed to refer the younger man to another teacher who actually knew her job, and because of a heightened sense of guilt, he had taken the following days to catch himself up on the differences in "past continuous" and "past simple," as well as the benefits and restrictions with each tense.

Smiling wider, Liam now realized he was once again unfamiliar with the terminology of either, and he wondered where that boy was today, more than a decade later. *He's probably a shit-ton better of an English teacher than I could've ever been.*

Soon after that teaching job, Liam had come to understand he needed to start a career, and because he had long ago decided he liked money, he knew he had to leave Sweden to get it. This country of wonderful people was a fantastic place, but if you wanted warm weather or to make lots of money, it wasn't the place to entertain such outcomes.

Feeling confused, Liam looked over to the entry slot on the carousel where luggage was supposed to exit, and he realized he was now the last person waiting to be graced by his bags. He really didn't want to pack much for this journey, but no matter how hard he tried, he found that it was always necessary to bring more than he had space for.

And now Liam was the last person here, and if it happened like it so often seemed to in the past, he would be without his personal things and would need to file a complaint in order to track them down.

Now, being a man of numbers, this didn't make much sense to Liam. The 787 Dreamliner (he knew and checked to make sure this was the plane to be used on this route, mostly because it was known to be a very safe model) could hold up to about 290 people, and his flight had been about seventy percent full, so about 200 people were on board.

What were the chances he would be the one to lose his bags, or barring that, would be the last person to fetch his items? *Probably the same percentage of chance I would be the one to find my wife was cheating on me, and worse, to come home early from work and almost walk in on the act. Thank God they at least got their pants up, and most importantly, thank fuck her kickboxer boyfriend ran out the back before he was forced to kick my ass.*

Suddenly, one of his bags, an old purple one that had been a wedding gift from his dad, emerged on the carousel. Feeling better about himself, Liam was equally happy to see a pink one emerge right behind it. Thinking for a moment, he realized that the second bag's color was even more gender-unsure than the first, but it was functional and worked, so if someone didn't like his luggage, then they could go fu—.

A strong hand grasped Liam's shoulder from behind. Surprised, Liam spun to look into the eyes of the person that grabbed him with that firm and somewhat painful grip.

Staring at him with a deeply smartass grin was Mattias Bergstrom, his lifelong friend and drinking buddy from those long-ago college years. Also in a living range that could loosely be called young, Mathias was a half-foot taller, wore wire-rimmed glasses, and atop his head, his dark and kinky hair was topped by a blond-dyed tuft of longer hair combed back with a generous portion of gel. With the sides of his head almost shaved to his scalp, the effect of his features made him appear like a human-sized quail. Adding his pockmarked complexion to the mix, he should have appeared ridiculous and somewhat insane.

Instead, the effect of Mattias' looks was instantly endearing, as for some odd reason, they made him appear both intelligent and interesting. Liam's features and mood became immediately happier as he awkwardly man-hugged his old buddy.

"Good to see you, Liam," shouted Mattias, grinning down in grand fashion. "It's been too long."

Struggling to pull himself out of Mattias' long grip, Liam nodded and smiled. "Dude, how'd you get in here? Don't you have to wait behind security?"

Chuckling, Mattias motioned towards the baggage belt, where Liam's things were soon to come into range. "Well, now you know the benefits of being a highly paid detective. We may not be able to solve a crime, but they let us go anywhere we want. Not sure why they let me in, but who am I to argue?"

Smiling, Liam hurried toward the belt, where he grabbed the pink bag first, hoping that doing so would make Mattias unsee the fact that it existed. Feeling better about the arrival of Mattias, Liam waited for his friend to grab the other as he hefted and tested the wheels on the gaudy luggage.

Moving close, Mattias gingerly took the purple bag, and, extending the bag's handle, turned towards a placard on the far wall that announced "Customs" and "Immigration." Pointing toward the sign, he looked down and wrinkled his nose at Liam's choice of ugly luggage before trudging toward the exit.

Chapter Three

Twisting through the rural countryside, the smooth but too-narrow highway was lined on either side with trees and bushes of red and golden hues. Late summer was a time of considerable beauty in Sweden, and the depth of color and changing landscape, full of green fields and clumps of uneven forest, made for an enjoyable driving experience.

As the car whooshed ahead, it passed several identical farmhouses of red siding and white trim. Staring straight, Mattias sat hunched in the driver's seat, focusing intently through his thick eyeglasses as he squinted through the dirty windshield down the two-lane road.

The vehicle he steered was a green late-model Saab, one of the last produced before that vehicle brand faded from history more than a decade before, and the venerable sedan currently barreled ahead at more than thirty kilometers per hour over the posted speed limit of "70."

Sitting in the passenger seat, Liam glanced uncomfortably over at the speedometer, obviously unhappy with the pace of the vehicle through the pleasant-but-isolated area. Around them, fields of different staple crops, from various grains to kludgy stalks of corn, stood unharvested and stretched out over the rolling hills of Central Sweden.

Unable to control Mattias' manic lust for speed, Liam took several loud breaths before accepting defeat and wistfully staring out his own window. They both knew Liam was a control freak when it came to driving, and Liam couldn't let Mattias win by begging him to slow down. Not only would that be unmanly, it would only make Mattias drive faster—if that was possible.

Trying to sound cheery, Mattias spoke in Swedish, almost sounding like he cared about a proper answer as he smacked on a piece of gum. "Are you keeping up on your Swedish? They say that keeping up on languages is a good way to keep the brain healthy. And your brain, I might note, certainly needs to avoid getting any more sick."

After a short grimace, Liam glanced over and shook his head. Speaking slowly, he annunciated carefully in English, trying to stress his native command of the language. Unfortunately, because Mattias rarely made grammatical mistakes, it was ineffective at showing him up. "Not really...I've decided that every Swedish person alive speaks English better than I can mangle Swedish, despite the years I lived here. So, the short answer is…no."

Looking confused, Mattias tilted his head and gazed over at Liam before returning his head forward. For some time, he watched a few cars whiz by in the other direction, and after careful consideration, he finally nodded. "Yeah, that's true, and a pretty good idea. Good thinking…and keep up with it. Don't continue embarrassing yourself."

The underlying mirth in Liam's face drained away, and he waited a while before responding, knowing he had to get the delivery and tone of his next words just right. "Mattias, did I mention you can suck my balls? I've noted in the past you had a particular skill for such things, so I thought I should just throw that out there. I'm willing to allow it if it means you finally getting what you most want in life—hairy nut sacks. What are friends for, right?"

Mattias raised an eyebrow at the insult, taking it in with clinical consideration, much like a scientist might examine a new and interesting form of the plague. After a while, the silence continued, followed by a mild grin from the tall man as he came to appreciate Liam's humorous achievement. Still, though, he remained silent to the offer. To respond with anything less than a witty retort would have been undignified.

While Mattias continued careening through the remote countryside, Liam sighed and leaned against the window, taking his time to catch a nap and reduce the jet lag pawing at his exhausted brain. There would be several days of joking and swearing in the near future, times that would require the best of creativity to denigrate his friend, meaning he had to rest himself to be in his best form.

#

While continuing to disregard speed limits, Mattias peered over at Liam. With Liam's head lolling and wedged between the window and headrest, he looked either catatonic or dead as the car bumped and veered around turns and rises on the narrow pavement.

As if he could feel himself being watched, Liam came awake, then blinked his eyes several times as he readjusted to where and when he was. Looking out his window, he smacked his mouth at the acrid taste brought on by airline food and the lack of a toothbrush.

It always amazed Liam how close humanity was to its roots; one minute you were flying across the world, and the next, you were one step from being a caveman because you didn't have access to a shower.

For a time, Mattias bit his lip and considered his next words, struggling in his thoughts with the best way to move forward. After some consideration, he tried to sound empathetic, but he mostly came across as sarcastic. "Liam, I was sorry to hear about Elise. I know you, umm…wanted to make it work out. I didn't realize she wanted out of the marriage."

Frowning, Liam stared over and sharpened his gaze on Mattias, as if he were unsure if his friend was sincere. After some indecision, he nodded and spoke guardedly. "Yeah, neither did I. You think you know someone…try to make a life, and then everything goes to shit. We even got a cat together, a Blue Russian. It was kind of like a prelude to having a real—."

"A Blue Russian? Those are a cool breed…and expensive as hell. What happened to it?"

"Well, to be honest, the little thing kind of creeped me out—made me think I was being watched by some kind of alien," Liam replied. "Whenever he'd sit on the counter and I worked on my laptop, he'd be staring at me with those weird eyes. It was like he was a lot smarter than he was letting on."

Looking intrigued, Mattias took his eyes off the road and glanced over. "So, it was kinda like a demon? I've heard cats were worshipped in several cultures throughout the ages. Maybe you got one of those holdover, sub-deity varieties? Could've been his way of telling you to make offerings to him. Like a daily fish or something to access his God-like powers."

Looking forward and unable to contain himself, Liam motioned to the road so that Mattias would actually look where he was driving. Acting chagrined, Mattias restarted his view of the road with a smirk—while also managing to speed up a bit.

"Anyway," continued Liam, "I would have given it to you, just to get the irritating feline out of my hair. But Elise kept the damn thing. Said I'm not responsible enough to have it. So, she kicks me out, then keeps my cat."

It was quiet for a moment as each of them thought about the direction of the conversation. Liam's frown grew more pronounced as he looked over at Mattias, who was struggling to keep a straight face.

"Spit it out," said Liam, waiting for the inevitable.

Trying to keep from laughing, Mattias spoke slowly. "I was just thinking, Elise's new and younger friend will be able to take care of your kitty. Pet it, keep it well fed, make sure it's always happy—the way you never could. I imagine her…I mean your…cat is in the best shape of its life."

No longer able to control himself, Mattias offered a grin that seemed to stretch from ear to ear. Much like a grinning puppet, he was immensely pleased with himself.

Lowering his gaze, Liam shook his head, all the while trying to keep from smiling himself. Despite the joke's brutal truth, it was a high-quality insult, and somehow, talking about it made him feel a little better, like he finally wasn't in the whole breakup thing by himself. "Dude, that's some cold-hearted shit."

Chuckling, Mattias held up a hand and extended two fingers, as if counting. "Bro, I told you the Golden Rules long ago…one, never get married, and two, never, under any circumstances, get married again. You broke the first rule without consideration of my advice; now, let's see if you wise up and remain happy and single."

"Uh huh, Mattias, spoken like a true dick. By the way, I noticed you're married?"

Raising his eyebrows, Mattias acknowledged his sin of marriage and sighed reluctantly. "Yeah, that's true, but she's even uglier than me, so the rules don't apply."

Grinning but not really sure why, Liam looked out the window, where a farmer who looked older than the ancient tractor he was driving puttered across a dirt field. Just now, that boring and seemingly nonsensical movement on the tractor looked vaguely fun, if only to take his mind off his messed-up circumstance.

"How far are we along?" asked Liam, at the same time wondering how a man that had to be at least a hundred years old could climb onto such a huge machine.

"About two hours," responded Mattias, and after hesitating, he continued in a cautious tone. "Listen, we have a surprise for you. We all decided to take you on a day trip to make you feel better. An old friend coming back to visit college friends—."

"We who?" asked Liam, raising his voice. "What did you tell everyone?"

For once, Mattias appeared worried. "Umm…we decided it would be nice to take you out to that island you always wanted to see: Vising Island."

"Shit, Mattias, what exactly did you say to everyone? I came here to have fun—not to be treated like a loser puppy dog. I could've hung out with my mom if I wanted sympathy. Are you trying to torture me?"

Licking his suddenly dry lips, Mattias avoided Liam's interrogating stare. "Well, Maria and Lilly suggested the island…"

Liam put his face in his hands and moaned at the mention of their two female friends. Mattias and Liam had known and loved them for more than a decade, but neither Lilly nor Maria were known for avoiding sappiness and emotions. Their unique brand of nonstop pity would not be what the doctor ordered for his marriage troubles, at least for more than a few minutes on the rest of the trip.

"Bro, it will be fun," said Mattias, trying to sound optimistic. "You always loved that history crap. We can have lunch out there and be back by night."

Liam let his hands drop from his face and then peered over at Mattias, like he was contemplating murder. "Did it occur to you that I would've preferred going to our rich friends' house on the coast?"

"Well, I thought—."

"Where we could drink their two-hundred-dollar wine? And have their cook make me a delicious steak with gravy and those mushrooms I like? The kind that I could never eat because they cost more than my shitty car payment?"

At a loss for words, Mattias mumbled to himself. He started saying something else, then thought better of it. The car went quiet, with Liam continuing his dagger-like glare in the uncomfortable silence.

"OK, we'll be in Grenna in about an hour," Mattias finally said, forcing a smile and abruptly slowing down to a normal speed. "Want to listen to some music? We got all sorts of…umm…"

Liam glared at Mattias as he reached for the radio. Thinking better of it, Mattias pulled his hand back and went quiet. Suddenly meek, he offered Liam an apologetic grin as he watched the rural farmland rush past.

As their dated car drove toward a meeting with the rest of their friends, Liam pressed his lips together in a controlled scowl. Even, or especially, after the long flight and scenic drive, his depressed mood wasn't getting any better.

Chapter Four

The ferry terminal was large, and plentiful parking surrounded it in all directions. The building, standing on the higher ground of a sloping and well-kept shoreline, had a walkway leading down to an open dock and loading area with several metal storage containers. Currently, there was a large and brightly painted yellow boat positioned in the water, and a host of cars were parked around its industrial-sized boating ramp.

Behind the gently bobbing boat was a vast lake, one that filled the entirety of the west-looking view from the terminal building. Lake Vettern, the second-largest body of inland water in Sweden, stretched across the horizon, and light from the early afternoon glinted on its undulating waves far into the distance. In that distance, an island hovered on the skyline, and the oblong piece of land rose unevenly from the water, as if it was beckoning all curious onlookers to visit its distant and vague outlines.

The day was a pleasant and bright one, and the hurried sounds of loud and flitting birds mixed with the occasional buzz of working engines to provide a lively environment for the small port. A few crowds of people gathered around the entry point for the ship, while bustling workmen moved around the dock as they readied the ferry for its journey to the island.

As Mattias drove down the long road leading to the terminal, both he and Liam focused on a group of people standing around a series of vehicles in the largely unoccupied parking lot next to the lake. Finally dropping his frown, Liam smiled and exchanged appreciative glances with Mattias as they drew closer to the expectant party of mismatched pedestrians.

Standing in smiling anticipation of their car's arrival were Lilly and Alex, Johan and Maria, Lars, and Karl. All in their thirties, they were fit and contented people, and each showed an eager smile as Mattias pulled close. Theirs were the anxious looks of longtime friends, and their beaming expressions grew even happier as Liam and Mattias exited the vehicle.

As Liam stepped close to the group, he flashed them a hesitant and self-conscious grin. "It's great to see you all. It's been too long; I try to come back every year, but things have been tough recently…."

Moving close to Liam, Maria and Lilly, who were attractive women with concerned expressions, began to embrace and dote on him, much like protective hens over a vulnerable flock.

"Liam, I'm sorry about Elise," said Maria, kissing Liam on the cheek and patting his head.

"Yeah, she has no idea what she's missing," agreed Lilly, and she rubbed Liam's back with a consoling smile.

Behind the girls, their husbands, Alex and Johan respectively, shook their heads and smiled apologetically at Liam. Each rolled their eyes at the spectacle, showing they understood the unique form of hellish sympathy being inflicted on their longtime friend by their nosy wives. If he had been a child, Liam would still have been embarrassed by the attention, but as an adult, the show of being comforted was made ten times more pathetic.

Still, for the moment, Liam wasn't quite able to cover up the fact that it felt good to be babied. His face flushed under the barrage of attention, and he quietly thanked the Gods for the burden of having friends that actually cared for him.

Raising her voice, Maria continued their adoring greeting with a mothering and tender voice. "Liam, don't you worry about it. We'll find you a Swedish girl that will appreciate you. Some girls don't know when they have a good thing going."

To the side, Mattias, who had been guiltily avoiding Liam's notice, now rolled his own eyes at Maria's proposal.

As the mood of communal sympathy continued, Karl stepped closer. He was a tall and strong man who held a satisfied grin at the situation, but there was also a certain hardness under his demeanor, like his eyes were somewhat removed from the present.

The hard edge of Karl's features didn't appear to be because of the current moment but was instead due to a sadness that lay just under his too-weathered skin. Like a boy that had experienced a life-altering event that forever changed his young view of the world, Karl showed that same expression in a far more intense and adult way.

"Uhh…I don't mean to interrupt this love fest," said Karl, flashing an understanding smile, with white perfect teeth and premature wrinkles around his eyes. "But the ferry leaves in about three minutes. Perhaps we should be going, so we don't miss it?"

#

Some time later, the solitary ferry plowed quietly across the surface of the enormous lake. Due to its odd coloring, the ship looked a bit like a floating banana as it cut through the mild swells of extended water toward the impending shape of Vising Island.

Above, the sun was past its midpoint for the late August day, and a brisk wind blew from the west overlapping waves as the boat motored ahead. The effect of the Swedish summer was on full and brilliant display, as the normally frigid and dingy weather of Scandinavia was momentarily replaced with the perfect lighting and temperatures of the region's most appealing time, late summer.

The top of the craft was open to the weather and elements, and the group of friends stood against the railing and watched the horizon with eager and happy faces. Behind them, several picnic-type tables were bolted on the outdoor deck, allowing for visitors to sit while making the crossing.

With a breeze blowing their hair and providing welcome refreshment from the warm day, they exchanged satisfied glances at the pleasant conditions and good company surrounding them. All was well in the sedate lifestyle of the thirty-somethings, and their moods, even that of Liam's, were for the moment extremely positive.

Standing at the very front of the ship, at a point where the railings came together in a "V" shape, Alex looked down into the frothy lake, then smiled to his right at Mattias. "Mattias, I can't believe you're still driving that old Saab. Didn't they stop making those in like 2011?"

Squinting ahead, Mattias frowned and spoke above the sloshing water and hum of the boat's engine. "Yeah, but see, I love that car. Besides, not everyone gets to inherit half of Southern Sweden as a career plan. We actually do something called 'financial planning,' which means the cost of running a car isn't based off what color of Maserati you want this month."

The rest of the group laughed aloud at those sentiments, including Alex, who puckered his face into a nonchalant smirk and nodded. After a deep breath, he spoke in a controlled manner to his friends, like he was imparting some age-old wisdom from a long-forgotten and enlightened prophet.

"Remember guys, the important thing isn't that some people are rich…it's that the right people are rich."

Alex's blue-blood statement of upper-class Darwinism wasn't well received, and a cascade of boos came from the rest of the party. Alex was just able to duck a croissant thrown by his wife, whose aim was surprisingly good from across the pitching deck.

For a time, the friends fell into personal stories and tidbits about their lives, and after several minutes of catching up with small talk, Liam decided to walk down into the passenger compartment for a bite to eat. As he moved toward the entry door that descended by steps into the interior hold, Karl took notice of Liam's intention and followed him down.

Inside the passenger confines of the ship was a table that held trays of sandwiches, mixed appetizers, and extensive finger foods. Around the offered snacks were tables full of locals and assorted workers, who spoke quietly as they munched on various portions of what was on offer.

To the side, next to a wooden door that led up to the captain's quarterdeck at the front of the ship, several men stood in a tight group and conversed. Jacob Aminoff was at the center of the group's attention. His clothing was contemporary with the current modern fashion of being informal, but he still evinced an odd combination of cultured breeding mixed with the unrestrained boldness of an alpha male.

Liam stepped carefully into the room, lining himself up to load some of the free food on a paper plate he grabbed from a stack of disposable dinnerware to the side. Falling in behind a portly couple, Liam smiled as he gazed at the food, which appeared to be very extravagant for such a normal spread on an everyday ferry. The meats, bread, side dishes, and fruits on display were of the highest quality and presentation, and their bountiful supply made Liam lick his lips in anticipation.

Behind Liam, Karl got into line and was likewise impressed with the culinary offerings. Even though he wasn't as hungry, he plucked a few morsels and added them to his own unplanned meal.

"So, Karl," said Liam, glancing over with a tentative grin, "I heard you made rank? Full captain, right?"

"Actually, that's Major to you," responded Karl, and for a moment, a flush of embarrassment covered his face. "It seems that the armed forces are even less of a good judge of character than when I joined."

"Impressive," Liam exclaimed, and he spoke a bit too loudly, so that some of the faces of the travelers in the dining area moved their eyes toward Karl and Liam. "What did you have to do to get that promotion? Surviving that United Nations mission in Afghanistan was a good way to jump-start your career, right?"

Grimacing, Karl's good mood soured a bit. "Not much that I want to talk about…especially with how things fell apart at the end…but, at least I got a higher grade out of it. It'll probably mean a desk job and a big gut, but I'll just have to take the bad with the good."

Frowning, Liam realized he was killing the good humor of the moment, and coming to think of it, the rather dour people in the room around him, shooting dirty looks and looking bitchy, made it appear even they were affected by the buzzkill.

Sighing, Liam dropped his gaze to the food and went quiet. He was really going to have to learn how to interact in the world without making the people around him unhappy. *Or make them sleep with strangers while I'm at work.*

In front of him in the food line, Aaron and Cindy Kauppila were the only ones left in the room that seemed to be in good humor, or even to be willing to talk. In their fifties and bursting at the seams of their already-large clothing, their appetites matched their prodigious girth. Leaning over portions of the displayed food, they picked over the foodstuffs and shuffled assorted edibles onto their plates.

"Well, this seems to be enough to tide us over until after the castle," said Cindi, speaking with a Finnish accent. "You can never be certain they will have a good place to get a good meal out on the island."

Glancing at Cindi and Aaron's robust bodies, Liam exchanged glances with Karl and stifled a grin at the mention of a lack of food. If not for the silence in the room, it may have been easier to avoid the smile that tugged at his lips, but Liam suddenly felt like a preoccupied boy at church who was trying to keep from laughing during a serious Sunday sermon.

"Yes, it will," replied Aaron, and he somehow managed to balance several wedges of melon on top of some scalloped potatoes.

Glancing back at Liam and Karl, Aaron flashed a grin and included them in the conversation. "Are you going to the castle? We've heard it's an amazing place. We've been wanting to go for years, but at the last minute, we found out they had a special offer for the ferry to go to the island for free. So, here we are. We even got lunch and a motel room thrown into the deal for a low cost."

Around them, the room continued its silence, and Liam cast his gaze around the place, peering at the locals as they nursed their drinks of soda and tea. The quiet seemed to him to be increasingly rude, and Liam was gratified when the groups of observers finally restarted their conversations and avoided his gaze.

Liam offered the Finnish couple a genuine smile and gestured to the west with a wave of his hand, indicating their upcoming island stop. "This wasn't planned by us either, at least too far in advance. But it'll be interesting to check out; I've wanted to see that castle for years."

Returning Liam's pleasant look, the couple nodded and continued finishing off preparations for their buffet feast. Stepping away from the serving table, they waved goodbye and moved to an empty table near the far wall, where they sat under a poster of a beautiful snowy scene in Lappland.

Motioning to Liam, Karl pointed upwards to the open deck area, where their friends awaited their return. Liam nodded and moved to the stairs. With his eyes glued to the food he carried, Liam relished the thought of gorging on the grub while taking in the beautiful view of the lake. *Life is going to get better. Now is the time to appreciate what is right in my life.*

As Liam climbed the steps, Karl moved to follow him, but his gaze briefly fell on Jacob, who was talking gently with two simply dressed men to the side. Something about Jacob disturbed him, and Karl briefly stopped and processed his sudden disquiet at the cafeteria-like setting around him.

Standing for several moments, Karl turned in a circle and took in the area with inquisitive eyes, like he was missing something. Taking an estimate of the normally dressed villagers and workers in the room, something tugged at his perceptions of the odd moment, making him focus on each person individually.

From one person to the next, Karl's well-trained eyes searched for something his unconscious mind told him was there. Something about the scene seemed to be manufactured in the way his military training and overseas experience taught him to be wary of. *But this was Sweden of all places, so what did I expect? The Taliban were not known for frequenting boring ferries or blending in with the rural Swedish countryside.*

Puzzled over his unusual paranoia, Karl finally shook his head and shrugged off the strange feeling. Taking the stairs two steps at a time, he exited the room and put the strange sensation from his mind. For the moment, his thoughts returned to his friends as he moved to the observation area above.

When Karl and Liam were gone, Jacob's striking gaze, formally disinterested in the pair, moved to the stairs, and he focused for a time on the spot they just occupied. Jacob's eyes, which were so recently dark and severe, flitted briefly to a deep and yellow tint, like they were suddenly powered from an intense light within.

Chapter Five

The remains of Vising Castle were a shadow of their former self. Set upon an elevated and grassy field, the defunct structure stood on an incline above Lake Vettern, and in the far distance could be seen the extended shoreline of Sweden's landmass encircling the water and island.

The main structure of the castle's central hall was the only portion of the keep remaining, with only distant rock walls and a stone arch passing through it as a reminder of its long-decayed outbuildings and towers. Time had whittled the massive complex down to a single building, and although it was in relatively good shape, the lack of a roof above its weathered stone walls made it seem eerie in the late-afternoon sunlight.

Surrounding the ancient building, growing in intervals from several hundred yards away, was a line of forest and undergrowth. The trees and brush that made up the sparse surrounding countryside were green and attractive, and they swooshed gently under the press of a cool westerly breeze.

The friends walked toward the old structure, their heads panning curiously as they took in the fascinating sight of a world long forgotten by current times. Lifetimes of toil, prestige, and power politics had passed around this abandoned location, and a certain sense of history seemed to lie under the surface of the now-dilapidated ruins. One didn't need to believe in ghosts to feel the pull from the silent remnants of the ancient stronghold, and the low howl of a passing wind only made the spirits of its long-departed residents seem closer still.

This mood of detached creepiness affected everyone as they drew closer to the building. The group had been jovial before, but now they trudged quietly as they considered the area before them. Fascination for the past filled their minds as their eyes swept over a structure that at one time had housed people of power, individuals that had shaped the world around them, and who perhaps even molded history itself.

Pointing to the side, Liam moved toward a plaque on a large rock on the ground near the building. As he got close to it, the rest of the party gathered around as he cleared his throat to read aloud. The panel below him, inscribed in English, had been created at some point in the recent past and was intended for tourists who frequented the island.

"In the years 1715-1718, the castle served as a camp for prisoners taken under Charles the Twelfth," Liam read, and his voice seemed to break the spell of melancholy, bringing the group back to the present from their morose thoughts about the past. "The prisoners, mainly Russians, suffered serious want, and the fire that destroyed the castle in 1718 was said to be caused by them."

Chuckling, Johan motioned to the quiet area around them, raising his voice in exasperation. "Well, that's pleasant. Not only do you get to starve in captivity, but you can also burn yourself up to escape your misery."

Liam nodded, sounding intrigued by those distant events. "That seems like quite a good set of options to choose from. You think they got like per diem for their suffering? If they ever got back to Russia, can you imagine the paperwork they'd have to file for reimbursement?"

With the mood momentarily lighter, Lilly stepped next to Liam. Showing him a frown because of his bad attempt at humor, she gestured to the wider expanse of the property. "What a wonderful way to spend the day…talking about starvation and death by fire. Maria, what do you say we go get some drinks at the restaurant, while the rest of the guys can mourn three-hundred-year-old dead people?"

Grinning, Maria moved close to Lilly. Arm-in-arm, she escorted Lilly away from the others, and the ladies picked up speed as they paced away from the castle ruins down the graveled road leading from the area. No longer interested in the historical site, they didn't look back with a parting glance, even to say goodbye to their spouses.

Frowning at suddenly being abandoned, Liam pursed his lips and motioned toward their surroundings. "Well, let's check it out. Never know when we'll get another chance to see something like this."

Breaking into groups, the men moved off into separate directions. While Liam, Johan, and Alex picked their way inside the building ruins, Karl and Mattias moved to the outside of the structure.

Working their way down the exterior wall, Karl and Mattias inspected various graffiti on the aged rocks, some of it ancient and some more recent. While the long-ago etchings in the stone were difficult to read, the more up-to-date scrawls of penises and crude language were much simpler to differentiate on the dark surface.

Grinning at humanity's capability to desecrate history—Karl had heard that some graffiti on Christian houses of worship in the Holy Land predated the fall of the Roman Empire—he turned to take in a view of the surrounding forest. There, the gorgeous outlines of clustered Spruce trees were jumbled in a line to either side of him across the open grass. Interspersed with the forest at the ground level were brightly colored bushes and flowers, making for a delightful backdrop to the green fields before them.

Stopping himself, Karl let his gaze linger over several spreads of the most dense foliage. Disturbed, he suddenly felt as if he was being watched as he peered into the groves of assorted plants. The thing about military men, at least those that were most successful and long-lived, is they tended to perceive when they were the object of attention.

This sense of unknown scrutiny was something hard to pin down but nevertheless felt real and very intense. Frowning, a clichéd thought crossed Karl's mind as his eyes sought the source of what bothered him: *Just because you're being paranoid doesn't mean they're not out to get you.*

From a copse of trees to the south of the ruins, a set of eyes returned Karl's gaze. Set amongst the thick brush under several overlapping branches, the eyes of the unseen face were yellow and feral, almost like those of an enormous predator cat. The owner of those pupils stood erect in the shaded area, and though remaining unseen, was focused completely on the duo. Remaining still, the observer studied Karl, Mattias, and their surroundings, as if gauging the level of threat the men presented. The breaths of the watcher, quiet but quick, were drawn in controlled gasps, as if it expected something while it watched.

After some time, Karl let his stare move away from the trees, and he arched his eyebrows as he worked through an inner sense of unease. Acutely bothered by something he couldn't quite see, his wary face took on the appearance of one who had an important duty to perform but had forgotten what he was supposed to do. As if missing out on a task he had trained for, Karl felt disconnected, and for the moment, his thoughts swam in a confused state.

Coming back to his senses, Karl looked at Mattias, who was staring at him from near the castle wall. Unsure of what was wrong, Mattias became hesitant and peered around carefully. With his own face becoming suspicious, it was as if Mattias was catching the scent of Karl's own nervousness. Like two people who could jointly perceive the weather was to worsen before a raging storm came into view, they both wrestled with a feeling of uneasiness while the moments ticked on.

Mattias' inquisitive stare made Karl feel defensive, and Karl showed him a feigned smile, speaking in a low tone as he tried to calm his frayed nerves. "Something about this place just seems...off. Can't really say that I like this old castle."

As if to answer him from inside the building, Liam shouted from the other side of the wall. "OK, let's meet up in here. You guys out there?"

Giving a last glance at the trees, Karl nodded and led Mattias a little farther down the exterior of the building, coming to a point with a small arched entryway leading to the interior of the roofless castle. Walking inside, they saw the others standing amongst some old, chiseled rocks and examining burn marks on a set of stones. The rest of the interior was laced with weeds and grass, empty of any furnishings or decorations that once made for an attractive residence inside these walls.

The light was beginning to wane for the day, but for the moment, it was adequately bright, and only a few shadows stretched across the barren area. The quiet, only intermittently interrupted by the low wail of a far-off breeze, evoked a sense of loneliness from the companions as they peered at what remained of the interior castle.

When Mattias and Karl got close to the others, Liam took a deep breath and smirked at Mattias specifically. "Well, this has been fun, but let's go join the girls. Getting drunk seems like a good plan, at least for me. I don't have to drive when we get back to the terminal on the mainland."

Each of Liam's friends returned the grin, with nobody in obvious disagreement about his proposal. Striding quickly away from the ruined stronghold, they fell into the relaxed gait of contented and worry-free travelers, like they finally decided to have some fun after the short inspection of the not-very-interesting medieval surroundings.

Everyone in the party anticipated a tasty meal and a mug of quality beer in the near future. Looking ahead, they moved with some purpose in their buoyant steps, and a time of partying amongst old pals seemed like the perfect ending for their enjoyable day trip to the island.

But for Karl—and to some extent Mattias—something else lay under their eager expressions. As they filed down the road toward their next destination, moving between dense trees and dark undergrowth to either side of the path, they couldn't quite shake a foreboding feeling that something was wrong at the end of their enjoyable day trip.

#

A few minutes later, the friends strode up a gentle rise on the unpaved road toward a combined inn and cafe. The cozy building, painted dark brown and built of sturdy wood, was two-leveled and immaculately clean. A sign, painted with green lettering over a white background in bold Calligraphy, hung on the side of the establishment and stated succinctly, "Vising Inn and Restaurant."

Next to the business was an asphalted parking lot with only one car, and a one-lane road led away from the area to the inner island through a collection of sparse trees. The sky above was taking on a darker hue as midday gave way to early evening, and the sound of chirping birds seemed to announce that transition with a barrage of pleasant chatter.

Straggling forward, Liam was first to enter the small diner through the main entrance. The place was a modest eatery, holding only a handful of tables and chairs to accommodate customers.

Sitting at a small table near the front window was the Finnish couple from the ferry, and they had several plates of European-style pancakes and a pitcher of orange juice set between them. Cindi and Aaron were enjoying the spread with bright smiles as they chatted, and seeing the men walk into the place, greeted them with happy expressions and friendly waves.

Toward the interior of the restaurant, near an inner hallway leading to the connected inn, sat Lilly and Maria. Showing they were prepared for their companions' arrival, several tables were pushed together to allow everyone to sit together for their late lunch. The girls grinned from the extended table, and each held up a glass of white wine, showing they had followed through on their promise for a head start on the meal and festivities.

To the side, behind a simple bar that held a row of mismatched glasses, stood an overweight bartender. The man had a serious demeanor and deep circles under his eyes, along with a shiny and shaved head. His disposition was not a friendly one, and he looked a bit out of place as he cleaned the bar top with a rag. Frowning down, he didn't seem to enjoy his mundane line of work.

Gazing at the middle-aged fellow, Liam got the impression that the man had seen a lot with those eyes, and his jowls and deep wrinkles appeared to have formed from a long and weary life. At some point in his past, Liam had come to understand that age alone did not make a person haggard, but also their stressful experiences tended to wear a person out—particularly if those experiences were traumatic. Staring curiously at the man, he guessed that to be the case with the bartender.

Setting their assorted bags and backpacks in the corner of the room, which in Alex's case included a waist pack made by Gucci, the party slid into their chairs and looked forward to a meal. As they relaxed from their sightseeing, mobile phones were laid across the table and they began with several loud conversations at the same time. What was formerly a quiet diner became boisterous and rather loud as the group settled in for a good time.

As the friends dropped into discussions of the castle and their brief expedition into it, the bartender began bringing trays of sandwiches, chips, and fruit to the table. Obviously ordered before the men's arrival, the food was not upper-class fare, but nobody seemed to mind as they joked and gesticulated about their trip to the old keep.

Deciding on something with a considered face, Alex took the opportunity to stand and clink his glass of water with a spoon. As he held it up, he raised his voice triumphantly. "I would like to raise a toast to my longtime friends in this wonderful…restaurant, and to say I am glad we can have this time together."

Murmurs of half-hearted agreement met his statement, but everyone soon moved back to their own discussions, as if Alex's words were appreciated but also an interruption to their personal anecdotes.

"I would also like to say," continued Alex, his grin broadening, "that all the food and drink you can manage are on me, free of charge, so eat and drink well."

A raucous applause then broke out, and even the Finnish couple, perhaps thinking they were part of the offer, also clapped at Alex's generous announcement.

The bartender, having already brought what made up the bulk of his available food to the party, came to the head of the aligned tables and cleared his throat. The pallor of his skin looked a little off, like he was a bit sick, but he tried to smile as he raised his voice in heavily accented English.

"As long as what you want for drinks includes the three beers we have on tap," he said, "or the one bottle of wine remaining, you can have anything you want."

With that, the man unceremoniously turned away from the table and retreated to the bar. Behind him, the room grew quieter and descended into a sad murmur as everyone digested what that exactly meant: *Only cheap beer and garbage wine for all.*

#

The party's impromptu celebration passed quickly, and in under two hours, the group polished off a gaggle of cold beers and the remaining bottle of wine. Across the tabletop, the cluttered space held numerous glasses vying for space with mobile phones and pieces of half-eaten food on small plates.

From everyone present, their faces had grown redder, their voices more slurred, and their eyes more engrossed with the pleasant company around them. For the moment, the times were good and carefree, full of hearty chuckles and endearing grins.

Looking tipsy, Liam's mood and tone were happy as he continued his cheerful interactions with his longtime friends. Though he had visited Sweden briefly several times since he left, it had been a decade since he had the opportunity to chat and enjoy himself in their company for this long. But now, swilling beer and discussing the local hockey team's chances at the championship made those college years seem like they passed only recently.

Growing sad, Liam wondered why it took so long to appreciate what you had in the past. It seemed now that chasing the mighty dollar and an engrossing career had captured all his attention, even when the important and joyful things in life were usually in the rearview mirror—which was precisely when he was at his most penniless. It was like a cruel joke from the Gods that, by the time you amassed enough money in life, you often had the least ability to enjoy it with those that mattered most.

Carefully standing, Liam motioned to the bathroom and said, "Toalett." As he stumbled toward the facilities in the hallway that joined the restaurant with the inn, he cursed himself for not pursuing the language over the years. Mostly it was laziness, but the other part was there was nothing like making an idiot out of yourself that forced you to give up, particularly when English was so common and widely understood in this country.

Besides, the Swedish language, although relatively easy from a grammatical perspective, was almost impossible for him to pronounce correctly. With three extra vowels and a "singing" way of stressing the words, it was next to impossible to properly sound like a native—no matter how well he spoke. He always dreaded that smile from the average person he interacted with, the one they used when Liam uttered a few sentences, that seemed to proclaim, *Bless your heart for trying, but we both know you will always sound like a moron when trying to speak. America may own much of the world, but we are always multilingual and informed here in the land of meatballs and ABBA.*

As he leaned his head against the wall and looked down at the urinal, Liam even remembered an older guy in the area he studied, Douglas was his name, that had lived here several decades and still continued to regularly butcher the language. It was like he finally gave up trying to sound like a homegrown resident and instead enjoyed using his shitty accent to make Swedes feel superior in their mellifluous speech.

After relieving his bladder, Liam stumbled from the bathroom with a strong buzz and partially dilated pupils. He was a happy drunk, but he was never able to master the ability to make himself appear sober when in this condition. Just now, his mind was stuck at the midway point of wanting to hug everyone on earth, mixed with thinking he suddenly had all the answers for world peace in his rambling thoughts.

Catching himself, Liam looked to the side and was briefly intrigued by a few photos hanging on the wall near the restroom. In three separate pictures were the images of a happy family, with a man, woman and child smiling from a shoreline, standing in front of a house, and dressed up in a variety of zombie Halloween costumes at a party. There was nothing quite as attractive as the faces of people who were caught happy in a snapshot, and Liam couldn't help but smile himself as he lingered in front of the photo frames.

"They are my husband and son."

Flinching at the sudden words, Liam turned to see a middle-aged woman standing next to him. Though now older, she was the same lady with the overwhelming smile in the photos. But now, Evelyn Anderson, who wore attractive, short-brown hair, returned his gaze with a haunted look. Liam had never seen or known her, but he could easily identify her as a person with emotional issues underneath her too-wrinkled face. Her eyes, though blue and piercing, held a sense of mourning and inescapable loss.

"And you are…?"

"I'm Evelyn. I run this little place," she responded, motioning behind her to the front lobby of the inn. Returning her eyes to the wall, she peered sadly at the photos, going quiet as her thoughts drifted elsewhere.

Knowing he wouldn't like what was coming next, Liam licked his lips, then pointed at the happy images. "They…you…look like a happy family."

"We were. The happiest people in the world. For our brief moment in time, everything in the world was…just perfect."

Such sad words, full of heartache and loss, were not what Liam wanted to hear, but here he was, half-drunk and stuck with this strange woman in a small inn on an island he hadn't planned to visit. There was nothing like foreshadowing and depressing words to turn good humor into a funeral-like atmosphere, just in time to ruin his otherwise-happy night.

Plunging ahead, Liam spoke guardedly, like he really didn't want to know the rest of the story—but was too far in to back out now. "Umm…are they…I mean, how are they—?"

Evelyn confirmed his worst fears as she continued staring, her mind lost in the pictures of a happier place and time. "They're dead. They've been gone a while now."

Stammering, Liam took a moment to respond. He was never one to dwell on emotions, at least those of other people, so he tried to inject some empathy into his tone. "I'm sorry to hear that. They seem…young."

Evelyn nodded, and her skin flushed under the interior onslaught of intense sorrow. "They were."

Sighing, Evelyn pulled away from her moment of personal anguish and redirected the conversation. "If you're going to stay, you need to reserve a room."

Relieved at the change of pace and the innkeeper's sudden move to a more normal expression, one that was more pleasant and less hopeless, Liam smiled. "No, we're going back to the mainland this evening—."

"The ferry leaves in twenty-five minutes. You'll need to hurry if you want to make it."

Alarmed, Liam's half-dulled senses grew sharp at this revelation, and his suddenly awake face focused on the diner. Looking back and forth, he took on a harried expression and nodded thankfully at Evelyn.

Waving goodbye, Liam paced into the restaurant and held up his hands. The group's enthusiastic conversation stopped when they noticed his panicked demeanor.

"Guys, we gotta go; the ferry leaves soon," said Liam, and he gestured out the window toward the not-too-distant ferry. "I hate to cut this short, but we're out of time."

The disappointed gazes of the party were immediate, but with impressive speed, they slid from their places around the table and began collecting their things from the table and the corner of the room. For people that were recently chuckling and sharing stories, the change to hurrying and quiet drunks made a jolting difference to the restaurant's mood, as if they were suddenly serious soldiers coming awake to move out for an upcoming battle.

As the guys prepared their day-trip bags and the girls collected their purses, Alex approached the morose bartender to pay the bill. While he swiped his card, not even bothering to check what amount was due, the party shouldered their belongings and prepared for the short hike back to the ferry.

Except, Lars was rifling through his man-purse, a small bag made of black leather, and was quickly growing frustrated as he hunted for something.

"I can't find my insulin," Lars said, his voice confused and high-pitched. "It was in here before I left the car…but I guess I could've left it in one of a dozen places."

Liam stepped close and peered into the open bag, like perhaps he could see something in the small confines that Lars had missed. Looking up at Lars, he frowned. "Geez, is it that important? Maybe we could—."

From across the room, where the bartender cleaned the same top of the bar that had been spotless for the whole meal, the chubby man interrupted. His coarse voice was matter-of-fact and not very polite. "You can go to our all-night clinic here on the island. They're sure to have your medicine there."

"But we'd miss the ferry," replied Lars. "Shit…"

Mattias, who was dutifully waiting for the order to head out to the boat, moved closer to Lars and Liam. Thinking for a moment, he spoke haltingly, as if considering their options and timing for the evening. "Well…we could just stay here tonight—after we got to the clinic. It's not like the night will be better by rushing back to the coast after we get off the island."

Karl spoke up from the corner, where he was peering curiously out the window towards the darkening sky and forest to the back of the inn. "Yeah, that's true. Tomorrow, we can get to Alex and Maria's place by late morning. We'll have plenty of rest in the meantime, and we might even sleep off that garbage beer."

Glancing around the room, Liam made eye contact with everyone, one at a time. The responding gazes ranged from skeptical to indifferent, but nobody appeared hostile to the idea. Whatever their driving focus for the short holiday trip, they didn't seem to mind a small change of plans.

Shrugging, Liam patted Lars on the shoulder and motioned to the hallway and inn beyond. "Alex, if you want, you, Lilly, and Karl can stay and rent rooms for everyone. The rest of us can keep Lars company at the clinic."

Relieved grins and good moods returned to the friends' faces. No longer in a hurry, everybody mentally adjusted to the prospect of a relaxing night at this simple and cozy motel.

Chapter Six

In the afternoon's decreasing sunlight, the clinic building was a stout and imposing facility, and above its gray exterior panels, subdued lights shone around a large neon sign that read "Vårdcentral." Though only two stories tall, the basic structure was buttressed by immense concrete columns, presenting a clean and sturdy appearance in an open clearing surrounded by darkening forests.

To either side of its bright and wide entrance, with several clean windows reflecting the illuminated lamps from outside, were collections of colorful shrubbery and perfectly maintained lawns.

Strangely, the parking lot in front and to the side of the building contained no cars at the moment, and the empty spaces and lack of vehicles, either from patients or workers, made the scene appear lonely. The incoming darkness filling the area around the clinic was quiet, making the whole environment, lit up like a Christmas tree, look otherworldly, almost as if it was a location abandoned in time.

Liam, Lars, Mattias, and Maria strode at a relaxing pace toward the front of the health center, and their voices, which joked about a wide-lipped and often-drunken man they knew in college called "Fraggle," pierced the silence surrounding the clinic. As they approached the entrance, mellow expressions filled their faces, and the companions smiled expectantly as they paced through automatic doors that eased open in greeting.

Inside, there was a large area filled with chairs and tables arranged at orderly intervals. The extended and open room was bright, and to the side of the large reception room was a small portion of colored carpet for children to play on. Scattered around the kids' corner were collections of play-blocks and other assorted toys, showing that the cluttered area was popular with youngsters while they waited.

But currently, there were no children or patients waiting to be seen, and only the friends' squeaking shoes on the tile floors broke the silence of the place. The antiseptic smell of the clinic's surroundings wasn't particularly pleasant but was appropriate for the hygienic setting.

The party, hesitant as they peered around, took in the scene with the eyes of people who didn't enjoy the idea of illness or injury that were often present in such facilities.

Behind a row of connected desks making up the barrier to the back of the clinic sat the only person in the building. In her thirties and with a dour look under her thick glasses, the receptionist, Natalia, wrinkled her nose as she took in the sight of actual customers at this late time of day. If there was happiness to be found in her mood from finally having people to talk to, it didn't show in her severe expression.

Walking carefully toward the plastic screen that separated the unfriendly lady from the new arrivals, Lars cleared his throat and spoke carefully as he leaned down. "Hi, it doesn't seem to be very busy—."

"How can I help you?" interrupted the receptionist, and by her tone, it was apparent that help was the furthest thing from her mind. In fact, if there was a modern face that represented aloof disinterest from the medical community, it was perfectly represented in her bitchy features.

Taking a breath, Lars showed a kind smile and pressed on. "Yes, I've lost my insulin and need to get a few days' supply."

Frowning, the receptionist thought for a moment. With a nod, she glanced down with undisguised reluctance and rummaged around on her desk. Clicking her tongue in satisfaction, she produced a collection of papers and arranged them on a clipboard. Happy with the presentation, she slid them through the opening toward Lars. "OK, please fill out these forms…and provide your health card. We'll have the doctor see you when he's…available."

Taking the forms, Lars returned her frown and glanced around the big room. The lack of patients indicated the doctor was probably more occupied with his phone or perhaps a video game in the back, but there was something about nearly every clinic on earth that made its gatekeepers happy to let you know you had to wait. Maybe it was about control and enjoyment of the power it gave certain workers to act this way? *As long as this witch helps get me insulin, I couldn't give a shit she hasn't been laid in a decade.*

Sighing, Lars took the papers and sat down to go through the motions of accessing his needed medicine. Meanwhile, Liam, Mattias, and Maria stood in a calm circle, chatting as they thought over their expiring day and looking forward to the next. The mood was buoyant as the longtime comrades considered their options for the near future.

"So, tomorrow afternoon," said Mattias, a big grin filling his unusual face. "You know who gets to drive Alex's boat first? The weather is supposed to be perfect, so I got first dibs."

#

Karl's bag lay on the bed, and he took his time arranging his things as he withdrew them from the military-style rucksack. Making sure that each fold in his packed shirts and underwear was aligned to perfection, he moved and stacked the clothing on top of a sturdy and shiny dresser at the foot of his bed.

Throughout the pleasant motel room, it was apparent that whoever had cleaned the place had done a thorough job. The floors were spotless, the bedding was clean and well-made, and the picture frames, holding images of far-off mountain ranges and river tributaries, were diligently dusted and without smudges.

Stopping in front of the second-story window, Karl peered outside into the incoming darkness. His face was firm and curious as he scanned the pockets of trees forming the darkening forest around the inn, and he tilted his head as he focused on the elongating shadows and colored underbrush of the sedate surroundings.

Karl was a man who liked to enjoy nature. Having grown up as a wandering and somewhat lonesome boy in Central Sweden, he had made a point of spending most of his free time by himself in such forest tracts that he now stared at.

What those relaxing and beneficial times had taught him was that nature had a certain pulse to itself, almost like a living and breathing creature in its own right. It wasn't exactly in a "mother-earth" manner, no, it was more like a way that the environment was in tune with the world around it, and if you were an observant-enough woodsman, it took little time to make your own perception of the forest blend with the wider area.

It was almost symbiotic, the relationship that formed, if a person concentrated enough to acclimate to the mood the natural environment exuded. The skittering of animals, the smell of the trees and flowers, the whole arrangement of animal trails and foliage, these things served to heighten the experience for anyone who truly endeavored to take them in. To make yourself part of the world around you wasn't that hard—if you listened to its cues.

Karl had honed this sense of being in sync with nature as he grew up, and in his time in the military, both in rigorous training in Sweden and on a few deployments attached to NATO, these outdoor inclinations had served him well. On more than one occasion, his closeness with and understanding of the physical world had kept him and his comrades out of harm's way, so he had grown to lean on his gut instinct when it came to avoiding danger.

And now that instinct was again telling Karl something was amiss in the surrounding woods. The forest looked friendly enough, even to the point of being attractive and inviting, but somewhere in the stands of trees, it seemed that something was off. The particular way that the environment encompassing the inn appeared almost to be an oppressive screen, as if hiding something—instead of the inclusive-feeling forest that he was accustomed to seeing in his normal routine—made him feel uncomfortable.

After some time probing the scattered trees and vegetation with his intense eyes, Karl shook his head and contemplated what could be wrong. Grimacing, he smiled to himself, thinking that perhaps his angst was due to some remnant of the counseling he had received from his stint in Afghanistan.

Maybe this odd, foreboding feeling he now felt was attached to some trauma from that deployment? Karl remembered a movie when he was young with Tim Robbins, "Jacob's Ladder," and in that film, a combat veteran spent decades of his future life battling demons from his time in service, almost as if the main character could never get away from his tortured war-time past. Of course, the film ended with Robbins discovering the time after the war was in fact only a mirage, and he was in truth dying on the operating table during the war, but the instructive idea that a horrific past could ruin your future was still a poignant one. *I better not turn into one of those nutcases that sees the enemy everywhere they look for the rest of their lives.*

Looking back to his bag, Karl frowned and walked to it. Reaching inside, he withdrew a long scabbard, one that held his trusty KA-BAR military knife. Made to endure the worst that field conditions could offer, the weapon or one like it was a mainstay of any fighting man, and pulling it from its sheath, he checked its sharpened perfection with a quick scrape of his thumb over the razor-sharp edge.

Tucking the knife into his waist, Karl pulled the door open and strode from the room. As he descended the scant stairs and pushed his way through the back door of the small inn, a worried frown crossed his face, like he didn't know what to expect next.

#

Minutes later, Karl kneeled on a path not far from the motel. Puzzled, he ran his fingers across the churned earth, which was marked by the passing of…something. Strange indentations in the moist ground indicated the presence of wildlife of some variety, but it was difficult to determine the precise animal that could have caused the tearing marks across the topsoil in an area so close to civilization.

Around him, the area was becoming dimmer, and an unseasonably chilly breeze rustled the cluster of branches in the forest cover above.

Looking up, Karl stared into the bright moon that already provided substantial illumination to the area. Glancing nearby, he took in the signs of other animal tracks that filled the soil, and a perplexed frown formed on his face. The indications on the muddy and upturned forest floor were not what he would have expected for such a location—or even would have thought possible. The signs he saw were like those from a zoo full of marauding animals, which made zero sense on Vising Island, a place with few wild creatures. *What the fuck?*

Standing, Karl spied and moved to a scratched tree that stood next to one of the nearby trails. Withdrawing his knife, he stuck the blade into a gouge in the tree's bark to measure the depth of whatever could have made such a mark. Pulling back the weapon, he noted the gash in the wood was substantial and deep, like it was inflicted by the claw of a large and predatory animal. The immediate thought that came to mind was that of a bear, but Karl had not heard of such beasts being resident anywhere close to this area—they were typically only in the northwest of Sweden.

Squinting into the deficient light, Karl looked up into the canopy of the darkening forest. Confused, he glanced around the gloomy environment as he tried to make some sense of the bizarre indications of animal movement.

With a frown and a shake of his head, Karl stared deeper into the forest, towards the area that would take him farther from the group's place of residence at the inn. He didn't really want to leave his friends alone, but in all his time living and exploring out-of-the-way landscapes, he had never seen something quite like this. Rural places with actual people and everyday commerce didn't show these types of wild habitation; in fact, no place he had ever seen in the past did either.

Curiosity getting the better of him, Karl came to an abrupt decision as he peered into the shadowy periphery of jumbled brush and trees. Steeling himself, he walked purposefully toward the deep interior of the spacious forest, intrigued with whatever lay in the forbidding and dense woods beyond.

Behind him, the last light of day fell off. Night was almost here.

Chapter Seven

Scrawling on the "medical history" portion of the clinic's paperwork, Lars continued his efforts to satisfy the Swedish state's demands for documentation to access his benefits by describing his symptoms, history of illness, and every possible allergy that could ever have affected a human being.

Lars wondered why answering a question about Dengue Fever was essential to obtaining medicine, much less whether he had recently been vaccinated for a host of barely pronounceable diseases. Frustrated, he flipped the paper over and, seeing that several more years of history were needed, let out an irritated sigh.

Behind her desk, the receptionist met his wheeze of annoyance with the first smile that seemed genuine since they had wandered into the facility. The twinkle in her eyes suggested she was more than happy his appointment would have to wait.

Looking back and forth between his friends and the woman, Lars frowned and wondered if his companions would mind if he screamed at the receptionist in an aggressive and full-throated bellow, just to keep her on her toes.

Swedish society was interesting in that overt displays of emotion were looked down upon in almost any social context. Careers could be lost in this country by something so simple as flipping out on a coworker, such was the social stigma attached to losing your cool.

Still, some people deserved to be awakened from being obnoxious on occasion, so it would serve the receptionist right to have her cage rattled a bit. Yelling at the woman wouldn't be fair, and indeed she might call the police on him, but at least she would think twice about being rude to the next guy needing his prescription filled here. Feeling adventurous, Lars flashed his own mischievous grin as he pondered the ways he could insult her and liven up this rather humdrum workplace.

Liam noticed the antagonism from the clinic worker, as well as the increasing annoyance from Lars, and he offered his buddy a placating smile to short-circuit any conflict that was soon to follow. Always the peacemaker in his interactions, whether with friends or at his work, Liam almost considered it his personal lifelong duty to tamp down such potential arguments, whether they were justified or not.

This want for peace and balance was a part of Liam's personality that often got him compliments, and he always prided himself on his desire for conflict resolution. He knew that it wasn't always possible to keep the peace, but he had learned that early action could sometimes preclude disagreeable situations, or worse, violence.

The clank of an opening door from the back of the clinic brought a strange sight into view, as a rigidly tall and completely bald orderly pushed his way into the reception room. Leaning over an empty gurney, the strange man pushed the squeaking apparatus at a slow pace towards the standing party, focusing ahead as if none of the friends were even there.

The seemingly preoccupied orderly, a bit out of place in the quiet clinic, kept his head down as he pushed past the circle of chatting companions. Maria, Johan, Liam and Mattias exchanged glances as they looked back and forth between the newcomer and each other, then shrugged as if assuming he was on his way to some indeterminate duty elsewhere in the medical complex. Meanwhile, Lars paid the tall stranger no attention at all as he finished up his paperwork while seated to the side.

Stopping behind Johan, the orderly moved aside a sheet that covered the tray of the gurney, revealing a long and thin sledgehammer lying on the shiny metal surface. The odd medical worker reached gently down and grabbed the tool, then swung it into an arc in one rapid and fluid movement.

Moving through the air, the dark metal end of the sledge was propelled forward. Catching the sight of the movement from the corner of her eye, Maria noticed the incoming assault and her face hesitated as she tried to comprehend the developing attack.

The dense metal thudded into the back of Johan's head, swung with such force that it planted itself partially into his skull. A spray of blood cascaded from the impact, with several droplets of gore thrown across the lobby and landing on Maria's shocked face.

Instantly incapacitated, Johan collapsed to the floor, his body slumping in an off-kilter way, his arms outstretched to either side. Unmoving, his brains were irreparably displaced by the solid weapon, and cranial fluid leaked copiously from the mortal head wound.

For the briefest of moments, there was no reply to the appalling assault. Maria's eyes locked open, stuck wide and confused, while Liam and Mattias' own understanding of the world seemed to go on "tilt," as if their brains had momentarily been reset by the horrific strike.

The face of the orderly, formerly clean-shaven and unemotional, became something entirely different as the friends stared in open disbelief. Now his features were smooth and white, with all-black eyes in orbs that were oddly distended on its angular, freakish face. His mouth was suddenly full of darkish teeth that seemed too long inside his bluish lips, and he snarled in an almost feline way as he moved his gaze between the dumbstruck companions.

Still holding the sledgehammer embedded in Johan's head, the hands of the orderly now showed long and black claws as it grasped the metal shaft of the weapon. The pallor of the skin above the vicious nails was milky white, and its limbs also looked chalky and pale on his just-visible forearms.

Coming alert, Liam was the first to react. "You...piece of shit," he screamed, and he surged toward the orderly, shouting in anger and hurling himself towards the huge creature.

The orderly met him halfway, adeptly backhanding Liam in a practiced and fluid movement. Even as he was a behemoth of a...something, this creature was clearly skilled in the art of personal combat. The SMACK of the blow was jarring, and Liam spun and pitched toward the wall, where he impacted and slid down the white-painted plaster.

Looking back at Johan, the creature now tried to dislodge the hammer from his skull. Once...twice...three times he yanked on the heavy tool, and the result was each time Johan's skull popped as he tried to extricate the metal end from his crushed brains.

Finally able to pull it free, the orderly faced Mattias, who seemed unable and unwilling to move as the creature raised its weapon and took a step toward him. A wicked scowl crossed the monster-like face as it moved forward to add another victim in the hideous attack.

From behind, a blur and a crash, as Lars smacked a wooden chair across the back of the aggressor. Falling forward, the orderly was briefly stunned as it sprawled on a tile floor that was quickly filling with blood and brain leakage. Continuing his fierce attack, Lars kept a piece of the chair leg in his hand, and he slammed the creature several times across the head as he wailed in uncontrolled rage.

Climbing atop the creature, Lars showed something like professional competency in Jujitsu as he inserted his hands under the thing's neck, then leaned back as he bent the orderly backward. The result was that, for the briefest of moments, it appeared Lars could snap the orderly's neck. As the thing was contorted against its will, it appeared helpless while its dark eyes stared searchingly at the ceiling.

Coming to its senses, the creature, wounded and bloodied by the savage attack, inverted one of its immense claws and pressed it into Lars' shoulder. The long, knife-like talon probed deeply into his flesh, and the creature moved the claw around in the joint, tearing through tendons and flesh as it scrambled the musculature underneath the skin.

Screaming and losing his grip, Lars recoiled in vivid pain, and trying to scoot away from his opponent, he grabbed at his shoulder, unable to feel or move the arm connected to it. Lars' face, full of emotion and want for revenge, became fearful as he grasped his inability to fight the creature off.

Capably inverting itself, the orderly focused on Lars. As Lars tried to move away, gasping and suddenly fearful, the creature's claws clicked on the floor as it scooted closer. Having dropped its weapon, it now appeared focused and cruel as it closed the distance.

Abruptly, a wail of indescribable mourning filled the room, sounding something like a wailing banshee. Maria, formerly stuck in a hideous and speechless fugue state, ran boldly into the bizarre fray of combat. Holding a metal paperweight above her head, she screamed at the creature, preparing to brain the thing with her makeshift weapon.

Unperturbed, the orderly stopped its advance toward Lars and crouched. Springing up, it ripped into Maria with its open claw in a brutal smack. Lifting her off the ground, Maria was thrown across several chairs and thumped headfirst into the baseboard of the wall. Quiet, still, and in an awkward heap, blood leaked from several scratches across her head and face.

Turning back towards Lars, the orderly seemed unbothered by any of the events; in fact, his bloody face, full of scrapes and gouges that created discolored furrows in its almost luminescent skin, evinced a sense of exhilaration at the tempo of the fight, showing happiness in his savage features at the chaotic nature of the pitched battle up to this point. Worse, his leering stare seemed to promise that the best was yet to come.

This unnerving confidence wasn't a good sign for the continuing fight, and Lars glanced left and right, looking for something else to use as a weapon or to put between him and the incoming predator. The ground around him was slippery and thick with liquids and blood, making his movement slow and ungainly as he backpedaled on his ass.

The crack of a gunshot filled the room. Shockingly, it was at first unclear from where the shot had come. Looking down at a bloody hole in its chest, the surprised creature arched his neck to see what had happened behind it.

Behind the orderly, Mattias stood with his gun drawn and pointed. Raising itself, the predator turned and faced Mattias, but its eyes were now confused as it moved to focus on the semiautomatic pistol in his firm grip.

Several more sharp pistol cracks followed as Mattias fired into the abdomen of the orderly, pulling the trigger mechanically and measuring the effect of each impacting round. The creature convulsed with each hit of lead that punched through its insides, filling its long white coat with circles of red and blowing chunks of flesh out the back of its body, but it didn't seem mortally wounded from the shots. Maimed and suddenly unsure of itself, the beast scanned quickly to the right and tensed its muscles to flee.

Raising his aim, Mattias continued pulling the trigger. Hitting the creature first in the neck, he kept firing until his bullets tore into its face, and with his last half-dozen shots, he blew the thing's frightening maw from its shoulders, leaving nothing but shreds of skull and brain where the monster's head had been.

Slumping to the ground, the now-dead creature was still. Gore leaked from its neck and gently pooled around the freakish figure, and both its whitish skin and jacket became soaked in dark-red blood.

Ejecting his spent magazine, Mattias quickly reloaded his pistol. For one who had been late to the fight, he was now aroused to danger as he racked a new round into the chamber of his .40 caliber Heckler & Koch service weapon. As he panned his head around, he searched for any new threat in the suddenly quiet room.

Natalia, the obnoxious receptionist, still sat behind her desk. Due to the inhuman and vicious nature of the fight, it should perhaps have been expected she would be scared or overwhelmed because of the combat. Instead, she had a sickened and unhappy look on her face, like perhaps she thought the wrong side had won the bloody confrontation.

"You," shouted Mattias, and he stared accusingly at her, his outraged face communicating his anger and disbelief at what happened.

Jumping up, the clearly upset receptionist fled from the office, ducking into the back as Mattias followed her with his aimed weapon. Confused at the chaos surrounding him, Mattias almost shot the woman, but decided against the rash action of killing someone without an imminent threat to himself. His police training was extensive, and whatever threat he now faced, executing bystanders was not part of his intended professional exploits.

Lowering his pistol, Mattias turned to take in the carnage that surrounded him. As he tried to come to grips with his surroundings, his fierce gaze descended into a sort of helpless gloom while he evaluated what the hell just happened.

#

Liam's eyes fluttered open, but he could see only blurry outlines of indistinguishable shapes as he sought to make sense of the fuzzy room. Groggy, he tried to raise himself up, but his leg muscles didn't fully cooperate, and he fought a wave of dizziness while grabbing at the corner of a nearby table.

"Take it easy, Liam, you've had quite a bash to the head," Mattias said, putting a firm hand on his shoulder and keeping him stable. "You're gonna be alright, I think, but you gotta move slow for a while."

Becoming more aware with each passing moment, Liam felt like he had gone the distance with Mike Tyson—but without any of the requisite skill it would take to keep from getting pummeled at will. His head thumped like it was being slammed between an anvil and a ball-peen hammer, while he also had the awkward feeling that his arms and legs were not his own, as if they belonged to someone outside his own bodily perceptions. To make matters worse, he didn't know where he was, or what had….

"Johan," Liam exclaimed, and he suddenly fought to stand, to push through the stupor and pain in his scrambled brain. He felt woozy and lost as he fought to overcome the effects of the creature's assault, but he still managed to come partially erect with the help of the furniture and Mattias' sturdy grip.

The room around Liam began to swirl, then came together, slowly taking on the appearance of the clinic that they walked into to fetch Lars' diabetes medicine. As the opaque shapes of the place merged to form the distinct items of the reception area, only now covered with splashes of blood, the entirety of the recent events formed into a clear memory…at least up until the point he had been bitch-slapped across the room by the orderly.

Staring at the shape of the dead animal-like person, then farther away at the form of his friend Johan, who lay silent and still under a blood-stained sheet, Liam's voice was overwhelmed and sounded unrecognizable to his own ears. "What…happened? What was that thing?"

Shaking his head slowly, Mattias continued holding Liam's arm, even though he now stood on solid and self-supporting legs. "No idea. It was some kinda monster. It's like some crazy dream…I can't figure out…."

Mattias' words drifted off, and Liam finally jerked fully aware and pulled free from his grip. Moving his gaze to the farthest wall, the one that Maria had so viciously been thrown into, Liam saw Lars bending over and tending to Maria's crumpled form. Lying on her back along the exterior of the tile area, she had some gauze on her head, which was affixed with several strips of elastic medical wrapping tape.

Mattias answered his unasked question with a hopeful nod. "Her pulse is strong. I think she'll be OK, but I don't know what to do about Johan's body."

Taking a deep breath, Liam steadied himself and focused on the covered form of Johan. Moving slowly, he grabbed a simple chair and shuffled next to the body. After seating himself, he stared for some time at the covered corpse. So recently this was his dear and cheerful friend, but now it was just an unmoving block of cooling meat. Johan's lifetime of being a good and faithful person had been distilled into a lump of flesh in a moment of violence, all occurring for some unknown reason in this horrible place.

Liam wept openly, unable to fully grasp the sudden loss. Reaching down, he touched the off-white sheet, and it almost felt like he could make him return if he willed it strongly enough. With his grief building in his tight chest, his mind struck out on a tangent of denial and overwrought sorrow. *This can't be real. I gotta be in the world's worst nightmare. Please let me wake the fuck up.*

Mattias walked carefully next to Liam, letting his own teary eyes move down to Johan's covered body. He gave Liam several moments of silence to take in what he himself had already internalized. Mourning had a different expression for everyone, but quietness was usually the best way to give space to those who were working through it.

Slowly, Mattias tucked his firearm into his inside-the-waistband holster, then gestured over to Lars and Johan's wife. "What…will we tell her?"

Taking his cue to join the conversation, Lars pulled himself away from the still-unconscious Maria and stumbled close to Mattias and Liam. His arm was in a makeshift sling, and he grimaced in pain as he adjusted himself under the bloody bandage.

Looking over to Johan's soon-to-be-distraught wife, Liam hesitated, then rasped his words out in a baffled tone. "Not sure what we're gonna do, but she doesn't need to see this when she comes around."

Mattias agreed with a huff as he peered cautiously towards the back of the medical center. "More important, I think, is we shouldn't be here if that thing has any friends coming. That receptionist was in on it somehow, and the building's now empty after she ran out of here. I checked the rest of the place while you were out cold—it's empty. We really need to get back to the inn and check on the others. I don't know what we're gonna tell them, though…."

Liam's face flashed in sudden anticipation as he remembered something. With a click of his tongue, he nodded and reached inside his coat. Producing his mobile phone, his eyes were momentarily enthusiastic as he peered down.

Mattias ended the hoped-for emergency call with a shake of his head. "There's no service. None of our phones work—I already checked. And if you think that's just a coincidence, I have a bridge to sell you that runs all the way to South America. Meaning, we're dealing with more than monsters, apparently."

Pointing to the dead creature, Mattias sounded sure of himself as he continued. "It's some kind of planned event, not the beginning of the apocalypse. I know a setup when I see it, even if that thing is…whatever the hell it is."

Liam frowned at this bit of unwelcome news. After thinking the worst was behind him, it suddenly dawned on him that their bad day, the loss of their friend, and their struggle to find out what the hell was going on could have just started. Being attacked in a random event was bad enough, but now they had to consider this was just the beginning of something that wasn't going to end any time soon.

An abrupt and unnerving thought came to Liam's mind, and it wasn't a pleasant one. He remembered the story about some soccer players that had crashed into a mountain while flying to a match decades ago in South America. Amazingly, they survived the initial horrible event. Unfortunately, though the survivors escaped instant death, it had been just the beginning, and several more team members died in the following weeks as they waited to be rescued in that freezing and remote mountain environment.

Eventually, after the pitiable athletes had been reduced to consuming the flesh of their dead teammates, the remaining survivors were finally saved, but it was brutal to imagine how wrong they were to think the worst was over when they had survived the initial destruction of their aircraft. Surviving a plane crash was an unlikely enough bit of luck, but the subsequent starvation and suffering of the group made the whole catastrophe seem even more unfair as it played out.

Liam had the disturbing impression he was in a similar struggle now, at least in the sense that their troubles had just begun. He was sure cannibalism wouldn't be necessary, but a feeling of abject and oppressive gloom, overpowering and very real, made him cringe in worry at what would come next.

Stepping as quickly as his unsteady legs would carry him, Liam moved over to Maria. Grunting, he carefully hefted her, all the while struggling to bear her weight. Despite her dainty size, the effort to carry Maria strained his muscles and made his head pound harder from exertion.

Sucking air through clenched and determined teeth, Liam pointed toward the entrance to the clinic and their eventual return to the inn. "With our shitty luck…it's up to me to carry her back. When we get help, we'll come back for…Johan,"

Motioning to Mattias and trying to adjust the dead weight as he cradled Maria, Liam explained his brazenness with a shrug of his sagging shoulders. "You got the gun, and Lars can't do it because of his injury. Makes me wish I had worked out like…ever."

With that, Liam moved clumsily through the automatic door in the front and stumbled out into the lighted parking area. His pace was slow as he moved, but he braced himself and focused as he took each step, feeling all the while that they had better move fast.

Glancing back to their dead friend and nodding a regretful goodbye, Mattias drew his pistol and followed Liam outside. As Mattias scanned the surrounding darkness for threats over the sights of his weapon, trying to keep a protective visual arc around Liam and Maria, Lars followed close behind.

Lars himself held up a sharp scalpel, one that he had pilfered from somewhere inside the building as he sought to acquire a weapon. For the moment he was silent, but determination dominated his face as he swept the shadowy trees for any further hazards to the group.

With the woods around them silent, the surviving companions, staggering and heartbroken, angled across the paved lot toward the dark trail that earlier brought them to this horrific destination.

Chapter Eight

The motel room was quiet and somewhat dark, with most of the moonlight filling the place coming from a partially curtained window with a view of the dark woods outside. Silence pervaded the area, both inside the motel and out, and only a methodical dripping sound filled the room, like that of a leaky faucet, making the room seem lonely and uninhabited.

Elsewhere in the room, along the connecting wall that faced another direction from the second-floor corner bedroom, a shadowed figure faced out a separate window. Standing still, the form was unmoving and quiet as it stared into stretches of gloomy vegetation under the moonlit perimeter of the property.

Hulking and focused, the large shape breathed carefully, as if he was fascinated with the forested area far beyond the walls of the well-maintained inn. Turning around, the quiet man was revealed in the errant light of a single lamp that shone from the corner table of the room. Weirdly, the illumination from the lamp was made less bright by a huge splash of dark liquid covering most of its lampshade, a fact that made the provided light orangish and splotchy.

The bartender stood there, thinking and surveying the bed under the off-color light. Formerly a somewhat overweight and dour man, his face would now have appeared calm if not for his savage and otherworldly appearance. His features were angled and fierce, with the same white and oily appearance as the orderly in the clinic. His lips were pursed around enormous, sharp teeth, and the lines of his heavy brows swept back in a menacing arc. His eyes, dead-looking and wholly black, were without orbs.

Pacing to the bed, the wildly altered bartender, clothed in a baggy long shirt and loose-fitting sweatpants that mostly hid his ferocious muscles, gazed down with an almost sorrowful frown at his recent work. Cindi Kauppila, the happy and rather chatty woman from the ferry and cafe, lay sprawled across the white covers below him.

On her back, Cindi's face stared to the side, like she was trying to peer out the window. Her throat was torn out, with two deep gouges furrowed into her robust neckline. To complete the tragic appearance, her too-white skin appeared almost like doughy putty that had been molded with sharp claws, severing her carotid arteries and causing her to bleed out from the gaping and deep wounds.

Blood pooled all around Cindi, soaking into the blanket in streaks, and several rivulets of her life force leaked off the side of the bed to the hardwood floor below. This was the source of the dripping sound in the quiet room, and her large body's blood capacity ensured there would be plenty more to disturb the silence for a considerable time.

On the floor next to the queen-sized bed, right next to the pool of her accumulating blood, lay her husband, Aaron. He was also silent and quite dead, but the cause of his demise was less messy, as his neck was bent to the side, causing his death-stare to face away from his oddly canted body. The savage nature that ended his life was readily apparent from his neck bones, which had been so shattered that several shards of their broken remnants poked through the skin of his neckline.

Extending his clawed hand, which was covered in a sheen of plentiful gore, the bartender appeared sad and dispirited for the moment. Running the sharp end of one black nail across Cindi's cheek, it was as if the creature was saying goodbye to an old and cherished friend, like he was heartbroken that the tourist had died. The silent moment stretched for some time, and the unhurried monster's movements showed some sincerity of his feelings for the deceased woman.

With a sigh coming out like an inhuman rasp, much like that of a beleaguered polar bear, the bartender suddenly rammed two of its long claws into Cindi's eyes. Driving his talons into her brain, he used the power and leverage in his long muscular arm to lift and drag her from the bed. The dead weight of her body thudded against the floor, and without slowing himself, the bartender yanked the corpse towards the door, using her head in a bowling-ball-like fashion as he pulled along her substantial girth.

When the creature exited the room, it continued to drag her, leaving a wide smear of her blood across the shiny wooden floor as it moved to the staircase. The hallway around the creature was pleasant and bright, full of attractive paintings of nature and open seas, making the violent movements of the strange monster a horrifying sight in the otherwise sedate area.

As the man-monster moved down the stairs, it did so with little effort, despite the size and ungainly effort of hauling a person that weighed more than three hundred pounds. The enterprise of transporting Cindi took on the appearance of a carefree person taking the garbage out, but in this case, the garbageman now had little regard for the humanity of his refuse.

After leaving Cindi at the bottom of the steps, the bartender retraced his steps, and coming back to the bedroom, stuck his claws into Aaron's head the same way. When he also hefted and lugged the unfortunate husband to his place alongside Cindi, sloshing the dead flesh in jerking movements as it thumped down the steps, the creature finally lined up the corpses at the bottom of the staircase.

Taking his time, the creature arranged the dead duo in peaceful postures, much like he was displaying them in an old western photo, just as if they were infamous gunfighters that had been slain and were now to be shown off to the world.

After staring at the deceased couple for some time, the bartender nodded and was happy with what he saw. Stepping forward, he now stuck Cindi again through her now-mutilated eye sockets, and gathering himself, kicked the door open behind him with his heel as he emerged to the reception area at the front of the inn.

As he pulled his bloody and unwieldy victim into the front reception room, and presumably on his way to some destination outside the motel, the sound of the front door clicking shut and a SCHIIKING of metal came from behind the bartender.

Spinning around, the creature was surprised, and the more-than-human bartender struck a combat pose with outstretched black claws as it faced the entrance to the quiet inn. Its pupilless eyes went wider, showing a bit of apprehension at the sudden intrusion into his strange efforts with the dead Finnish husband and wife.

Karl stood there, and the military man had an astonished and disbelieving look on his face from no more than twenty feet away. Like a man witnessing the first arrival of predatory aliens from outer space, he blinked slowly, hoping this was some bizarre ghost that would soon disappear in a wisp of smoke.

But this hideous enemy was no spirit, no figment of his bruised memories or his less-than-perfect mental state. The creature met Karl's eyes with the unmistakable appearance of one accustomed to fighting, and to make matters more worrisome, winning. With eyes that suddenly flashed a yellow and wicked tinge, this beast oozed confidence from every pore of its grotesque features.

Taking a step back and collecting himself, Karl held out his enormous military blade, dropped his sheath, and faced off with the former bar worker. Glancing at the dead woman on the ground behind his bizarre opponent, a disgusted grimace came over Karl's resolute features. What was in front of him couldn't be real, but the malicious gaze of this sudden enemy was striking and intense, making the horrid thing's features more of a reality than anything he'd ever witnessed.

As Karl prepared to do battle with the creature, he tightened his grip on the cold-steel KA-BAR knife and held up his left arm at a defensive angle. Keeping his weight in a firm and balanced stance, he positioned his feet and was poised to react at the proper angles for both effective movement and close combat. Letting himself relax in his core, his long-trained muscle memory allowed him to get ready for what came next.

Keeping his voice low, Karl spat out a question, though he knew there wouldn't be a reply. "What…the fuck…are you?"

#

The extensive and attractive estate was a wonder of modern construction and impeccable design. The two-story residence, built with sturdy pillars buttressing its clean-lined concrete exterior, embodied Scandinavian style and understated elegance.

The oblong main structure, its exterior fronted with coverings of occasional light-red bricks to enhance its whitish color, ran on top of a hill, the highest elevation on the entire island. Below it, in the pale light of moon-brightened darkness, gentle whitecaps on the surrounding lake offered a pleasant backdrop to the calm nighttime environment.

From inside, whoever was resident in the home could easily gaze over the rolling water's surface—as well as the surrounding land—and ensure that any prospective visitors to the mansion would be known well in advance.

A large and green lawn, filled with occasional Renaissance-style statues, encircled the residence, and coupled with solar lighting that illuminated pleasant pathways through several gardens and numerous hedges, provided a sophisticated ambiance to the sprawling property.

Covering several acres, the entire estate was designed with the best and most expensive tastes, such that even a Silicon Valley billionaire would have found the surroundings difficult to replicate in all its well-heeled glory. With a multi-level roofline topped by gray tiles and shiny windows set in harmony across twenty thousand square feet of immaculate habitation, the entire property showed an owner who knew how to present his wealth and prestige in a classy and endearing fashion.

Walking determinedly down one of the well-lit paths, Stanislav approached the steps to the main entry of the formidable home. His face was a mix of consternation and grave concern as he focused on the door.

Such a look and bearing were something that Stanislav had perfected over several centuries, always making sure he was prepared for the worst by expecting it, and he made it a point to flash an indifferent grimace to the two armed guards standing to either side of the heavy wooden door, barring entry to the house.

These men, dressed in dark suits and outfitted with submachine guns and wary stares, nodded respectfully. The older guard, with a half-bald head frosted in gray stubble, spoke carefully into a wrist-mounted communication device.

The massive oak door, an ancient-looking portal with a strange insignia of a sword held by a bloodied and gauntleted hand, clicked open, and Stanislav stepped through it without further deliberation.

Facing back outwards, the rather serious-looking men reassumed their probing stares of the quiet and dark area around the house, showing the look of individuals that took their security duties seriously.

Inside, the clean walls of the home were no less attractive. Paintings were spaced at sufficient intervals, showing views of stormy seas and snowy mountaintops, that they offered just the right balance of decor without the hindrance of being overwhelming or flashy. As with a pretty woman that shouldn't use too much makeup, or a handsome man that shouldn't reveal his material wealth too overtly—lest either be considered arrogant or overly showy—the point of design in expensive houses was to know when something was too much and to pull back before crossing into tackiness.

As Stanislav made his way down a hallway and past a piano room with various sculptures of long-forgotten Roman statesmen, his mood darkened. His day had been a normal one, at least as normal as could be expected for one who was the right-hand man to Jacob Aminoff, but it was now to become increasingly stressful.

Striding to a large door flanked by two further guards, Stanislav tapped once on the white and heavy barrier to Jacob's workplace. The thud of his firm rap indicated the thick and protective nature of the entrance, showing that Jacob, in all things, was careful to make certain he was protected from unwanted outsiders.

"Enter," came the muffled-voice response, and taking a considered breath, Stanislav pushed inside.

Jacob's working area to administer the island's affairs was surprisingly austere, especially considering his otherwise opulent house. The walls were filled with simple prints of Rembrandt and Van Gogh, while a rather long wooden table ran the length of an attached living space. That area, clean and open, had a large bay window looking over the garage and a grassy area to the front of the enormous home.

The floor was an expensive and deep-grained wood of a variety that must have mandated the early death of some priceless old-growth tree. Several 75-inch flat televisions were spaced throughout the enormous set of open, attached rooms, and international news programs in several languages droned quietly from each of their screens.

A well-appointed kitchen with a large black marble island lay next to Jacob's personal headquarters, and specialist pans for cooking hung from the area over the high-priced stove that was part of its center. The effect of the large space was to show the area as a self-contained inner core of the larger facility, with everything Jacob would need, from extra bathrooms to plentiful accommodation for guests, within easy reach.

Jacob was staring out a side window, one that held a beautiful view of the shoreline to their south, and in the far distance across the lake could be seen the lights of the mid-sized city of Jönköping. He turned carefully to look at Stanislav, and his eyes took in his subordinate with some curiosity.

Motioning his head, Jacob waited for Stanislav to sit on a leather sofa near an alcove by a window farthest away from the kitchen. The mild smile on Jacob's lips wilted a bit as he noted Stanislav's controlled and dour mood.

When Stanislav had taken his seat, Jacob began speaking in Russian, the language of all their personal interactions. "Stan, do tell me the news. I hope that all is well with our plans?"

Stanislav shook his head, making sure to avoid eye contact. "It's very bad. We moved on them, at least some of them, when they went to the clinic."

"And?"

"Radomir took them by surprise but was slain in the fight," Stanislav said, and his expression became mournful. "He managed to kill one before—."

Jacob muttered something under his breath, and his expression, always controlled and focused, grew exasperated. "Radomir is dead? How did they…?"

Stanislav stayed quiet as Jacob's confused voice drifted off. Not accustomed to relaying such news, Stanislav glanced up and finally met Jacob's gaze. "One of the group was armed. He…we…weren't prepared for that."

Collecting himself, Jacob thought for a moment. His was not a face that often betrayed surprise or grief, and in a few moments, he mastered these emotions as he considered the developing situation. Lacing his fingers behind his back, he turned and walked the length of the room, taking his time to move his gaze outside and over the detached garage that housed all his precious automobiles.

Stopping at the end of the table, Jacob's voice was monotoned. "Continue, please."

"Natalia saw everything at the clinic. Radomir would have easily eliminated them all but was shot down by the tall one in the group. We are recovering him now and…cleaning the area."

Nodding, Jacob turned and walked near the couch. Motioning to a decanter with expensive bourbon inside, Stanislav responded to the offer with a polite shake of his head.

"You said that one of their party was killed?" asked Jacob.

"Yes, he will be processed in accordance with your wishes," replied Stanislav, but he didn't appear enthusiastic about that small victory.

"Well, at least we have that," Jacob said, and he moved to pour himself a drink of whiskey. Taking his time, he used small metal tongs to place one ice cube in a glass from a chilled container, then splashed some of the fragrant liquid inside. After raising it to take a sip, he grew thoughtful. "How long has it been since we lost…a member of the family?"

"Fifty-two years, Jacob. More than a half-century since one of us…perished."

Holding his glass up, Jacob stared into the rusty-looking liquid. As he focused, his expression became worried, and his dark-brown eyes hardened into a scowl. "Stan, I want to apologize for this. This turn of events and loss of Radomir are my fault. I took a risk to fill our collective pantries with food, and this…tragedy is the result."

"Jacob, you couldn't have known," said Stanislav, trying to sound reassuring, but he mostly came across as anxious.

Shaking his head, Jacob stepped away from Stanislav and moved again to the window with the expansive view of the lake. "Yes, but we have still lost one of our own, and this is a trade I never would have been willing to make."

After working through his peculiar grief, the type that seemed to apply to considerations of his own men but not their victims, Jacob changed the subject. Raising his voice, his intense eyes flitted over the dark water below. "Have we heard from Ivan at the inn yet?"

"Not yet. I'll let you know as soon—."

"Then we may assume he has failed, as well," Jacob continued, and his voice became contemplative as he ran through in his mind the prospect of an unexpected and skillful foe, right here on their own island, in their place of refuge from the wider world. "Our prey appears to be far more dangerous than we imagined. We mustn't underestimate them again."

Pacing carefully back to the couch, Jacob set his glass on a coaster on the glass table in front of Stanislav. Looking carefully at his friend, he spoke in a low and considered tone, one that was full of warning. "Send four of our best fighters to the inn. Have them bring justice for our family's loss. Make certain they show no mercy to these 'people.' We can only hope Ivan has already done so, without injury."

Nodding, Stanislav rose and made his way toward the door. Preoccupied with his orders and plans, he was somewhat surprised when Jacob stopped his departure by raising his hand to preempt his departure.

"Stan, before you go, please keep something in mind," said Jacob, his tone and demeanor becoming even more serious. "A wise man, if he indeed was a man, once said that in order to overcome his enemy, the sheep would lie down with the lion."

Getting the biblical reference, Stanislav nodded and waited.

"For us to win…in this world of men," continued Jacob, "we must live with the sheep—without their knowledge. Let us be certain they remain ignorant of our presence."

Considering Jacob's words, Stanislav nodded again. Pulling the door open, he strode from the room, his mind full of what was next in their suddenly worrisome situation.

Moments later, Stanislav exited the building and walked down the pathway near the brightly lit garage. From his window, Jacob watched him go, and as his outline disappeared into the dim night, Jacob spoke worriedly to himself. "Be careful."

Chapter Nine

The ferocious creature was the first to attack, striking out and raking its deadly claws forward. Its speed was such that it seemed a blur in the sparsely lit front of the inn, and Karl had to pivot and throw himself out of the way to avoid being torn across the face and abdomen.

The bartender, surprised at coming up short in his bid to quickly eviscerate Karl, glared at him. The black and savage eyes of the monster showed no feeling or inclination towards caution, but it now moved carefully as it looked for the best way to defeat this upstart man.

Karl abruptly lunged ahead, slashing his knife in slanted thrusts towards the beast's midsection and important organs. The bartender responded by angling away from the determined attacks, then tearing its talons in a wide arc across the smaller man's limbs.

The jagged wounds from the assaults on Karl were not deep, but now blood flowed from his muscled forearms, dripping through the wool fabric of his long, dark-green sweater. The creature had drawn first blood.

Pulling back and trying to balance himself, Karl's eyes narrowed as he recognized the danger of his precarious position. His enemy was stronger and faster, as well as having more means to inflict damage than Karl's own single blade. He would have to land a killing strike inside its rapid attacks if he was to prevail in the uneven battle, but that would be no easy feat, considering what he faced.

Any man who carried a knife for defense knew that using blades against a similarly armed opponent, not to mention this raging and deadly creature, was a difficult endeavor in the best of times. The truth about bladed combat, without armor or means to easily defend yourself, meant that to win would require getting stuck at least a few times, so the important thing was to protect your own vital organs until you had the chance to skewer your adversary with a lethal thrust.

The bartender growled a wild, animal-like battle cry and lunged forward, swiping his arms in a flurry of savage attacks. Karl retreated under the deluge of swings, deftly avoiding the worst of the blows—but still taking stinging hits to his arms in the brutal process. Blood now seeped freely from Karl's wounds, making him grimace as he circled and looked for his opportunity.

In an explosion of violence, the next moments of melee combat moved in rapid succession. More slashes from the creature created trickling gouges on Karl's head, shoulders, and arms, while Karl's thrusts across the bizarre limbs and torso of the creature caused only superficial wounds. Karl's attempts at feints to open up the bartender's defense were not working, and it appeared the beast was falling into a comfortable rhythm as it measured Karl's potential and fighting style.

Two times Karl was slammed against the wall with jarring force. On each occasion, he barely recovered from the impact before being swarmed and finished off by his larger opponent's body.

As time wore on, Karl began to heave for air. Out-mastered in combat, he also lacked the stamina to endure a protracted fight with the bigger creature. Struggling for breath, his bloodied arms drooped lower, and he blinked blood away that dripped from his wounded forehead and scalp.

The emotionless eyes of the creature went wide in expectation. Clearly, the beast saw its chance to end the fight, and in a blinding rush, it threw itself forward, seeking to end the hand-to-hand exchange in a merciless strike.

Karl's tactics of playing weaker than he actually was had worked, and as the bartender flung itself on him, he ducked inside his opponent's guard. As the creature rained slashes on his shoulders and back, Karl thrust his blade up and rammed the knife into its midsection.

While squeals of base anger and surprised agony bellowed from his adversary, Karl used his lower leverage to push the monster back, and again and again he pierced its bloodied torso with jolting thrusts. Crunching against the wall, Karl drove the metal blade upward, forcing the knife deep into the taller figure's fleshy neck.

Screaming and in the fight of his life, Karl continually jabbed his weapon forward, all the while receiving horrible and deep cuts from claws into numerous parts of his wounded physique. The struggling duo, looking like a stuck-together mass of humanoids bathed in gore and wounds, clutched at each other on the wall in an escalating crescendo to their dance of violence.

Out of other options and with his energy waning, Karl thrust his blade up a final time, cupping his hand around the hilt and using all his strength to shove it through the creature's flailing defense. Ramming through the clammy and moist flesh underneath the creature's chin, the knife punched through the bottom of his horrid enemy's toothy mouth. The length of the weapon plunged up and into its skull in one explosive, quick motion.

Instantly rag-dolled by the mortal stab, the bartender's arms went wide and convulsed, its fearsome mouth locked open, and its body began to slide down the wall under Karl's pressing force. Karl, gravely wounded himself, with a host of frightening gashes across his body and head, slid down with it, having expended all his remaining energy in the barrage of attacks.

As the creature slumped to the side, Karl fought to stay awake, to overcome the sudden need for rest. Instead, darkness began to take him, but as he passed out, he muttered a small claim of victory to the bestial corpse he leaned against. "Got you, fucker."

Chapter Ten

Liam peered down, dread and incomprehension filling his troubled features. Overwhelmed, he stared up to the ceiling's wooden beams, then ran shaking hands over his face and through his dark hair. His temperament was caught in an odd moment of aimless sorrow and astonishment, like he was waiting to be awakened from a dream that had come apart at the seams and morphed into a horrid and inescapable reality.

Below him, Aaron and Cindi Kauppila were laid out on a fresh blanket, one that Liam had fetched from an unoccupied guest room in the motel. Out of respect for their dignity, he had covered their faces with another small blanket, but the bloody hands of the couple were just visible outside the covering, their clenched fingers locked in testament to their sudden and terrifying deaths.

To the side of the couple lay the body of the abhorrent bartender. His distended corpse, with a wicked and dangerous appearance even in death, was not positioned in a way that evoked respect. Instead, his whitish skin and fearsome appearance, full of bloody gouges across his exposed abdomen and freakish features, stared up and to the side. The odd death-pose of the beast, slain and sprawled at such a weird angle, made him appear like a fictional wax figure set up to be ogled by curious onlookers.

Finally able to collect himself, Liam gazed over at Karl, who was propped against the wood-paneled wall to the right. Unconscious, Karl was being worked on by Mattias and Lars, whose quick movements, along with Karl's plentiful bleeding, suggested his numerous injuries were serious.

At the back of the room, near the hallway leading to the cafe where they had recently celebrated their short vacation, Alex and Lilly sat on two chairs. Their eyes, open and haunted, glanced around the room in a confused daze.

To their side, Maria was also sitting in a chair, but from her appearance, even though awake, she was less aware of her surroundings. Her vacant stare peered at nothing in particular on the blank wall ahead. Her head, still wrapped in Lars' makeshift bandage, covered her wounds, and no further blood had soaked into it from the deep scratches across her pale skin and matted scalp. Lilly had her arm protectively around her friend, but Maria didn't appear to notice the caring gesture.

"Could someone please tell me," asked Liam, and he paused and pointed to the arranged bodies, "what the hell happened?"

Speaking from his chair, Alex spoke in a soft voice, and his bearing was defensive, as if he had become uncomfortable with himself. "We were in our room and heard all these crazy sounds…screams and grunting. We barricaded the door and decided to wait for help. Like you, our phones didn't work, so we thought it best…"

As Alex's words faded off, Lilly nodded in agreement at the tactics she and her husband used to survive the violence from the bartender. But she also glanced uncomfortably at the dead Finnish couple, appearing worried they may have been able to help the tourists if they had chosen their actions differently.

In response, Liam nodded his understanding and patted Lilly on the shoulder. Moving over, he peered down at Maria with empathetic eyes. When she didn't look up to meet his gaze, he crouched down and gave her a long hug. Unfortunately, his efforts didn't seem to change the dynamic of grief filling her crestfallen face, and she didn't return the embrace.

As he pulled carefully away, he tried to offer encouragement and sympathy for Maria's loss with a simple, reassuring smile. Liam was no counselor, but basic human logic told him that people, themselves included, needed close friends around in times of such horrible trauma.

Standing from where he was bent over Karl, Mattias cleared his throat and walked near the rest of the group. His tone was grave, but underneath the heartache was some optimism. "OK,

I think Karl is going to make it. He's got more wounds than I thought possible, but he seems to be hanging in there."

"Thank God," replied Liam, but after an uncomfortable moment, he frowned at the wider implications of such a pronouncement. "For that, anyway."

While Lars continued with first aid on Karl, Liam motioned towards the corner, out of earshot of the traumatized Maria, Lilly, and Alex. Nodding his quiet agreement to avoid upsetting them more, Mattias paced over to chat with Liam near the welcome desk at the front of the inn.

"So, what could this be?" asked Liam, unsure of himself and glancing over to the rest of the group. "Is it the end of the world? Space aliens?"

Mattias chuckled and shook his head. "I dunno, Liam…there's certainly something going on I don't understand."

"You think?" asked Liam, and after a sarcastic pause, his face grew serious and thoughtful. "OK, let's address what we do know. One…these creatures can look normal, and two, they can act normal. The orderly at the clinic was chilling out at one moment, showing us a regular mortician vibe, then wham, he's throwing us all against the walls like toddlers. Here, this dude was serving us drinks a while ago, and now he looks like Nosferatu's cousin."

"Which means," responded Mattias, nodding as he absorbed that line of reasoning, "anyone on this island can be one."

"Exactly, but why attack us now? Why attack us at all?"

"I have no idea, Liam. But there's no cell reception, even though there certainly was earlier…both here and at the clinic. It's got to be a coordinated attack by someone, or something?"

Liam, frustrated and confused, answered with a shake of his head. Grappling with their situation, there appeared no good explanation for how they ended up in their current predicament, as well as no good prospects for what should come next. The chances for their survival hinged on understanding and overcoming unknown and perhaps unknowable threats.

Propping Karl in the corner with a blanket and pillow, Lars stood up from his medical duties. Their large friend, bound up with cloth-sheet bandages, remained unconscious.

Thinking for a moment, Lars chewed on his lip as he considered something. After walking over to Liam and Mattias, he spoke with a curious voice, while also making certain it was only them that could hear him. "What happened to the innkeeper? What was her name, Evelyn, right?"

With that, all three of them turned to look behind the motel's reception desk. A single dark-wood door was there, and it suddenly appeared forbidding in the ensuing silence.

Mattias slowly drew his pistol and waved it toward the door. "She's either dead or…one of them?"

Meeting gazes, the friends went quiet. Walking back to Karl, Lars picked up Karl's knife for self-defense, while Liam searched the lobby area for any other object to use as a weapon. Grabbing a rather unconvincing broken leg of a chair, he hefted it and frowned at its less-than-imposing size and weight. It wouldn't strike fear in the heart of an enemy, sure, but it was certainly better than nothing.

Moving behind the counter, Mattias stepped carefully toward the door, while Lars and Liam followed close behind, their faces a mixture of worry and expectation. As an armed investigator, Mathias was trained and competent as he prepared to seek out the motel desk agent, but Lars and Liam, looking unready and awkward, appeared a bit ridiculous as they crept forward.

Gripping the doorknob, it turned easily, and the door creaked open. Rearing back, Mattias kicked it fully open, and moving quickly, rushed through the doorway and leveled his pistol, scanning for whatever awaited them on the other side.

The spacious apartment he hurried into was pleasant and clean. A well-appointed kitchen was attached to a huge front room, and in the kitchen area were arranged polished and metallic appliances and a table set upon an expensive tiled floor. The walls held several family photos and prints of animals in the wild, evincing a certain natural-park-like motif to the eating space.

To the side was a comfortable living room with a huge flat-screen TV and several shelves of oriental-style sculptures on each side of it. Furniture there constituted of a matching black-leather couch and loveseat near a glass coffee table, all arranged on a pricey white shag carpet. In the far corner of the area, a dark hallway led to what must have been bedrooms and a toilet.

Evelyn sat on the loveseat, and on her lap was a family album. Not paying attention to the newcomers, she continued staring at photos of her and her family in various outdoor environments.

Wary of what they were walking into, Mattias, Liam, and Lars flooded carefully into the open room around her.

Looking up, Evelyn offered the friends a mournful smile. Her eyes were puffy and red as she spoke. "Took you long enough. I was beginning to wonder if you'd ever visit me."

Advancing near to the table, Mattias peered down his open gunsight, fixing the point of aim on Evelyn's forehead. "Lady, if you move in any way that I don't like, you're going to be shot."

Not looking surprised or particularly intimidated, Evelyn pursed her lips and raised her hands in mock surrender. "You're the boss."

Liam crept in from the side, moving to a vantage point where he could make out the main photo under the glossy cover of the album on her lap. In it were Evelyn's husband and son, both of whom he had already seen in the photo frames on the hallway wall near the small restaurant.

Stopping, Liam held up his wooden furniture leg and focused on Evelyn's sad eyes. "Are you one of those things?"

Evelyn shook her head, a resentful flush coming over her face. "No, most certainly not. But, if you want to know about them, get the rest of your friends together. I'm not going to say everything twice."

After blinking away her sadness, Evelyn's face appeared strange as she looked at each of the people surrounding her, like she had suddenly come to a new and life-altering decision. Something like relief, mixed with controlled despair, was evident as she nodded at the looming strangers. "This is like nothing you've ever heard before, so you'll want to keep an open mind."

#

The front room of the inn now had a decidedly isolated feel to it, making it seem like a modern version of the doomed frontier fortress in Texas, the Alamo. Most of the lobby furniture, including a long blue-velvet couch from an alcove near the front, were now piled in front of the business' entrance, while tables and chairs from the connected restaurant cluttered the hallway to prevent entry to the motel from that direction.

To the back of the inn, the entrance was also barricaded with bed frames and assorted knickknacks, including a large exercise bike wedged against the outer door frame. The party had spent their recent time ensuring no easy access would be found into the now-cluttered location, with the result that the whole area now resembled a hastily assembled flea market.

Evelyn sat in the middle of the lobby, where she was tied in a chair where she had spent the better part of her life working as a receptionist and host. Cords and packing tape affixed her legs and arms to the sturdiest chair that could be found, and several of the impatient friends surrounded and looked down at her with varying degrees of suspicion and open hostility.

Evelyn didn't seem bothered by the attention, nor was she openly worried about her current status as a prisoner of the besieged tourists. Moving her gaze to each of the party members, she raised her eyebrows in anticipation for the upcoming interrogation, like she wanted the group to get on with it.

"OK, talk, Evelyn," said Liam, doing his best to sound reasonable in this most unreasonable of times. "When you're through, give me a reason we shouldn't kill you. We lost our friend, and you didn't do shit to stop it."

Evelyn's facial muscles tightened as she took in Liam's open threat, like she had just swallowed a bite of rancid food. Keeping her voice measured, she didn't like the mention of her potential execution at the end of this questioning process. "They tell me nothing of their plans, and I have no input at all with what they do. I host tourists for a living, and they've never done anything like this—at least while I've been here."

"They?" asked Mattias, and he moved to her other side, forcing Evelyn to rotate her head to keep him in her field of view. The effect of not being able to keep everyone in direct line of sight, especially while she was tied up and helpless, caused an even deeper frown to form on her pale complexion.

Plumbing new depths of discomfort, Evelyn sighed. "To start with, these creatures have been here on this island," and she pointed to Liam, the only American in the group, "longer than his country has existed. They're as much a part of the world as we are."

Liam looked at his friends, starting with the groggy Karl, who seemed to be coming awake near the wall, to Mattias, who merely shrugged at the mention of murderous and unknown creatures in their midst, as if to say, *better than space aliens, anyway.*

Attempting to find her mental footing in this uneven and multi-partied inquisition, Evelyn bit back her fears. She tried coming across as nonplussed as she spoke in a matter-of-fact tone, like she was describing a boring history lesson pertaining to the Industrial Age. "They've been here in Sweden for three hundred years—give or take."

From the far corner, Maria stood from her chair, a place where she had been perched for some time, silent and unmoving—even as the group had been setting up their defense of the motel. Everyone now looked surprised, though their happiness at seeing her awake was offset by concern for the malice radiating from her expression.

Maria stepped closer to Evelyn, and her eyes narrowed as she focused down. "Sounds like bullshit. You better do better than that, or my husband's death will seem like child's play compared to the pain I will bring to your…pathetic life."

Evelyn, evidently not ready for such open aggression from a new source, nevertheless showed a defiant streak as she met Maria's stern gaze. "Ah…more threats…lovely. Listen, I've lived with evil most of my life, so please drop the Rambo routine."

Maria stepped closer, and looking around for a weapon, appeared ready to make good on her threat. Mattias, flashing her an understanding smile, stepped in between the seated woman and his friend, politely stopping any rash action on Maria's part.

For some time, Maria thought through her options, and the area was silent as each friend gave her heartfelt and sympathetic looks. Finally, she collected herself and moved back to her chair, where she sat quietly. But her expression, the unflinching one that harbored a vicious desire for vengeance, did not recede. If anything, her look of open hatred was made worse by the verbal exchange with Evelyn.

In turn, Evelyn now appeared less sure of her prospects with the group. Still, it was too late to turn back, so she plunged ahead. "You people should know that you have stepped into a place that few people know of—an island filled with nightmares. And the nightmares want you as food."

Awkward silence filled the room. Each friend, momentarily plunging into their chaotic thoughts, absorbed the information with searching eyes and baffled expressions. Like a puzzling theorem that made no sense to new students in an advanced math class, they were collectively confounded by this new and bizarre problem.

Liam was the first to respond. "They want to eat us…why?"

Evelyn shook her head, showing her frustration at the pace of the conversation. "Because they need human flesh to survive. It has to be recently killed—but not too fresh. And they have to prepare it somehow. They never age, so the food does something to keep them youthful. Whatever and however they are made, human tissue allows them to remain vigorous. You are what you eat, as they like to say, something about taking in the life force of living people."

As one, the party was revolted, and now Alex and Lilly also stood to join the ranks of the hostile. With her narration not winning her any friends, it looked like Evelyn was the one to soon be eaten.

"They don't give me all the details, and I wouldn't want to know, even if they offered," exclaimed Evelyn, growing even more defensive. "I've never seen them hunt anyone local, anyway."

Staring down, Liam was exasperated. "So, we're dinner for these monsters? What about you, why aren't your teeth sticking out?"

"Because about eighty percent of the island is normal, I think. We are kind of like their treasured pets; they take care of us completely," replied Evelyn, speaking normally—as if such an arrangement wasn't all that odd. "They see to all our needs."

Rubbing his less-than-robust facial stubble, Liam shook his head. "You…serve as pets to a group of cannibal creatures? You sound like a great person…Charles Manson would have been so proud."

"They never feed off islanders," replied Evelyn, raising her voice. "And the people here get whatever they want. Safety, money, whatever—,"

"Well, that's convenient," interrupted Lars, and moving from the front entrance, where he had been carefully watching the area outside, he joined the circle of companions around Evelyn. "It's like a collection of lunatics surrounding a group of monsters. What could go wrong?"

Evelyn met Lars' sarcasm with a considered nod. "Most of the people here are fanatically loyal to them. The cops, the public works, they're all aligned with them. Especially their leader, Jacob. I'm not justifying anything; I'm just telling you how it is."

Remaining in her chair, Maria leaned forward, her glowering expression growing ever angrier. "So, my husband is being eaten as we speak by ancient monsters that…have people as pets and walk around, acting like normal humans?"

Hesitating, Evelyn thought a moment, then nodded. Glancing around the room, she looked wary, as if she worried this might be her last living action.

With a frustrated grunt, Liam threw his chair leg against the wall, where it careened with a thump and landed unbroken in the corner of the room. The fact that nobody present seemed to be overly worried about his little temper tantrum didn't dampen his aggravation, and he raised his voice at Evelyn. "What do we do now? How do we get out of here? And be very specific, if you can manage that."

Evelyn waited a moment, clearly unsure if there would be any more thrown items. When there were none, she took a deep breath and spoke lower, her voice assuming a more confident tone. "You have more time before more will come to kill you.

But it won't be just one this time; Jacob is known to be thorough in everything he does. We once had a fishing derby on Drottning Lake in the center of the island, and he planted so many fish there that the kids would have caught their fill with bare hooks. When he decides something, he leaves nothing to chance."

From her left, Lars moved suddenly close to Evelyn. Holding up Karl's borrowed knife, he leaned in and uttered his words through clenched teeth. "I'm still not getting why you're talking to us now, you evil…woman. Why the change of heart, after being such a 'treasured pet.' What do you want now?"

"When my son drowned six months ago, money and comfort stopped being enough to pay me off," replied Evelyn, and her eyes teared up at the boy's mention. "I can't be around this…place, with those things, anymore. I need a normal life away from this."

Maria huffed and shook her head, sounding skeptical. "So now you want off the island? Out of this nightmare?"

Evelyn nodded without hesitation, suddenly appearing servile as she panned her head to each of the companions. "I can help you. I'll report by radio that most of you are dead, and the survivors are in the reception area. Your only chance, and it won't be a big one, is to catch them by surprise when they come."

The party took their time for a response. Liam looked from one pal to another, trying to estimate the support for their next move. Eventually, all but Maria nodded hesitantly at Evelyn's proposed course.

Shaking her head, Maria stood carefully, making clear her position with a hateful glare towards Evelyn. As she spoke, her face reddened and her jaw quivered, making her words halting and full of grief. "So now we have to kill some monsters, and this bitch gets to live, even though she knew about everything? After she let Johan get killed?"

From behind everyone, Karl leaned up and tried to stand. Grunting, he came to one knee, gradually rose, and managed to balance himself by keeping his hand against the wall. Considering his injuries, the rest of the group was surprised, and they moved their shocked gazes between each other as they tried to determine if he should even be allowed to move on his own.

Karl nodded with a grimace, showing a weary grin that implied *it's only a scratch*. He then pointed to the corpse of the bartender and muttered in an emotionless voice. "She could've run back to her bosses when I killed smiley over there. So, we better at least keep her with us until we can find a way off this island."

Taking his hand off the wall, Karl shook his head and, pushing fatigue away from his mind, gradually walked toward the others. His steps were not carefree or easy-to-make, as each focused foot placed forward was slow and painful, but neither did he look to be at death's door from his fight with the creature. For those around him, the fact that he was awake and moving, much less talking, continued to make everyone astonished—even Evelyn.

"In the meantime," Karl continued, his voice and bruised face growing more alive and earnest, like he had suddenly taken charisma lessons from Sean Connery, "we need to get ready for them. Anything can be killed; we just have to be willing to do whatever it takes to win."

#

Over the next several hours, the group worked to prepare themselves for the formidable and ferocious beasts they soon expected to arrive. Such was the breadth of danger these creatures offered, with their inhuman strength, fearfully fast reflexes, and focused and violent capabilities, that the friends moved with panicked and rushed movements.

In the dim garage of the inn, which was located to the back of the establishment and contained Evelyn's not-often-used Volvo S60 car, Karl conferred with Liam, talking and motioning to a range of gasoline containers on the floor. Pointing to the largest of the petrol cans, Liam nodded and bent down to insert a large rag into its top.

Contented with their proposed course of action, Karl moved carefully behind Liam, where he peeled off a long strip from a roll of duct tape. Stooping down, he carefully bound together several of the other cannisters holding the fuel. Though injured, Karl moved with methodical patience and didn't appear overly bothered by the limitations of his recent injuries.

Elsewhere, in Evelyn's kitchen, Maria and Lilly had set out a collection of cutlery, from sharp and expensive-looking steak knives to sturdy and broad cleavers, small paring blades, and a host of chefs' knives. Testing each of the metal cutting tools, the ladies practiced driving the knife points into a wooden cutting board to test for proper cutting edges. Encouraged by the heft and sharpness of the utensils, they appeared hopeful and motivated.

Digging through a closet in one of the upstairs rooms, Alex sorted through and cast aside several items such as a bowling ball, old fishing rods, and mismatched boxes of clothing. A grin suddenly filled his face as he worked his way through the last of the junk, and nodding, he reached to the far end of the dark space. Withdrawing an aluminum baseball bat, he held it up approvingly as he estimated its length and potential to bludgeon an opponent.

Stepping back into the bedroom, Alex took several practice swipes with the bat, smiling to himself like a contented kid. He showed substantial agility with the item, evidently from having some experience with the sport in his not-too-distant past. Whomever was on the receiving end of his violent attacks would be quickly incapacitated, or even better, instantly killed when he caved their heads in.

Near an unused fireplace in front of the inn, Mattias and Lars had moved a table into the area underneath the main chandelier. On its surface were several items that could be used for self-defense, from a collection of fireplace pokers to some dark iron rods of indeterminate purpose. These things had been found in an old workshop in a small building to the back of the motel, and they were now arranged to allow a range of choices for the party to defend themselves when the time came.

Reaching to the side, Lars picked up a solid wooden stud, and in the old lumber's end were driven several nails, allowing the item to be used as a makeshift spiked mace. The sharp and long nails, bent in odd directions to ensure they wouldn't dislodge when impacting an enemy, made up-close combat seem like a winnable option. Lars smiled as he turned it over in his hands.

Lars almost felt sorry for the enemies he intended to make pay for Johan's death, yet he also felt enthusiastic for the opportunity to bash their ugly faces into pulp. Grinning at the thought, he glanced over at several more pieces of wood leaning against the hearth next to a bucket of nails. This was not the only spiked and blunt weapon he and Mattias intended to make, and the process of constructing weapons to maim and kill their strange adversaries was therapeutic for the trauma already inflicted by the bizarre monsters.

Some time later, after each of the party had done their part to assemble and prepare, the party stood together again in the front lobby area. Evelyn was tied up in a far-back bedroom, while the rest of the group stood and waited near the reception desk, the same place the friends first arrived for their quick holiday jaunt a mere few hours before.

Now, their entire prospects and hopes for the rest of their lives had changed, and looking somber and anxious, the companions moved their gazes towards the front entrance. It wasn't an optimistic feeling that filled the air, making their collective mood somewhat like condemned inmates waiting for the hangman to escort them to the scaffolds.

But at least they could face the end together, however disturbing the prospect of imminent attack seemed. The human condition was in many cases plagued by selfishness and outright wicked behavior, but in this matter, amongst longtime friends banding together for a chance at survival, the comfort of friendship and hope could push back the darkness, at least for a while.

Rubbing his hands together in a mock-confident gesture, Liam broke the silence with a not-too-serious tone and a mild grin. "Well, maybe after they see what we have in store for 'em, they'll just run away in fear?"

The others in the room returned the joke with hesitant smiles and nods. To the last person, however, nobody believed anything of the sort would really happen.

Chapter Eleven

Stanislav looked uneasy as he stared ahead. Rotating his gaze, he took a deep breath and breathed out in a controlled rasp, like he was exhaling air that was too noxious for his reluctant lungs.

Around Stanislav were four of his men, grizzled veterans all, who wore curious expressions as they looked at him for guidance. These "people," who each had lived for several hundred years and had accompanied one another on a multitude of dangerous tasks, waited expectantly for directions to their next mission. As a group, they fixed their questioning eyes on their leader.

The five men stood in the middle of an elegant armory, one filled with all manner of spears and medieval-looking polearms at spaced intervals on clean racks lining the walls. Farther down the extensive room, which altogether ran for at least fifty yards, were yet more collections of swords, knives of all varieties, maces, and even a small collection of scythes. Such a vast display of old-looking armaments would have seemed exquisite in ancient times; in current periods, they made for a one-of-a-kind exhibit.

At the end of the armory were several smaller weapon shelves holding more modern armaments, with shotguns, hunting rifles, and several Kalashnikov-type long guns aligned in pristine condition. Though these modern firearms seemed more dangerous and effective, their location and relatively fewer number in the arsenal suggested they weren't the most popular choice when it came to the business of doing violence.

"Alright, pay very close attention to our situation," said Stanislav, and he lowered his gaze for a moment, waiting to deliver the bad news to his subordinates. "We've lost two of the family up to this point, so it's essential that we quickly destroy the prey—while also not getting harmed in the process."

Startled looks came from the men, and their groping eyes couldn't grasp what Stanislav exactly meant. Hearing about the death of one of their own, much less two, wasn't something they were accustomed to or ready for. Like a group of tourists that couldn't understand a nearby foreign language being spoken, they fixed their stares on Stanislav, as if paying closer attention to him could make his words make sense.

Sergei, middle-aged looking and with gray streaks pulled back in long hair, was the leader of the four fighters that had assembled. Looking first to Stanislav, then to the rest of his trio of men, he scowled and waited for an explanation.

Stepping near several long lockers close to the armory's entrance, Stanislav pulled a metal door open. Inside were several leather-armor shirts with slots down their front—providing a place for knives to be inserted and easily carried.

Moving carefully, Stanislav pulled four of the rough armor-tops out and distributed them to the group. With the practiced movements of professional soldiers, they pulled the ancient outfits over their loose shirts and tightened them into place with leather ties.

Gesturing to a collection of knives, Stanislav spoke curtly. "Outfit yourselves with several daggers. Leave nothing to chance. Do not assume you are dealing with incapable enemies. Because of the need to keep our prey's corpses intact and uncut, Radomir was killed at the clinic while only using a sledgehammer as a weapon. It's not a mistake we will make again—the first goal is to kill, and we will worry about our nourishment at another time."

The men, taking their time, rummaged through the rack and collected several vicious-looking blades. The ease with which they tested the knives' strength and balance indicated high weapon proficiency, and in a few moments, each had collected a brace of daggers and inserted them into their hardboiled shirts.

When they made themselves ready, Stanislav looked them over, assuming almost a motherly bearing as he ensured all were in good fighting order.

Raising his voice, Stanislav spoke cautiously. "Evelyn has told us that most of our quarry has been slain and only four remain in the inn."

Stepping away from the group, Stanislav assumed a serious appearance, and his firm jawline clenched in deep thought. Walking to the entrance of the armory, he peered through the open metal door into the hazy night outside. His vision, enhanced by his inhuman condition and ability to see clearly in the darkness, focused on several stands of trees as he thought through their current situation.

"But something doesn't feel right," Stanislav continued, shaking his head slowly, "so make sure that Evelyn comes back with you when you have…disposed of our visitors."

A moment of silence passed, such that Stanislav turned around to make sure the men had heard and understood their orders.

Meeting Stanislav's stare, Sergei spoke up, getting to a point that was clearly bothering the others. "What about this 'prey,' Stan? How have normal people bested two of us in combat?"

Stanislav nodded, taking on a contemplative tone as he peered from man to man. "Yes, good question. One of the party was armed, so pay close attention that he is destroyed first. The rest, try to keep intact—as much as is possible. We can at least put their bodies to good use."

As the fighting party finished their preparations, Stanislav stepped closer and exhorted his men with some heartfelt support. His words were genuine, as could only be the case for companions that lived with a shared history over several lifespans. "Our human friends have short lives—and they endure a high degree of pain and sorrow. It is a sad condition that they must persevere in, and we all remember such times."

The group nodded in agreement, looking expectant and motivated.

Stanislav clapped Sergei on the shoulder, half-hugging the brawny man before continuing. "We know the feelings they have, for we were once in their shoes. Our enhanced longevity makes us appreciate the value of life more than they ever could from their own limited experience."

More nods from the fighters, and each appeared happy for the pep talk. Stanislav always had the gift of commiseration with the common man—both before and long after the ancient change he went through with Jacob.

"So, do your job, do it well, and use your heads," said Stanislav, and he showed them a disarming smile before getting to the next point. "Most importantly, make certain you come back alive. You are needed and valued in our community."

Offering a final appreciative nod, the war party filed from the room and walked silently into the night. Their movements, controlled and easy, showed no hesitation as they jaunted across the damp forest floor.

After they were gone, Stanislav stood in the doorway and watched them blend into the tree line. Slowly, a worried frown replaced the determined look he had maintained for the benefit of his men.

#

The area was quiet, with no sounds filling the trees surrounding the plush lawns leading to the peaceful-looking inn. The lodge was illuminated by generous lights, both from inside and out, and it presented a welcoming and attractive face to the night's intrusive darkness.

With not a chirp of a bird or the skittering of a nocturnal animal, the calm area around the motel appeared almost as a frame-stopped video, frozen in time for the purpose of a pleasant nighttime scene. Between the sedate backdrop and enjoyable weather, represented by a comfortable temperature and a mild breeze, any observer could be forgiven for thinking such a location was a relaxing place of retreat.

Above, the starry sky was shrouded by a collection of dark, meandering clouds, while the full moon cast a vigorous glow at intervals across the wooded countryside nearby.

Crouched some distance into the tree line, Sergei concentrated intently on the silent structure. His fierce image, now fearsome and changed into that of a predatory animal, roamed over the exterior of the building, looking for some indication of what awaited him and his men.

Sergei's terrifying face would have made any sane person flee in fear, but his was not the visage of an unthinking animal; instead, his probing black eyes, backlit with a yellow tint, displayed caution and intelligence as they scanned their target. These traits of his character, heightened through innumerable days spent living through and carrying out dangerous tasks, had served him well throughout his vast lifetime.

As one of the trusted few who would lead hunting packs in a wider society that didn't believe they existed, Sergei was a fierce yet careful arm of the family's interests. Carving out a place and manner of living in a world such as this, amongst a more numerous but weaker species that would never be comfortable with their presence, required a steady and careful consideration of risks and rewards. He was neither brash nor reluctant in performing his duties, and Sergei always preferred to make bold moves only when the odds were carefully stacked in his favor.

Using hand signals, Sergei motioned back at his comrades, who were also now changed and malevolent-looking monsters as they hunched under more stands of trees behind him. With fluid movements and easily understood pointing from his thick black claws, he silently laid out the plan of attack for the fighting group.

When he returned his gaze to the inn, Sergei thought for a moment longer. Coming to a quick decision, he moved back and crouched amongst his fellow fighters.

With an unearthly and brusque voice, somehow sounding both vile and tepid, Sergei gave out some final advice. "Stan said they would be injured and weak. Do not slow until they are all slain. Make this quick and painless—and we can return to our comfortable lives. They must all die now."

With not a hint of hesitation, the three creatures agreed and spread out from their shielded position deep within the forest foliage. Assuming a slow-creeping stature, one that looked a bit like a two-legged cat being quiet as it stalked its unsuspecting prey, they each took a different route to get into position for their approach to the inn.

As they prepared to dispense a quick end to the human party, using force and violence they had perfected over a lifetime of superior strength, speed, and skill, each of these beasts moved with absolute certainty and confidence. In the matter of close battle, they had never had a peer challenge them, and as they now focused ahead, they were fully confident of a predetermined outcome.

Chapter Twelve

The group stood quietly in the middle of the cleared-out front section of the motel. Anxious and peering at one other, they looked unready and worried about how this nightmare would play out. As they mulled over their harrowing predicament, dread filled their anxious faces.

All the friends held a makeshift weapon in their hands, and though they were openly committed to surviving what lay before them, none of their grips appeared overly strong on the implements they carried.

"Are we…ready?" asked Liam, and from his uncertain tone, it seemed obvious his own answer was far from a resounding *yes*. As he peered from one lifelong friend to another, he hoped for some reassuring replies but mostly got blank stares.

Collecting his courage, Liam gestured to Lilly and Alex. "Don't mess around, guys. Get back inside quick. They're faster than you'd think possible."

With hesitant nods, Alex and Lilly walked near the front door, where they stayed within a few feet of Lars, who scanned worriedly out the windows to the front of the property. Outside, the night seemed quiet and peaceful, but recent events had shown how deceitful such appearances could be.

Clutching their weapons of knives, clubs, and in Mattias' case, his firearm, the rest of the party moved back into the hallway that connected to ground floor rooms and the inn's rear exit. With anxiety filling their features, each appeared resigned to their fate.

Mattias spoke loudly, making sure his voice and intention were clear for the three companions in front. "OK, be careful."

Smiling at Mattias' well wishes, Lars motioned to Lilly and Alex. His voice was kind but worried. "Move fast, and we'll roast those fuckers alive."

Grinning, Alex showed a brave face to the rest, but his eyes appeared unsure of his part in the upcoming struggle. "Will do. I have a yacht to get home to. If something happens to me, no one else will know how to sail it."

From the back doorway, where a still-woozy Karl leaned against the door jam, he spoke up. Even while grinning at Alex's joke, Karl still sounded like a high school basketball coach that wasn't certain his players had the talent to win the big game.

"OK, guys, this should do it—we just need to wait. Lars, make sure to light the bottle as soon as you hear them coming in."

Patting Karl on the shoulder, Mattias nodded and gently pushed the injured big man farther down the hallway, away from the perceived incoming danger.

Placing himself at that chokepoint at the back of the motel lobby, Mattias checked that his pistol was fully loaded and motioned for Liam and Maria to get behind him. Somber, those two filed by and went all the way to the end of the hallway, where they waited nervously for what came next.

Now came the moment when all the party's plans were laid out, and they just had to hope everything would turn out for the better. With everyone in place and ready, Mattias raised his voice. "And remember, we need to get them all. None of these things can get out alive."

In the lobby, Alex pulled out a pack of cigarettes and offered a smoke to Lilly. As a person who never had the habit, she still grinned at her man as if to say, *what will it hurt, now?* Taking it, she popped the cigarette into her mouth and awkwardly lit it from a Zippo lighter she had found in one of the bedrooms.

Stepping through the front door and moving outside, Lilly and her husband made a great show of having a relaxing smoke break, even as their paranoid eyes scoured the wooded perimeter around them.

To the far right of the couple, hidden in the brush and watching them carefully, Sergei and two of his hunters waited.

Being masters of camouflage and in easy control of their observable profiles, they crouched unnoticed behind dense bushes as they evaluated the duo.

Sergei was not impressed with what he saw. Two lazy people puffing clumsily on cigarettes did not inspire fear or worry, and his eyes roved between the two, as if estimating how soon it would be before each of these pathetic humans would be dead. *From the looks of them, not long,* he thought.

In all things, there was a time to move forcefully, to grasp your responsibilities, and do what needs to be done. All the family had spent their extended lives nurturing this form of independent inclination, and Jacob had always made sure to drill this approach into how they operated and harvested their kills. Sergei knew that their moment of action had come, and he hissed out the order. "Now, go."

A slight rustle of nearby vegetation accompanied two of the creatures as they broke from cover. Surging into the open, they ran at high speed, their elongated and claw-tipped arms outstretched and pumping, toward Alex and Lilly. In just a moment, they had closed the distance to the inn's well-lit entrance and their waiting victims.

Lilly's eyes locked open, and she hesitated at the dark shapes running for her. Alex, similarly scared, took a second longer before catching himself and casting his smoke to the side.

"Shit, here they come. Move," shouted Alex, and scrambling as fast as his quivering legs would allow, he clapped his wife on the shoulder and flung the door open. Pushing her inside, he was just able to get through the entrance before the incoming beasts were on them.

Careening through the doorway and panicked, Alex shouted over to Lars, who stood under the chandelier next to the table full of hand weapons. "They're here. Do it!"

Holding up his Molotov cocktail, Lars began striking his lighter, and with each click of the striking mechanism, time seemed to stand still. The cloth hung from the bottle's top, soaked in gasoline, waiting for the christening spark from the cheap lighter.

Breathing hard, Alex and Lilly ran up next to Lars. Trembling, Alex grabbed the aluminum baseball bat from the table and spun towards the incoming creatures. Lilly, after plucking up two sturdy kitchen knives, hurried to her husband's side.

Time continued its slow march, and after a moment, the two monsters leapt through the front door, breaking through the glass with their massive physiques. Landing at a crouch, they looked up to see the flame of the lighter ignite the firebomb, and their surprised stares showed their fear of Lars' weapon.

The window at the side of the room, formerly covered in a gray curtain, burst in, and the third creature rolled into view. The effect of the immense impact stunned the three friends, and Lars was just able to hold on to his burning cocktail.

Crouched and ready, the monster's white face and clicking black teeth faced Lilly. With a flick of its wrist, there was a

THUK sound, and Lilly stumbled backward, a long knife buried to the hilt in the front of her throat. Blood poured from around the wound, and she gurgled as she vainly tried to stem the sheets of it pumping from her severed carotid artery. Unable to stay conscious, she stumbled backward and collapsed against the wall.

Stunned, Alex's eyes went alive with hate, and he rushed forward, swinging his metal bat in wide and deadly arcs. The creature nimbly dodged the attacks, stepping back with agile movements, and after the third swoosh of air by its head, it stepped inside the manic swings.

Once…twice…three times the creature stabbed out with fearsome quickness. The first two jabs of the double-sided blade pierced Alex's chest, driving into his lungs and heart and severing multiple essential arteries, while the third thrust shucked into his throat and sliced through his trachea. Blood sprayed from each of the horrific injuries, but with the speed of the attacks, Alex's shocked face didn't even register his own death as he toppled onto the floor.

From the back of the room, Mattias leaned into view and began cracking shots from his semi-automatic pistol. The .40 caliber rounds blew chunks from the chest of Alex and Lilly's killer, but the beast turned toward him without obvious mortal injury.

Unnerved and overwhelmed, Lars glanced up at the two remaining enemies moving from the front. They were wary of the fire weapon he held, but they were also seasoned and prepared to end his existence with the blades they had withdrawn from their chest rigs.

Crouching down, Lars looked back to his dead friends, who now lay at odd angles in expanding pools of their own gore. Sounds of gunshots boomed through the room, and for a second, Lars made eye contact with Mattias as the man screamed something inaudible across the chaotic space.

The exchange of information in their locked gazes sent a jolt into Mattias. Trying to pull the door entirely open, he made a fierce try to wade into the room, to stop what was happening, to save his friends from the fate they had already met.

A faint smile crossed Lars' face, and he raised his fiery weapon, casting the flaming bottle just as the sharp points of two well-thrown daggers buried into his chest. The projectiles from the incoming creatures plunged lethally into his essential organs, causing instantly fatal wounds. Lars crumpled to his knees, slumping over while holding the hilts of the knives that had skewered him.

As if in slow motion, the bottle turned over in the air, flying past the incoming creatures as their eyes darted back to watch its tumbling path. Seeing what was coming, Mattias pulled himself into the back hallway and yanked the door shut, just as the Molotov cocktail exploded against gasoline cannisters that had been tied in several bundles near the front of the inn.

The room erupted into a vicious inferno, with flames exploding across the interior of the formerly cozy motel lobby. Burning liquid erupted into a cacophonous conflagration, burning over everything…and everyone. The destruction of the fire was absolute, and nothing inside the space was spared from its scorching intensity.

From outside of the inn, Sergei watched the shadows of the fight develop. From his hunters making entry, to the screams of the dying humans, to the worrying sounds of gunfire, he was still confident in both his men and the result of their work. Firearms could be dangerous, but to his rapidly moving men, a kill shot was difficult for the very best of marksmen, and his fighters' attacks would terminate the shooter long before the creatures could actually be threatened.

Creeping forward, Sergei withdrew two daggers from his vest, and holding them deftly in his clawed fingers, prepared to join the fray—just in case. With the lives of his men his full responsibility, he could never be too careful.

When gouts of fire gushed from the building, with huge and deadly bursts of flame surging from every point of entry to the inn, everything suddenly changed. Sergei's mortified eyes, eyes that had witnessed the birth and death of nations and had known friendship and camaraderie more than any mortal man ever would, simply could not understand what had happened.

Stumbling forward, Sergei saw the burning body of Anatoly, an esteemed and irreplaceable friend, leap from a window. Making it only a few feet from the building, the creature's corpse was consumed by flames that quickly fed on the remaining flesh of a man he had known for centuries. Peering down, Sergei witnessed his dying friend's last moments, and he quickly knew the same fate had also fallen on the other hunters inside.

Sergei now pulled himself erect, and those same fully black pupils, the ones that usually held little pity for his victims, were now moist with anger and sorrow. He had not known such abject catastrophe since that long-ago time in his mortal life when he was captured by the Swedes as a common soldier.

But now, incomprehensible sadness and anger filled his mind, forcing him into a terrible place of inconsolable grief and detached bitterness. Several minutes passed, and Sergei struggled to contain the rage coursing through his monstrous form. His chest heaved with the effort at self-control, forcing him to stand in place and control his desire for vengeance.

Snapping back to the reality of the tragic moment, Sergei surveyed the nearby area. As his mind grappled with the enormity of his and his men's failure, he understood the news of the catastrophe must quickly be relayed to Stan and Jacob. Recovering his composure, he turned and fled into the now-brilliant night.

With flames engulfing the building behind him, his outline was soon lost in the flickering shadows of the surrounding forest.

#

Liam rushed up to Mattias, who cowered and coughed from smoke leaking under the savagely hot lobby door. Grabbing the crouched man by the shoulder, Liam shook him vigorously, checking to see that he was unhurt.

Mattias had his head buried in the sleeve of his light coat, hiding from the fierce heat radiating behind him, and when he looked up at Liam, tears and terrible distress were evident on his disturbed face.

"Let's move," screamed Liam, his voice barely audible above the roar of flames on the other side of the door. "We gotta get to a safer place."

Half-dragging his tall friend away from the now-burning front of the inn, they struggled down the hall. The sound of the fierce blaze from the lobby area was buttressed by the audible shriek from an alarm system that accompanied the inferno.

Already knowing the answer, Liam stopped for a moment, and his horrified stare focused on Mattias. "Lars…Lilly…Alex?"

His face still overwhelmed by the enormity of their loss, Mattias could only shake his head at Liam, and as they came closer to Maria and Karl, he continued his grief-stricken movements. Still quiet, his shocked features made obvious the fate of their beloved companions.

Stunned, Liam nodded and motioned towards the blockaded exit at the end of the hallway. "We need to get out of here. The whole place is comin' down."

Karl, though supposedly the one injured and needing help, moved up and grabbed Mattias under one arm. As they leaned on each other and stumbled past Maria to the back exit, the flames behind them, licking at the thick oaken door, were slowly eating through the wooden barrier.

Tossing aside their makeshift barricade of chairs and tables, Maria, Mattias, and Karl hurried to clear their way to safety. After creating a breach in the clunky barrier of furniture, they scrambled through the disassembled blockage and out the back door.

Forgetting something, Liam caught himself, stepped to the right, and hurried into the last guest bedroom near the exit. Inside the simple room, Evelyn was tied to a chair, and she glared in confusion as Liam moved close.

"Did you get them?" Evelyn shouted, keeping her voice loud to overcome the clamor of the raging flames and siren. "Is everyone OK?"

Liam hurried to untie the innkeeper, even as his teary eyes answered Evelyn's query with a decisive and depressing *no*. Cutting her bindings off with quick slashes of a kitchen blade, he hurried to extract her from her prisoner status in the dim room.

Because Evelyn's limbs were without proper circulation for some time, in addition to a pronounced limp slowing her down, Liam struggled to help her through the back door to the remaining friends. As they trudged through the smoky hallway and out the exit, their panicked eyes searched for the rest of the group.

Outside, Maria, Mattias, and Karl sat at a picnic table close to the structure, and they each met Evelyn and Liam with disbelieving looks, showing the faces of bereaved and bewildered victims.

Carefully setting the limping Evelyn next to Maria, Liam raised his voice and scanned the lamppost-illuminated area. "We need to get outta here, guys. The whole place is burning down."

Looking crestfallen, whether due to her recent visitors' deaths or to the destruction of her inn, Evelyn shook her head. "I don't think it will. The fire-suppression system is top-notch. Only the best things are installed for Jacob's lapdogs."

Looking from Evelyn, Liam met gazes with Maria, Mattias, and finally, Karl. They were all absorbed in the enormity of their loss, and they appeared lost and uncomprehending, like they were not yet able to interact with reality. Pangs of anxiety and distress filled their eyes, and their bearings were detached from the present as they processed the horrific attack and its devastating results.

After a brief silence, matched with the raging fire apparently dying down in the doomed motel, Karl was the first to recover. Standing cautiously, his face assumed a deadpan and emotionless mask, and he held out his blade defensively and strode around the side of the building towards the front of the inn.

Sitting next to his friends, Liam fell into his own thoughts, and sorrow pushed him into a sort of fugue state. For the next minutes, not a word was spoken or a thought exchanged between the survivors. They merely sat quietly, lost in personal considerations of grief and despondency.

More time passed, and Karl finally walked slowly from the front of the building. Formerly he had a limp, but that weakness in his posture seemed to have dropped away. Now he walked with firm steps and serious purpose, and a hard expression had replaced the momentary weakness of personal sadness from the death of his pals. The scratches across his face were still deep and noticeable, but color had returned to his pale skin tone, making his expression determined and vaguely hostile.

After gingerly taking a seat, Karl put his hands on the table and leaned close to the others. Keeping his voice low, he met the group with an intense stare devoid of feeling. Emotion tugged at the corners of his eyes, but he fought through the clear desire to rage against the trauma he had just witnessed in the front of the motel. "Doesn't seem to be any more of those freaks around. The fire is dying and most of the lobby is destroyed, but a bunch of sprinklers have beaten down the flames."

Karl took a deep breath before continuing, and his voice cracked as his tone dropped to a whisper. "They…are gone."

Looking up, Mattias nodded. His haunted features were lost in a sea of grief, and he held the faraway appearance of one who is preoccupied by interior torment. "Lilly and Alex were killed before the fire started…and Lars sacrificed himself to save us. One of those snaggle-toothed cunts came through the side window, and Lars was trapped between them."

Pulling herself from the table, Evelyn came to her full height and tried to sound sad, even as she appeared unsurprised by the information. "They don't live hundreds of years by being stupid. We're lucky to make it through a fight with them. Probably…nobody else ever has."

Sighing, Liam pressed his hands on the table, focusing down on the thick veins that ran across the back of his thin hands. As he moderated his breathing, he struggled with the sorrow of a young man who only knew self-satisfaction in life, not the torment of losing friends he thought would be around for decades longer. Taking this tragedy in made him realize just how sheltered his selfish life had been up to this point. "What…now?"

Evelyn's compassion for the group seemed to dissipate as she looked around the clearing behind the inn. Peering up at the starry sky, she took some time before answering. "We can't stay here. If any of them escaped, or even if none did, the rest of them will be after us now. And next time there'll be no ambush to spring on them. They'll tear us apart."

"How do we do that?" asked Liam, and his voice was a bit hysterical, like his mind was losing its moorings to the normal world. "What the fuck does that mean? How the hell do we get off this island?"

More silence came from Evelyn, and she moved her eyes along the tree line, then to the north of the motel, where an extended forest stretched into the unlit interior of the island. "We must go north. The main harbor would be a trap for sure…but on the coast, there's a small dock with several small power boats. They use it to bring meat from the outside."

Maria, finally emerging from her deep interior pain, responded with a forceful and accusing voice. "Meat from the outside?"

Looking down at Maria, Evelyn sounded apologetic, but not overly so. "Yes, they can't have normal tourists seeing bodies coming onto the island from the usual harbor. That dock is far out of the way, and I've never seen it guarded."

Motioning to the north, Evelyn breathed deep as she worked through some mental calculations. "It's about eight kilometers through the forest. But we have to hurry. Nobody has ever outsmarted Jacob. It's like we just took up tennis, and now we have to beat the world's best player in our first match. He's the smartest 'man' I've ever met."

As the reticent companions took in the recent events, a sense of detached calmness fell over their distraught faces. After a moment, Liam stood and moved close to Evelyn. His face was sad, but his eyes sharpened when he leaned close to stare into her surprised features. "Everything that's happened here to me and my friends…is your fault, Evelyn. In fact, everything that's ever happened to anyone who've been victims to these monsters is also your fault."

Stepping back, Liam's voice grew more aggressive, and he raised his tone to match his burgeoning outrage. "Those things are animals acting on…instinct or whatever, but you KNOW better."

Defensive, Evelyn was quiet. Leaning her hip uncomfortably against the table, the former innkeeper crossed her arms and considered Liam's words.

After thinking through his pointed accusation, she nodded and spoke delicately. "That may be true. But right now, I'm the only chance you got if you want to escape the hell that's coming for you. I have to live with my past, but I can also make a difference for all of us now—and in the future."

Rubbing his hands over his face, feeling frustrated at the unfairness of it all, Liam had no reply. Too sad to argue with the truth of her logic, he deflated as he panned his head towards her suggested path to the far-away dock. Staring into the darkness and shadowy outlines of endless trees, he fell into momentary despair.

Grunting from the effort, Karl now stood, and in tight control of his emotions, he nodded down at Evelyn before turning to his friends. His demeanor had become that of a professional, and now he was entirely in his element. The change was startling, as if his sorrow had been abruptly transformed into a carefree and even eager competency.

Karl was now a soldier with a mission, and like all his missions, he didn't get to pick the difficulty level they would need to complete it. His voice came out as oddly reassuring, even considering the heinous situation the party found itself in. "OK, we got to make it through five miles of unknown territory, and we got a horde of monsters on our tail. At least they won't know where we're going. We can survive this; we just need to avoid stupid mistakes."

Taking several strides towards the dark forest, Karl turned around and motioned to the front of the smoldering inn. "With a little luck, they won't know how many of us are left because of the fire."

With that, everyone stood and looked into the gloomy night and gently swaying trees. The friends pondered their chances of staying alive, and their hope for escape from this hideous circumstance briefly overpowered their considerable grief.

Whatever their pain, the truth was they all wanted a chance to survive; coming so close to death had a way of intensifying the will to live—no matter what already happened or how dim their prospects were for the night ahead. Exchanging worried glances, they nodded their individual agreement with the plan to flee for the remote location on the north of the island.

Mattias, who had been silent and stunned for some time, spoke in a calm voice, revealing what each of them inherently knew to be true. "Yeah, Karl, we better hope so, because I got the feeling we just stirred up a nest of hornets, and I don't think those stinging bastards are going to be in a forgiving mood."

Chapter Thirteen

Sergei stood in front of Stanislav in the bright lights of the otherwise-empty armory. The weathered veteran, a longtime survivor of the family's turbulent past, peered at Stanislav with a mix of worry and exasperation. Devastated by the ambush at the inn, he held his now-normal hands to his sides, continually flexing his fingers to relieve the tension in his powerful forearms.

Stanislav glared back with incomprehension. Frustrated, he breathed his words out between gritted teeth. "They're…all dead? They should have been enough to kill twenty men. Such a thing is…beyond…."

As Stanislav trailed off, Sergei continued his brooding demeanor, and he idly thrummed his fingertips against the hem of his loose-fitting pants. He was clearly at a loss for what caused the debacle, but his strong jaw and fierce eyes showed a man unbowed by his failure to destroy Liam's party. "Stan, when we normally hunt, we are assured of success. This wasn't what we thought awaited us."

Stanislav's expression sharpened, but he didn't respond to the unexpected course of the conversation. He urged Sergei to continue with a wave of his hand.

Stepping close to one of the racks, Sergei produced his unused knives and returned them to their slots in the brackets. When he looked back at Stanislav, his voice grew more cautious. "When we take a dementia patient, we face little danger. And when we harvest a camper far from civilization, dragging some poor dreg from his tent in the middle of the night, there's little chance of something going wrong. It's like 'shooting fish in a barrel,' as the Americans coined the expression so long ago."

Stanislav looked dubious as he considered Sergei's point. Unconvinced, he motioned toward the door and the wider world. "Is that an excuse? Should I tell Jacob that, in the future, we will only fight nursing home patients? Or lonely backpackers in the mountains? Do you think that is what Jacob will expect from his trained fighters? Are we to fear partying tourists that vacation on our island?"

"No, of course not, Stan, but it could be it has been too long…that we have become too comfortable in our ways. We never fight anymore—or take chances. Any of us. How else could you explain being bested multiple times by…normal humans?"

Stanislav thought for a moment, and though he didn't overtly agree with Sergei's sentiments, he nevertheless saw truth in his words. Staying quiet, he moved to another of the racks and extracted his own preferred weapons from the ancient grooves in the well-ordered display. Swinging the blades in tight circles, he practiced cutting the open air with two long and vicious-looking knives.

"They were also ready for us," added Sergei, and he pointedly made eye contact with Stanislav, letting his pronouncement hang in the air. "It's not an excuse that I'm offering—but merely a statement of fact. We've been betrayed, I fear."

Stanislav's eyes widened, and he turned to face Sergei directly. Moving close to him, he continued arcing the blades with rapid and dexterous movements between them. Sergei didn't appear worried by the proximity of the knife practice, but he still kept the movements of the wicked weapons in his low peripheral vision.

After some consideration, Stanislav sighed and slipped the sharp knives into custom sheaths inside his long leather coat. Taking a last step, he moved very near Sergei, looking down at the shorter man with a solemn stare.

Suddenly allowing an ironic grin to cross his lips, Stanislav continued studying his subordinate. "Fair enough, old friend. I hope that Jacob will accept this. It is not news that I have ever needed to bring him in the past, but you can be certain he will not be happy. His displeasure will have no end."

Turning around, Stanislav moved to a nearby wooden table that contained an attached metal press and an ancient-looking anvil. The solid slab of black metal looked unusual in the room, like it had been left there to add medieval decor to the armory.

Lifting two throwing daggers from the table, Stanislav tested their weight, and, spinning one in each hand, he twirled them like a stage magician might manipulate his playing cards. Letting the rotating knives come to a stop, he held the weapons by their polished metal edges, with their hilts facing outward.

In deep thought, Stanislav contemplated his options. As he worked through the specifics of the recent violence, as well as the potential problems if their prey managed to escape, he realized there were few outcomes that were pleasant. He would have to be very careful with his choices, both because of the physical danger the interlopers presented to his people, as well as what would happen if they attracted unwanted attention from the wider and unknowing world throughout Sweden and beyond.

Coming to a decision, Stanislav's eyes moved to Sergei, and speaking in a firm voice, he gestured outside. "Go get everyone ready. If anyone survived, including Evelyn, we will have a long night ahead of us. I do not know how far this event will proceed, but I can assure you, we will solve this problem with utmost severity."

After some hesitation, as if he wanted to say more but thought better of it, Sergei nodded, then spun and exited the room. Trudging into the night, he picked up speed and broke into a run towards the nearby village and the location of most of the family.

Inside, Stanislav was left alone in the vast arsenal, and he spent a considerable time pondering the near future. Unhappy and torn with grief, he deliberated the best approach in informing Jacob of what transpired. It was a delicate matter for sure, and though Jacob was his closest friend, his temper could be extreme when matters did not develop as he pleased.

Shaking his head at the bizarre events, his frustration boiled over. Moving his hands in a flash, he cast his blades across the room. Thunking into a wooden practice target some thirty feet away, they stuck perfectly straight and deep into the dark-grained timber, making a perfect bullseye into the outline of a human head against the wall.

Dispirited, Stanislav emerged from the armory, where he closed the clanking metal door and secured it with a thick chain and enormous lock. Stopping himself, he ran his fingers over the massive links and large padlock, admiring the craft and materials that went into creating it. Such quality work was long lost to this modern world, and he had grown to truly appreciate the skilled efforts from the past that went into making long-lasting objects.

Turning around, Stanislav collected himself, then walked down the cobblestoned path toward the far-off ridgeline. From there, he would make his way down the extended trail to pay a surprising and unwelcome visit to his lifetime mentor and boss.

#

Walking to the sturdy door in Jacob's personal living area, Stanislav noticed a difference in the atmosphere of the house. In front of the entry, in a place where only the human guards usually stood watch over the entrance, there was also one of their own, Fedor, who was one of the family's strongest fighters. The calm but watchful man noted Stanislav's approach to the door, and showing a polite nod, motioned for the regular guards to open it.

As Stanislav passed through the doorway, the whole home seemed to be different in its makeup and character. Far down the hallway to the back of the main room could be heard loud voices arguing in both Russian and Swedish, while from outside, the sounds of a running generator and multiple car engines provided a lively atmosphere to the compound. Whereas before the place could have been described as sleepy and calm, it was now wholly awake, with a bustling and hectic vibe throughout the extended property.

Jacob stood in his customary place, standing at the corner of the living room and kitchen, where he could overlook the extensive front yard of the property, as well as view the dark surface of the lake to his left. He didn't initially comment on Stanislav's coming into the room, and he stayed locked in a contemplative pose as he stared into the gloomy darkness outside.

When Stanislav stopped a few feet behind him, Jacob spoke without turning around. Talking slowly, his voice was bitter and worried. "You might as well ruin the rest of my night, Stan. What tidings do you bring?"

Taking a deep breath, Stanislav relayed all that had happened at the inn, up to and including Sergei's guess about the reason for their ineffectual efforts to destroy the humans. He did, however, leave out that the ambush on the hunters may have had its origin from treachery amongst the family's human allies. Such notions could be a dangerous topic, especially with such a volatile background as now existed. Taking a cautious approach, he decided proof was needed before he could discuss that matter openly with Jacob.

At first, Jacob seemed unaffected by the information, but after absorbing the news, he cried out. The sound he emitted was both base and uncontrolled, almost like that of a wild beast that had lost its offspring to a predator. Still not turning around, the whine of misery in his inhuman growl carried on for several moments.

Spinning around, Jacob's face was fearsome and vengeful. His features, though seemingly human, were dominated by his eyes, which shone a piercing and intense yellow. Such a visage would have made most people, either from the family or human, flee in fear, but Stanislav was able to keep his composure by dropping his gaze to the ground.

After a moment, Jacob managed to control himself, and focusing on Stanislav, he uttered a question between sharp and gasping breaths. "You have more, I presume?"

"We don't know how many survived the fire," Stanislav responded, and he carefully raised his eyes to Jacob. "Sergei came back immediately following—."

"You mean fled back?" interrupted Jacob, a frown crossing his lips. Meanwhile, the unnatural color receded from his eyes, and his pupils returned to their brown color. "What else?"

"Evelyn called me by radio to say there were only four of the tourists left. It should have been only…."

Jacob held up a silencing finger, forcing Stanislav to abandon his narration. Turning around, Jacob focused his now-calmer expression out the window again. "Interesting, Stan. This is a new wrinkle in our lives. We've been…betrayed."

Unconsciously shaking his head, Stanislav spoke quietly. "Jacob, I'm not sure about that. She could have been tortured, or—."

"Why would Evelyn do such a thing?" asked Jacob, continuing his one-sided conversation.

Knowing enough about his boss to keep quiet, Stanislav kept his thoughts to himself. His place in the hierarchy meant he should listen and take in Jacob's instructions, not risk further belligerence from the family's founder.

"I think it is because not all pets appreciate their comfortable lives," continued Jacob, and a flash of recognition crossed his face as he grabbed onto some important memory, "and perhaps she feels a need to separate herself from our happy tribe."

Turning to the side, Jacob paced carefully to the long table fronting the main bay window. The lights above produced bright illumination, and on the table, a large parchment was laid out. Picking it up, he stared at the aged document and crinkled it in his hands. As he held it for several moments, his face took on the appearance that his mind and thoughts were somewhere else.

When he came back to the present, Jacob spoke intensely, as if he was pleading an important case to the highest court in the land. "We have never liked what we must do, Stan. And we have always been kind and loyal to our humans."

Ruffling the parchment, Jacob dropped it back on the table. Facing Stanislav, he raised his tone. "Even with our victims, we have killed humanely and without malice. A hunter that needs to feed his family never apologizes for harvesting a deer, correct?"

"Yes, Jacob."

Jacob's face flushed, and his voice grew loud. "This is the way of things if a family is to survive. It always has been thus and always will continue to be so in the future. But now…the fucking DEER are killing the hunters."

"Yes, Jacob, but—."

"Silence," Jacob shouted, his voice booming through the room, and likely, the rest of the house. Outside, the shuffle of feet preceded Fedor sticking his head in to see that everything was okay.

Waving Fedor away, Jacob returned to the window, and looking towards the house's large separate garage, peered down at several men loading supplies into a pickup truck. As he watched their efficient movements, he comported himself, and after an extended silence, his features softened.

When he turned again to Stanislav, Jacob's demeanor was now apologetic, and he gazed kindly at his old friend. "We've now lost five friends, Stan. Five men that I have known and relied on for more than three hundred years. They were part of my heart."

Jacob's tone wavered, and now his eyes watered. His voice became so low that it was hardly audible. "And they are irreplaceable."

Dropping his gaze back to the floor, Stanislav nodded.

After running a hand through his dark hair, Jacob became animated, and grief transformed his expression into a serious and determined scowl. "There will be no more half-measures with this."

Motioning out the window, Jacob assumed an emotionless voice, one that was commanding and without reservation. "I have already got things rolling, as you may have noticed. I did not anticipate your failure, but, as with all things in leadership, I made plans to ensure our interests are protected. Send out the entire family, and make sure all our most loyal humans are armed. We shall treat these strangers as the dangerous enemies they are, and we shall have no mercy on them."

Moving near Stan, Jacob's attitude was grave, as if what he was about to say was pivotal to their survival. "Bring me the bodies of all our prey, even if they are only ashes and bone. If you cannot account for even one of them, then search every inch of this island. Nothing will be left to chance from this point forward, Stan. The mistakes stop now."

Nodding, Stanislav met Jacob's gaze. He appeared respectful but was also undaunted, as if he knew only he could make the proper preparations for what came next. He was one of those people that always put his best into his work, and so never felt regret if matters went wrong. "I will do as you say."

Stanislav turned and hurried from the room. As his footfalls receded down the hallway, Jacob returned to the table, where he peered down again at the ancient document. The parchment showed a medieval scene of four men and two women being burned at stakes, while a crowd in peasant clothing seemed to cheer on the spectacle from the front of an old church behind them. The drawing was crude, but it was also effective at conveying the brutality of a terrifying moment.

Tapping the painted figures in the scene with his fingertip, Jacob huffed as he concentrated on the image. His mind, full of the considerations and memories from so many lifetimes, was briefly lost in that specific and traumatic episode depicted on the parchment.

With his mindset now brought to a sad but stable state, Jacob moved to the wall near the entrance to his private abode. Taking his long and expensive coat from a shiny metal peg, he carefully put it on, then strode out the door to join his family.

Chapter Fourteen

Down a remote trail and through a brace of tightly packed trees, the moon's streaming light made visibility tolerable, and only a shrouding mist prevented a deeper view into the depths of the sprawling forest. To either side of the way forward, the woods were relatively quiet, with only the occasional skittering of some small animal to break the nighttime silence.

Karl walked first down the path, holding his knife warily in case there was a need for violence. As he scanned the brush and thickets in front, his eyes dropped intermittently to the forest floor to check for traps or any recent tracks of the creatures. His professional gaze took in every aspect of his surroundings, and the party was making good time.

Stretched out in an offset line behind Karl were Mattias, Liam, Maria, and finally, the hobbling Evelyn, who seemed overwhelmed and unsure of the rapid pace the group was keeping. None of the remaining friends seemed to care that Evelyn wasn't matching their pace, and frustrated, she stopped and coughed loudly to announce her displeasure with the hurried situation.

The noise she made was not pronounced, but in this quiet environment, it sounded to Karl that she was as loud as a blown trumpet in church. Glaring back, he fixed Evelyn with an impatient stare.

Shrugging, Evelyn met Karl's gaze and pointed to her arthritic hip, the source of her agony and the obvious limitation to their timely journey to the coast. Unapologetic, she was contented with the knowledge they required her to make it to their destination. She even managed to smirk as she motioned for the need to take a break.

Grimacing, Karl looked around the forest for a proper spot to rest, then gestured to a raised and open area of rocks that provided cursory protection from being too easily noticed.

"We can stop for a quick bite to eat and drink. We should be way ahead of them, and it's a good idea to not wear ourselves out. Although…I've always tried to keep two steps ahead of the enemy," explained Karl, and he frowned at Evelyn, who was leaning against a rock and sipping from a water bottle, "apparently we aren't in a big hurry."

Evelyn stared back at Karl's undisguised insult, and shaking her head, she offered him a fake smile before taking another swig. The other companions, uninterested in arguing, spread out and found a place to rest.

Mattias, crouching next to a tall Birch tree, kept his pistol gripped in his lap and scoured the area for any signs of danger. Nothing forbidding answered his diligent and paranoid search, and for the moment, their surroundings were without evidence of their formidable adversary.

Maria, pulling her loose summer coat closer for warmth, sat on the cold earth with her back against another tree. Dropping into her personal thoughts of loss, she continued her descent into listless silence and internal suffering. Karl tried to cheer her up with a squeeze of her shoulder, but there appeared little to be done to alter her foul and withdrawn mood.

Farther in the trees, Liam found a rock that appeared comfortable to rest his ass on. Breaking out several packets of salted peanuts, things which were now undoubtedly the last remaining snacks from the extinct bar, he perched on the hard surface and chewed in silence.

For several minutes, Liam did not look too hard around, and his depressed demeanor suggested he didn't much care if the creatures found a way to track the party down. Engrossed in his sorrow, both from his dead friends and his fucked-up domestic situation at home, nothing really mattered at the moment. Absently sucking on the salty treats, his mind was removed from the present and unable to bypass the stultifying barrier of misery that blocked his emotional way forward.

This is the way of the nice guy, Liam thought, and he gave himself up to his self-pity. Reality in his life had always been disappointing, and in most of the things he did, he underperformed or failed outright.

As a student in a small town, Liam had always been picked last to partake in sports at recess, and later, when high school reared its ugly head, he didn't even get the benefit of being picked last. Instead, he failed to even make the team. He still often thought about the look of revulsion he got from his school's fat basketball coach as the man wrinkled his nose when looking at Liam's smallish frame and normal height. That humbling event had taught Liam to only do what he was good at and never take chances.

In higher education in Sweden, Liam continued a solid if unspectacular academic career as he sought to become a doctor. Unfortunately, he had neither the temperament nor the intellectual skills to bring that quickly to fruition, so he instead moved on to a marketing degree. When things got tough, this was the way Liam handled it, by finding something else that offered less difficulty or effort. *Better to never truly try at something than to fail spectacularly.*

When he returned to the US, Liam tried his hand at a few jobs, but he soon found he never was quite able to fit into a normal career path, at least as defined by the office worker and IT jobs that his friends often gravitated towards. Eventually deciding he wanted to follow something that interested him, he got into writing about and handicapping sports betting, and though it wasn't a typical nine-to-five job, he found he really enjoyed it.

Liam remembered the first time he actually understood that sports betting was one of the few things in the world where the odds could be overcome—if you knew what you were doing. He had focused on NFL football as his favorite game of choice, and that is where he subsequently built up a solid following of folks that listened to his thoughts and paid for his prognostications. He was not always right in his predictions—nobody ever was—but he was prescient enough to make his clients money, and that was always something that ensured he would be forgiven for his mistakes.

In this pursuit of excellence at his job, Liam found people actually listened to him—for once in his unremarkable life. He never became rich or formed his own top-of-the-line company, but at least he found something he was good at and would leave him regular funds in his bank account.

But then there were the relationships, or more accurately, the lack of them in his rather calm life. From the time he was a teen until his thirties, like most boys he was girl-crazy, and he spent most of his time thinking about who his everlasting love would be. Whether it was the blond girl named Heather in the eighth grade or that gym-goddess Ulrika in one of his failed chemistry classes in college, there was always a beautiful girl to show him just how out of his league the ladies were that Liam most hoped to partner with.

The biggest problem was, though Liam was liked by everyone, he was also somewhat plain-looking and without interested counterparties in the competitive game of love. It turned out he was always the better friend to lean on and not the object of affection with his cross-gender relations, which was a humbling fact of life that made his dating life a lonely endeavor.

Liam had thought that changed when he met Elise, and he was certain his personal prospects were bound to improve from that point onward. This gorgeous and seemingly sincere woman, full of life and always willing to try something new, would be the answer to all his riddles about females, and indeed would bear him children and make a household. They would become a happy family unit, and whatever happened elsewhere in his life, they would always lean on each other to make their next day together better than the last.

All of Liam's considerations of happiness were made whole when he looked into Elise's blue eyes, and moreover, he never felt attracted to another woman after meeting her, at least not in any genuine way. She was the shining star in his limited and untraveled galaxy.

As a result, Liam showered Elise with love and praise, making her his queen in their simple and mundane lives. He brought her flowers, cooked for her, and made it a point to be interested in all her womanly pursuits, however much he personally loathed them. With him, she would always be looked after and made the center of his world, which was something that most women claimed they wanted.

Of course, the result of this pandering was, like with the rest of his romantic interests, she got bored, and the writing was soon on the wall for the end of their short-term and unsatisfactory (at least for her) marriage.

And now, as Liam sat in the woods and grieved over his dead friends, she was probably getting pounded like a cheap rug having the dust beaten out of it.

For some reason, the rug idea made Liam smile, as he remembered Elise hated the rug his mother had bought for their apartment after they were married. Grinning further, he hoped she got a horrid rug burn from the thing as she writhed on it and screamed for more from her new man, Serge.

The thought of Elise's handsome new man made his heart tremble, and Liam's smile sagged as he considered that thieving bastard. There was just something that the woman could do to twist the knife a little deeper into Liam's back, and her new love interest certainly did just that.

Using her charms and trim physique, Elise found a fit and undoubtedly virile man, and now she seemed completely contented to jettison Liam from her life without even the mildest of regrets. It was almost impressive, if he was brutally honest with himself, how easily she had disposed of Liam, so at least he had to give her respect for dumping and moving on from him in the most efficient and ruthless manner possible. The world was full of people that avoided hurting others because of their sensitive feelings, but in Elise's case, she made no effort to lighten the emotional murder she inflicted on his fragile psyche.

In a way, that was more humane than dragging the process out; it was kind of like a pet owner that put down a suffering animal in order to save it from the drawn-out agony of a lingering death.

Interrupting his moment of self-pity, Liam saw that Karl was making his way over after he had been talking with Mattias. Liam's pathetic inner thoughts melted away as his large friend came near him, met his eyes, and squatted down.

"How are you doing, Liam?" asked Karl, and it seemed to Liam that Karl's face was worried in the way that concerned family members might be when checking on the mental status of a known-to-be-crazy uncle. "You feeling okay?"

Surprised by the query, Liam stumbled through his rambling, traumatized thoughts. "Not really, Karl. I can't believe…Johan…Lilly…all our friends."

Karl nodded in empathy, but his eyes showed a man that was accustomed to loss and trauma, a man who knew how to put aside bothersome emotions when necessary. "I know. It's beyond belief. Literally the worst thing in the world."

"Then why are you so cool? We'll never see them again. All those good times, days spent hanging out and partying, sightseeing all around Sweden, visiting family and going to hockey games. All of it…for what?"

Liam's eyes teared up, and his grief bordered on the unendurable. Fighting the urge to bawl like a child, he looked shamefully away.

Karl smiled in a passive way, like he was sorry he had to witness Liam's emotional meltdown. Letting his voice drop to a whisper, he spoke so that only Liam could hear. "Liam, I'm going to be honest with you, so don't be offended. I'm not trying to make you feel bad."

Looking back to Karl, Liam was surprised, but he stayed quiet as he waited for the meat of Karl's point.

"When I was in Kabul," Karl said, and his eyes became detached from the moment, lost in his troubled memories, "I once responded to a suicide explosion that targeted westerners in the capital. It used to happen pretty often, and the sick fucks would set off an explosion to indiscriminately wipe out a few aid workers, people that were just there to help Afghanistan—not even soldiers."

"Shit, sorry Karl, I never knew—."

"Let me finish. I'm not just here to swap war stories or depress you. Anyway…so I arrived on the scene of what was a market, where people brought their families to buy and sell food, supplies, whatever they might need to make their humble lives a bit better in that wretched place."

Interested, Liam's silence and attention were absolute. Not one to hide his emotions, he couldn't deny this was an interesting interaction, whatever his own pain.

"And when I arrived, there were sons and daughters, men…women… all blown apart. Some were living, some dead. It was strange watching family members going through such a thing, in some cases trying to put their loved ones' bodies back together."

"K…Karl, that's like the worst thing I've heard in my life."

Karl nodded, and though obviously disgusted from his memories and their retelling, he assumed a businesslike expression. "So, these types of things happen all the time, every day even—all across the world. Even in the United States and Sweden, people go through the most horrible things. It seems to be part of the human condition, this violence and killing thing. No country avoids it."

Growing curious, Liam stewed in his thoughts. Perplexed, he gave Karl a questioning look. "OK…but what's your point?"

Offering a gentle smile, Karl leaned closer. "Now YOU are in one of those terrible stories you've always read about. You're the one you never thought you'd be, a victim of something far worse than you'd ever imagined possible."

Liam scrunched his face up, trying to understand Karl's intent. Unsure of himself, he appeared despondent and tense.

"So, you have to decide how this will end, and what part you're going to play in this, Liam. I'm telling you from experience, your actions had better be quick when we get our chance to move. Your life—our lives—depend on it."

Doubtful, Liam shook his head. "So, I need to be a gung-ho soldier to survive? I was never even a cub scout."

Karl shrugged. "You look like you already want to give up. I'm telling you, and I want to be clear, survival is a choice. If you want to make it out of this, drop the puppy-dog eyes and man up. You have what it takes to be a fighter, even if you don't know it yet. Choose to live, for you and our dead friends."

Coming fully to his feet, Karl patted Liam on the shoulder and smiled encouragingly. "We'll have the rest of our lives to cry over them. They are still with us and always will be. But that doesn't mean we need to join them just yet."

Flashing a sincere smile, Karl turned to the others and made a motion with his hand to pack up and get ready to move. Walking away, he didn't turn back to see the effect of his pep talk on Liam.

Liam, considering the direction and specifics of their conversation, made ready to move again. Stuffing the plastic wrappers of his small meal back into his pockets, he realized that something so small as a remnant of his snack could allow their disgusting adversaries to track them. Something he never had to worry about, even the unintentional act of littering, was now a matter of life and death.

Regarding Karl, Liam of course knew that the professional soldier was correct about everything—he really couldn't remember a time when Karl was wrong about even one important matter. The only issue seemed to be, *what exactly can I do to get home?*

Thinking harder, Liam worked through the evidently low chances of their success, as well as the unbelievable and wicked nature of their pursuing enemy. This evil batch of bestial monsters was straight out of a children's horror story, but they were also not invincible—they could be killed with applied violence. Both Karl and Mattias had proved that, and both were still alive after winning their encounters with the deadly fiends.

Looking around at his friends' dark shapes amongst the dim woods, Liam suddenly realized how important it was that they, and not just he, survived this nightmare. They were still here and trying to escape, trying to work as a team, and they now needed Liam as much as he needed them. However small the group had become, they were still alive and fighting to make it past the abominable odds staring them in the face.

Coming to a personal decision, Liam's face finally showed something from his character that had been missing for a long time: determination, and for the first time since the terrible attack at the clinic, he felt hopeful.

#

The raging fire had severely damaged the front of the building, but the main face of the inn was still largely intact. The windows, formerly pleasant and clean portals to the cozy motel lobby, were now gaping holes in the forward part of the scorched building, while the glass doors of the main entrance were also broken and burned out. The ferocity of the flames, aided by the propellants used by the friends, had reduced the formerly attractive business to a burned-out shell.

Two fire engines with flashing emergency lights were now parked near the front of the place, and lazy jets of water squirted from their cannons to bathe the smoking ruins. There were no more flames in the remnants of the building, and not-very-busy firemen walked in and out of its openings as they worked to ensure the fire was completely extinguished.

Other figures, undoubtedly specialists from the family, picked through the piles of charred wood and the remains of interior furnishings, looking for anything that could help them understand what precisely happened during the violent clash and subsequent fire.

Stanislav stood near the front entrance where he chatted with two serious-faced firemen. The men, clearly working to ensure they were doing their jobs with the utmost care, motioned to the interior of the motel as they explained what had been discovered so far.

From the night, far away from the structure, bright headlights suddenly came into view, and after banking from the simple paved road, a black SUV pulled up to the smoldering property. Not bothering to use the parking spaces to the side of the establishment, the vehicle drove to a stop on the matted grass near the entrance of the building.

Peering from the front passenger window, Jacob extracted himself from the cab, and focusing on Stanislav, walked slowly toward the assembled group. The firemen, who had been acutely interested in their conversation with Stanislav, used the occasion of Jacob's arrival to make themselves scarce, suddenly finding other cleanup duties to keep them busy.

As Jacob paced closer to Stanislav, he arched his head towards the blackened building and made an insincere attempt at smiling. "So, Stan, what is the situation?"

Stanislav answered with a grimace. "We aren't completely sure. It seems some of the prey are still missing; we have found five human bodies…as well as four of our own. Three of our hunters that accompanied Sergei are among the dead, as well as Ivan, who worked at the restaurant. The results are as bad as you presumed."

Jacob's eyes locked on the building, and his mind processed the scene as he specifically sought out what had happened. "Show me."

Nodding, Stanislav strode through the front entrance, where he kicked aside some burned-out wood to make the way clearer for Jacob. Inside, the front lobby was soaked from thousands of gallons of water, both from the sprinkler system and subsequent fire engines, which somehow left the interior surprisingly intact. The burned remains of the conflagration were extreme, but there appeared no immediate possibility of structural collapse.

Stanislav motioned to bodies on the floor, which had been arranged in order across the center of the lobby. The first four were the crispy remains of the family, with trunks and claw-tipped limbs longer than normal humans, while the remaining corpses were of their intended prey. All the singed bodies were barely identifiable, with mouths open wide and odd-angled poses caused by extreme heat that had contorted their forms and roasted their insides.

Staring down at the deceased, Jacob's expression was contemplative. "So, we have at least four of the group, and I am assuming our own Evelyn, that are still alive somewhere on our island?"

"It seems that way, Jacob. We have yet to discover how they managed to come out on top in the fight—."

"They lured our hunters in," said Jacob, and he motioned to the front of the room, where the burns on the wall appeared more pronounced and the fire damage more intense. "Apparently, it was some kind of fire trap—they were certainly informed of our coming and ready for us."

Looking down at the deceased, Jacob scowled at the waste of life—at least the lives of his own. "Our men managed to kill a few, but the overall results were not favorable...."

Raising his gaze, Jacob stepped away from the bodies and moved to the back of the inn, where Evelyn and her family had lived for many years. Moving carefully through the doorway and into the charred interior, he studied the seared debris throughout the living area. Following behind, Stanislav also examined the scattered remains of the apartment.

After a visual inspection of his surroundings, Jacob noticed a framed photograph on the ground, where it was sticking out from a pile of charred rubble. Picking it up, he held it up to light streaming from headlights through various holes in the inn's front wall.

The picture was of Evelyn's husband and son, and the teen and his father stood at a beach somewhere on the island. Smiling, the duo looked in the prime of life, happy with their circumstances and environment. The glow of their smiles as they looked affectionately behind the camera indicated it must have been Evelyn that took the photo.

Jacob looked closer at the background of the picture, and he brushed away ash to get a clearer view of the area. Thinking for a moment, his face locked in recognition, and he gestured outside as he turned to Stanislav. "She is leading the group to the north dock, where we often bring our food from the outside world. Send out the hunters and make haste to ensure our humans block all the approaches to that location."

Nodding quickly, Stanislav turned to leave, but Jacob caught him by the arm. Leaning close, Jacob's words were precise. "Tell everyone that under no circumstance are they to attack—unless they have an overwhelming advantage. I will not lose another life to this fuck-up."

Letting his words grow even graver, Jacob dropped his tone, making certain only Stanislav would understand what came next. "And Stan, do try to take Evelyn alive. We shall have to make an example of her. In all this time, we have never been betrayed, and it is not a situation I wish to experience again."

Stanislav agreed with an awkward nod, but there was some hesitation in his demeanor. "I will do as you say."

Jacob noticed his uncertainty and was curious. "What is it?"

Taking a moment, Stanislav thought through his words, making sure he wasn't out of line or being too bold. "A couple things are worth mentioning—if you do not mind me being honest."

"When have I ever asked otherwise?"

Stanislav ran his hand over his stubbled face. "Well, the men are feeling a bit…apprehensive. They are wondering if we are perhaps taking too many risks."

Jacob frowned. "In what way?"

"In trying to take too many prey at one time, and from a source we were unfamiliar with, they think we have…erred."

Jacob broke into an unamused grin. "Is that it?" and he pointed his long index finger directly at himself. "We have indeed erred. I have erred. This whole debacle is my fault. Tell them that—without reservation."

Looking pained, Stanislav nodded, but he didn't appear eager to press the matter.

Jacob's dark eyes grew animated as he softened his voice. "But also tell them, Stan, that I have taken care of them before. And I will continue to do so as long as I live. You know that they always come first in my calculations."

Stanislav's features warmed, and he offered a face that wasn't critical or angry. "Everyone knows that you have their best interests at heart. But it has been an extended time since we have been at war, or at least fighting for our lives. It is like we are coming back to our roots with this awful matter."

Agreeing with a cursory nod, Jacob motioned for Stanislav to continue. "What else?"

Stanislav dropped his gaze to the floor, clearly unhappy with the next topic. He spoke very quietly now. "Nobody will like to hear about Evelyn. Her treachery will worry…."

Jacob spoke curtly, cutting off the continuation of that thought. "I agree, Stan, it is a sensitive matter that goes beyond our normal interactions. Our 'partnership' with the humans requires a great deal of trust, from both sides."

Jacob hesitated, then spoke in a voice thick with seriousness and warning. "Stan, make certain all our people know they are not to touch a hair on the head of our human friends…not a hair. They are never to remotely consider taking revenge on another for the betrayal of Evelyn. If there was a conspiracy, we will ruthlessly tear it from our community, but there will be no guilt by association."

Now looking up, Stanislav's eyes brightened. Though he remained quiet, his face grew calmer, and he stifled a smile.

"And tell them all to stay strong," continued Jacob. "We have endured and outlasted kings and rulers throughout Europe. Our future remains bright."

Nodding, Stanislav finally did smile, and after gazing around the destroyed room, his eyes became distant. "Remember when Andrey thought it a good idea to join the Axis during The Great

War? When he thought it would solve our food issues forever—by picking the winning side in that horrible conflict?"

Jacob grinned, his face resuming a normal expression. "Yes, I do. It was one of his many bright ideas, and it was a bit of advice I am happy we ignored. He was never good at choosing the victor, whether in horse races, battles between noble houses, or as you've noted, between doddering empires. We were lucky to avoid being drawn into either of the great European wars last century."

As they stood staring at each other, a moment of kinship came over them. Despite the difficult situation and sorrow, they shared several moments of respectful silence. Being friends over such a prolonged period enabled them to understand and enjoy one another's company, much more than others—even their own kind—could ever understand. Their relationship was more than leader and follower or boss and employee, but instead had the markings of brotherliness, with all the genuine feelings attached to such a heartfelt relationship.

Taking a calming breath, Jacob mastered his feelings of loss and betrayal. A good leader knew how to focus on the matter at hand, without letting peripheral considerations take away from achieving a necessary goal.

Composed, Jacob motioned toward the front of the inn and the tasks that awaited them across his humble island domain. "Let us find the rest of these wretched people, and we can then get on with the rest of our lives. In time, this will be but a 'bump in the road,' and we can return to less onerous means of assuring our food supply."

Spinning around, Stanislav retained his grin as he walked quickly from the motel into the darkness. His steps were jaunty and happier, and a renewed sense of completing the mission filled his mind. The way ahead for the family would not be easy, but Stanislav's ruthless plans for their island guests would soon ensure a deserving outcome for these upstart humans.

Chapter Fifteen

Karl, still taking the lead on the shadowy and ill-defined trail, crept gently across the damp ground. Trying to ensure absolute silence, he stepped across the earth without the slightest disruption of the assorted twigs or low-lying bushes beneath his feet.

Behind him, the others were less careful, but the gist of their efforts was the same: silence was essential, and to a person, they all knew that remaining quiet could be a matter of life or death. Moving his eyes back to the other party members, Karl nodded and appeared contented with the efforts the group members were making to avoid undue noise.

Up ahead, radiance from the stars and moon illuminated a large graveyard, one that almost seemed to hover out of the foggy environment. There was a large stone wall to either side of the entrance to the cemetery, and the arched entrance and iron gate looked as if crafted from a particularly poignant ghost story. Beyond the entry, rows of old Orthodox grave markers, with the bottom of the crosses offset by slanted crossbeams, receded into the misty background.

A plaque hung from the top of the entrance, showing some bold writing in Cyrillic on the wooden panel. Turning back, Karl returned to the rest of the party, where he set his curious gaze on Evelyn.

Answering Karl's unspoken question, Evelyn whispered. "This is where most of the soldiers were buried. After becoming prisoners, they were brought to Sweden in the early 1700s."

The eerie effect of the cemetery's appearance on their journey was not an encouraging sign, and the group swapped surly expressions as they peered at the rows of old graves. Dead people, even long-decayed ones—as well as creepy burial grounds they were interred in—had a way of acting like a wet blanket on burgeoning feelings of hope and internal fortitude.

Pointing to the plaque above the graveyard's entrance, Liam sounded dubious of the date Evelyn mentioned. "That sign isn't from the 1700s."

Evelyn agreed with a raised eyebrow, somewhat surprised at Liam's meticulous observation. "No, it's updated every few years. It says in Russian, 'They could never go home.'"

Considering those words, Liam grew somber. "That's really kinda…sad."

"I somehow find it hard to feel sorry for people that are killing us," interjected Maria, and the party all looked at her with some surprise after having grown accustomed to her not talking much.

Reaching down, Karl picked up a piece of oddly shaped wood, which looked a bit like a gnarled fist. While turning the dried chunk of tree over in his steady hands, he nodded understandingly at Maria. "Whoever died back then, it wasn't their fault their friends—and our current tormentors—became cannibal mutants."

Liam chuckled, then offered Maria a conciliatory smile to lighten the mood. "True."

Trying to ignore Maria's bitterness, Evelyn continued. "The conditions they had as prisoners were apparently quite bad. To hear them tell it, all their compatriots were dying of disease and starvation in some noble's dungeons."

"Lovely," interjected Mattias, and he didn't hide his lack of sympathy for those involved in those long-past events.

"So…Jacob started making the survivors into 'family members' in small groups," continued Evelyn, and she pointed to the cemetery. "Now they treat this place as some kind of shrine. It's maintained and kept in excellent condition, despite the age of the graves."

Karl gestured to the creepy entrance, his voice and bearing intrigued. "How many of this 'family' are there?"

"At least sixty or so," replied Evelyn. "They never gave me a roster or anything, and I doubt I met them all. It's not easy to feel like they're good friends, if you get my drift. So, most islanders keep a respectful distance and just act nice all the time."

Rubbing her leg defensively, Evelyn pointed to the side of the entry gate, where several wrought-iron benches of exquisite design, with ancient-looking gargoyles of amazingly sharp detail were fashioned on the back supports. "If you don't mind, I need to rest for a while. They won't think we came here, I hope, so it should be safe—for a while, at least."

Several minutes passed as the party collected themselves and spread out to sit on the ornate benches. As they tried to get comfortable, no words were exchanged, and the creepy environment just became more acute as they peered into the spooky surroundings. As if made from a fog machine, sheets of stagnant mist appeared to cling to the surrounding undergrowth and around the grave markers.

Clearing her throat, Evelyn grew uncomfortable, evidently unenthusiastic about what she wanted to say next. "I didn't want to say anything until I was sure, but I think you all should know…Karl and Maria are going to become those creatures. I'm pretty sure of it, anyway."

Shocked, everyone responded to Evelyn's observation with open eyes and disbelieving stares. That was, everyone except Karl, who somehow managed to appear unsurprised and self-controlled while munching on a granola bar.

"What?" asked Maria, who was finally emotional and ready to talk. "I feel normal…this can't—."

"Because of our wounds?" asked Karl, and his mechanical chewing continued.

"Yes…it's why we can't live too close to them," said Evelyn, and in contrast to her normal expression, she appeared genuinely sympathetic. "One infection, like from a cut or something, and you end up like them."

"And they won't allow anyone else to turn," continued Evelyn, and looking serious, she made a cutting motion across her neck. "Guess they would need all of Sweden to feed them if their numbers kept growing. Population control is a major part of the family's way of doing business, apparently."

"I'm not going to eat people for a living," said Maria, and with that, she dropped her gaze to the ground, her mood becoming depressed and docile again.

"Me neither," Karl said dryly, finishing up his snack and not appearing too disturbed by the revelation.

Evelyn pointed to Karl's and Maria's wounds, which now seemed like mere scars compared to the deep gashes that were oozing blood before. "Look at your injuries. They're all practically healed, despite you both being seriously wounded. So, it may take a few days, but you'll turn into them. You'll feel normal and keep all your mental capabilities—."

"Wonderful," said Karl.

"And you'll never age," said Evelyn, flashing a worried glance at Karl.

Liam looked between Karl and Maria, as if to say, *well, that's not bad, at least.*

"But you will grow claws and teeth at will, like you've already seen, and need to eat their sort of human meat-food as long as you live—though I've never seen how they prepare it or what it looks like. You'll also be faster and stronger than normal people, which you also witnessed."

Looking up to the sky, Mattias blew out a long, dismal sigh. "Is there any way to prevent or treat this?"

Thinking for a moment, Evelyn shook her head. "Not that I know of, but I'm no doctor. I think once it's in you, there's no way to stop it. I heard that one of the islanders was infected in the 1800s, and they had to kill him. They're very strict about who gets to join their 'club.'"

As Maria stayed locked in her own thoughts, Karl continued his evaluation of their surroundings. While deeply disturbed with Evelyn's insights, Karl affected a carefree disposition, almost like he had just ordered a random pizza and was curious what type of pie the delivery person would bring.

Pressing his lips into a tight scowl, Liam stood and paced several yards, pondering the group's delicate position. Unhappy with the news, he still tried to sound encouraging. Whatever they faced, sitting here for too long a time wasn't going to make them any safer. "Well, this sucks, but it doesn't change our situation much. Evelyn says you'll keep your mind and thoughts, which should mean you won't eat us."

Evelyn nodded. "They've never been anything but nice to us, so they can control themselves."

"OK then, so let's get the fuck off this island and then sort it out," said Liam, and he tried out an optimistic grin as he scanned the others' dire expressions. "We can get you both treated somewhere when these monsters are far in the rearview mirror. As an added bonus, if Karl starts to grow fangs and wants to munch on us, it should be easy to convince the rest of the world this crap really is happening. Who gets to be the one to inform mankind there are real creatures among us?"

Continuing his uncertain smile, Liam stared around the gloomy woods, all the while trying to stay upbeat. Unfortunately, nobody else appeared amused by his sense of humor, nor were they particularly excited about what the night had in store for them.

#

Some time later, the way through the shadowed forest had become thicker with trees, and the companions' pace slowed as a result. Around them, although the obscuring mist had become less dense, Karl was reduced to walking carefully and checking near each trunk root and small bush for anything hazardous as he crept forward. Whatever his current health status or potential for changing into a creature, his longtime woodsmanship skills were on effective and open display.

Evelyn, struggling in the back of the line, where she still limped and sucked for air, managed to keep up with the others, but perspiration had soaked into her beige long-sleeve sweater. Tugging at her constricting collar, she huffed with fatigue, and with a sweaty and pale face, she looked in danger of collapsing.

Stopping, Evelyn coughed to get the others' attention, then spoke in labored gasps. "One more break…please. We're only about an hour from the coast. We just need to climb the next ridge and follow it down to the right."

Disappointed frowns greeted Evelyn's suggestion, and the friends traded annoyed glances due to their concern she was slowing them down yet again. The likelihood of escape for the group seemed to decrease in their collective eyes with each new stop, however much their weary guide needed the rest.

Karl moved his eyes around the woods as he contemplated what they should do next. "Not the best time, but unless we are gonna leave you here, we might as well take another…break."

The way Karl inflected his words about leaving Evelyn disturbed her, not the least because it appeared that possibility wouldn't bother him too much. Sitting on a mossy area next to some thick brush, she tried hard to imagine it was only her paranoia, and not Karl's actual intention, that left open the possibility.

Mattias, showing a half-sincere smile, moved close to Karl and nodded toward the path. "Let's check out the area ahead. No use wasting time on our ass when we're so close to the coast."

Nodding, Karl led Mattias into the darkness, and with Karl making it a point to move quietly, Mattias followed his lead and kept his firearm ready as they stepped into the dark woods.

As Mattias and Karl's forms melted into the forest's ever-present fog, Maria and Liam frowned. Leaning against two separate trees, neither said a word to Evelyn, but speech at this point was unnecessary to register their unease with having to stop. Time was slipping away, and the reason for the delay was a woman who could have prevented their friends' deaths, even if she was personally unaware of Jacob's impending attacks on the party.

After several minutes of catching her breath, Evelyn rose shakily. Appearing contrite, she tried to smile and gestured to the side of the trail. "I need to go to the bathroom. I'll be right back."

Liam, agreeing with a brooding nod, whispered back. "Don't go far."

Moving in starts, Evelyn worked her way towards a stand of trees, looking for a place that could offer her some privacy to do her business. Walking around the stand of heavy firs, she disappeared behind a wedge of shrouding branches.

After a quiet moment, a loud clack emanated from that spot. A scream, one of agony and shock, rang through the quiet forest, "Ahhhiayy, help me."

Eyes going wide, Liam rushed toward the shielded area, and he held out his humble kitchen knife in tentative self-defense as he peeked behind the bunched-up vegetation.

Evelyn screamed as she met his eyes. With her pants around her ankles, she breathed in raging, panicked rasps, drawing in air and bellowing in tormented pain. On her back and sprawled out on the dark soil, her leg was caught in the maws of a vicious-looking bear trap, with thick metal points fully buried into the spot below her left calf. Blood surged from the horrid wound, and the size of the trap made her limb appear almost severed between the trap's ragged teeth.

"Shit, you've got to be quiet," urged Liam, and he bent down, trying to figure out how to retract the teeth of the ungainly contraption. After having no luck, he settled on working to stem the flow of blood from the nasty injury.

Joining Liam, Maria peered down at Evelyn. A long and heavy chain, which must have weighed fifty pounds, led from the trap, where it circled around a tree trunk and was secured by a metal peg driven into the thick base of the tree. Whoever had set this trap made it a point to ensure whoever was ensnared wouldn't be able to carry it away.

Evelyn continued her screams, and the silent night seemed to amplify her terrified and pained shrieks. In a moment, the sound of rushing feet through the brush was accompanied by the form of Karl, who hurried into view, followed closely by Mattias. Bending down, Karl quickly examined the trap, running his hands over its metal parts to examine its condition and means of attachment.

Scowling, Karl looked up, and his features were neither pleased nor optimistic. Staring first into the forest, his gaze then moved back to Evelyn. "The trap's been modified. It has some barbs in it to keep the teeth from being retracted. Some kind of locking device to keep it from being tampered with. I've never seen anything like it."

As moans continued from Evelyn, Maria made a shooshing sound as she vainly tried to quiet the woman. The effort was wasted, and Evelyn's eyes, delirious with pain, showed no inclination or ability to control her agony.

Frustrated, Liam pulled his belt off and ran it around Evelyn's leg, where he tightened it in a bid to contain the bleeding. As Liam cinched the leather around her calf, Karl leaned very close from the opposite side of Evelyn. His calm eyes meeting hers, his tone was gravely serious. "You need to be quiet…now. You'll bring them all down on us."

Evelyn's expression was locked in rigid shock. She had never felt such pain or physical trauma, but Karl's icy stare convinced her to dial down the noise. Nodding, her pronounced shrieks devolved into dazed groans of misery.

Standing, Karl looked again into the surrounding darkness. Processing their situation, his mind raced to find the best way forward. Panning his head between the way towards the dock and from where they just came, indecision filled his face.

From the night, from a far distance but closer than any of the group would have wanted, a distant cry came. The sound was oddly human, even as it also carried an animalistic base in its prolonged cry. The odd screech reminded Karl of that accusatory wail from that grief-stricken woman who, witnessing the death of her family in the long-ago market in Kabul, wanted revenge. Except, the vocal cords that could make such a sound were beyond anything he'd ever known.

"They're coming," said Karl, his face frustrated as he worked through the problem. "No normal animal makes that sound."

Crouching back down, Karl met Evelyn's terrified stare. For a moment, some sympathy bled from his expression. "Evelyn. We have to leave you. There's no way to get you out of this, and I think you deserve to know that. Do you want me to…kill you?"

The friends around Karl, serious and confused, didn't quite grasp what he meant. Unable to understand his intent, they became incredulous. They had been focusing on the task of getting out of this predicament, but now they stared like he had lost his mind. Even Maria was unsettled by the cold-blooded offer.

Karl shook his head, addressing their concern with calm candor. "It's far more cruel to let her fall into their hands. We don't know what they'll do to her, but it'll be horrible. I've seen what depraved humans will do to a prisoner. These…things will probably be worse. She'll wish she were dead."

Nobody responded to Karl, and when Karl looked back at Evelyn, her whines of pain had stopped entirely. Her eyes were now full of fear as she considered his words, even as she grasped their brutal truth. "I want…to live. I want to have a life. This can't be the end. I'm not supposed to die this way."

Breaking down, Evelyn began to sob uncontrollably, and grabbing a branch, she managed to raise herself to one knee on her good leg, as if making to rise and escape from her current dilemma. Here she was, blubbering and helpless, but even hopelessly trapped, she intended to survive.

With a flash of movement that would have been impressive for a professional fighter, Karl cracked Evelyn across the chin with a powerful right cross. Without a sound, the woman crumpled to the ground, her body instantly rag-dolled by the vicious punch.

Mattias came closer, his face contorted and confused, as if trying to comprehend what had just happened. Maria, also overwhelmed, took a step back from Karl, unsure of whom might be assaulted next.

Liam, reaching carefully over and grabbing Karl's shoulder, spoke in a shocked voice. "Shit, Karl…."

Peering first at Liam, then up to Maria and Mattias, Karl spoke in a whisper, but his patience with the situation was wearing thin. "I had to knock her out. They'll know where we were going in any case, but this is the best we can do for her. Her fate is obvious, but at least we have a chance—if we move our asses."

Standing, Karl patted Liam on the shoulder. He exuded calmness and control, just as another cry from their distant pursuers resounded through the crisp night air. Though still far away, the strange call now seemed a bit closer. "We're now alone in enemy territory, guys, without a map or guide."

Pointing back to the trail, Maria spoke up, her face full of warring emotions, from sadness for Evelyn's plight to astonishment at Karl's brutal and unrepentant actions. "We can stick with the trail—."

Karl shook his head. "No way. They'll take her, but even if they don't, there's zero doubt where we're going. We gotta come up with our own plan. A new one. There's always another way of doing something; it's just a matter of using our brains and intuition to figure it out."

With no response to his proposal, Karl took a couple steps away, where he peered into the forbidding trees and misty undergrowth of the untraveled and trail-free part of the forest. Nodding, he turned around, and true to his nature, still managed to sound calm. "Let's head west. We need to find a new way off the island. And now we can't stop, even for a minute—no matter how tired we get."

Chapter Sixteen

Jacob walked with the saunter of a composed and self-assured predator. Not that he was intent for the moment on violence, but the very way he carried himself, with his heavy steps and self-confident swagger, said that he owned anything and everyone he placed his eyes on. Here was a man with the means to do as he pleased, and he wouldn't hesitate to reveal that fact to anyone who ventured a glance his way.

But his face was quite discontented now, miserable even. Nothing about his expression could be confused with happiness, and as he strode toward the front of the still-smoky inn, his pace increased in anticipation of something he had never expected to happen.

Walking through the tattered and broken front door, which now had most of its scorched debris cleared away, Jacob moved to the back hallway and across the filthy carpeted floor towards the rear exit. There, next to one of the guest room doors, stood two of his guards, one from the family and the other a human. Stepping aside, they avoided his gaze.

Turning into the bedroom, the exact one Liam had used to house the innkeeper and one of the few left in the motel that could offer a semblance of normalcy, Jacob's eyes fell on that same Evelyn. Tied to the queen-size bed, she was completely immobilized by ropes, and her mouth was stuffed with a dirty rag. Her leg was bandaged well, and in testament to the medical care she received, it appeared she would recover from the serious bear-trap injury.

Evelyn's eyes, set in her ghost-white face, were awake and in terrible fear. Paralyzed, she focused on Jacob with alarm and trepidation.

Standing near the bed was Stanislav, and happy to see his arriving boss, he nodded at Jacob with subdued respect. Still, he had the weary appearance of a man who was there to do a job, but beyond that, he didn't appear overjoyed with the task awaiting him.

"Hello, Evelyn," Jacob said, and his voice was thick with irony. "I imagine you never considered the possibility you would see us again? Life has a way of offering such surprises. This I can say with utmost sincerity, since I've had a lifetime of dealing with events I never fully expected."

Evelyn's rigidly fearful gaze focused on Jacob, but after a moment, a mild change came over her. Formerly pitiable, an undercurrent of defiance became evident in her unflinching stare.

Jacob noticed the subtle change, and moving to the bed, he allowed a malicious smile to fill his pretentious face. Reaching down, he removed the rag from her mouth and held a finger over his lips, indicating silence was her best option for the near future.

"Evelyn, I am going to tell you a story," said Jacob, and he looked at her sincerely, almost as if he was talking to an old friend, which until recently would have been the case. "Please follow along and do not interrupt. This story is a tale none of your fellow islanders has ever heard, so you should feel some fortune that I have deemed you worthy to hear it."

Jacob's eyes locked on Evelyn for a second, and feeling enraged, his hand shot down and grabbed her face. His impossibly strong grip encompassed her jaw, and his thumb and middle finger were placed to either side on her cheeks. On those fingers, black claws began to grow, and after a moment, he tapped each claw on her white skin, as if he was deciding whether to tear her face off entirely. The edge of each razor-sharp nail bit into each of the cheeks, forcing a small spot of blood to come to the surface.

Above her, Jacob's eyes shone a deep yellow, and the fierceness in his stare was wicked and horrifying. Evelyn trembled as she awaited her death, which was unlikely to be a pleasant one.

Suddenly releasing her, Jacob's eyes and hands were again normal, and he resumed a false smile towards his defenseless prisoner. Turning around, he paced several steps before spinning again to restart his speech. "It was my mother that showed me this long, long life. She was a difficult person, brusque and impatient, and she spent a life of toil in Russia at a time when it was recovering from the continuous depredations of the Mongols. That plague of a people tortured Russia for almost two hundred fifty years and made life unbearable for many, especially my ancestors."

Slipping into his memories, Jacob smiled to himself, then glanced over to Stanislav, who appeared very interested in the developing story, even though he had heard it many times. "She saw death and wanton misfortune on a scale that nobody would understand today, for that was a time when war and violence were very personal things. Regions and towns were often depopulated without the slightest hesitation from conquering armies or warlords. In our current day of 'human rights,' free health care, food subsidies and such, those distant times would seem positively barbarous."

Flashing a mirthless grin, Jacob continued in a steady tone. "So, my aged mother received this gift of extended life from a traveling band of entertainers, which in that time went throughout the countryside offering simple carnivals to the rural masses with games, juggling acts, magic shows, and other forms of showmanship.

"These entertainers ran a portable version of 'Las Vegas,' and unlike many performers in our modern productions, there was some amazing talent to be had from this wandering band. Fortunately, one of these gypsies was infected with this condition I now carry, and he decided to pass it on to my extended family through my dear mother. Subsequently, the rest of my blood relatives were soon included in this new way of living."

Moving to the back of the room, Jacob showed some interest in a simple calendar hanging on the wall. The photo for this late summer month showed a horror image from the movie *The Thing*, a classic film from 1982. The movie was a favorite of Jacob's, and he smiled as he played through the events in his mind of a plot that saw visitors from outer space infecting and destroying a remote scientific base in Antarctica. *If only they knew of a real infection that lives among them*, Jacob thought, *they might not feel so secure in the reprobate world they call home.*

Turning back to Evelyn, Jacob continued with a detached and morose bearing. "But my family was not able to continue their lives of feasting on their neighbors for long. Within just a few months, when multiple people from our local village came up missing, they were found out and burned at the stake in a most horrible display of humanity's tolerance for…us."

"Thereafter," said Jacob, seeming miffed but not particularly upset by the telling of his family's demise. "I alone was able to flee farther into the provinces, and I never was able to return to that village. It was fortunate for me that my mother taught me the proper recipe to 'cure' my food before I went on my way—before she met her end in the blistering fires of our neighbors. Anyway…I was left alone with my condition, and for decades I lived as you see me now, traveling across the vastness of Russia and taking my food where I could. It was a lonely and delicate life, without friends or attachments to things that you take for granted in your shorter lifetimes."

Walking near Stanislav, Jacob now nodded affectionately at his friend, and his face became happier as his mind moved to more recent and pleasant memories. "I then served in several militaries, from those of the first Tsar to several Eastern European duchies, where I had access to food without the attached interest humans got when I preyed upon simple peasants. It was a safer way of living, and though not a great existence, I was able to form my time into something that approached a normal manner of conducting myself."

"But this time in my life, where I was alone and without love or direction, taught me that I had to have friends and family if I was to keep living at all," said Jacob, and he now sounded like a preacher, one that showed a sort of intense and devout faith. His stare, formally noncommittal, became that of a righteous believer awakened to something new and wonderful. "So, I decided to change my ways."

Snapping his fingers, Jacob raised his voice, and he fixed his suddenly enthusiastic eyes on Evelyn. "And I did change. I became an officer and began having real friends. I began to accrue wealth, which is not too difficult a thing when one lives over such long periods. I also learned that my words had to be trusted when I gave them. Most importantly, I came to understand that the most essential traits to a 'person' such as myself were loyalty and trust."

Walking back toward Evelyn, Jacob peered down mockingly at his distraught captive. She was now to do with as he pleased, and the joy of his control over her doomed destiny was obvious and exhilarating. Basking in his moment of glory, he felt better than he had in a very long time.

Such was the breadth of Jacob's life, filled with so many mundane matters of business and leading his people, that he rarely had the chance to indulge himself in this way. Just now, he felt like a professional sports player who had spent many years away from his sport, only to again discover he loved to play his cherished game every bit as much as when he was younger.

However, with his soon-to-be victim, some measure of a different emotion began to show itself from under Evelyn's terrified features. What had been there before was Evelyn's abject desire to escape her condition and retain some hope for survival. She of course feared Jacob, but the most important thing to her psyche was a desire to live. All people, to more or lesser degrees, always wanted a chance to make it out of their dire situation when cornered, and in this horrid circumstance, she was no different. Hope sprang eternal, even while she suffered in her inescapable predicament.

But now she saw in Jacob, despite his droning story about his distant past, the utter ruthlessness and lack of mercy that had always informed how he dealt with his enemies. She had never seen his lust for violence turned against the islanders, but here he now was, positively happy to play with her feelings and ultimately dispose of her. She also knew that the end, however he decided to snuff her out, would be painful and unimaginably cruel.

And so, Evelyn saw with sudden fatalism what was soon to occur, realizing that today, and specifically soon, would be her last day on earth. Like the flip of a switch, she knew her life's end was now inevitable and imminent. A new sense of stoicism made her jaw harden, and she suddenly didn't see Jacob as a demigod, like so many of the islanders always had in the past. Now he just seemed like a vicious and pitiless creature, one that was spawned to inflict pain and agony on the world.

Jacob continued, and for the moment, he hadn't noticed Evelyn's hardening resolve. "As my wealth grew, so did my need to feel engaged with the wider world. Deciding to never again return to Russia because the Orthodox Church was aware of my special abilities, I ended up in this beautiful country, a place I have grown to love. Here, my circle of friends grew, and I counted the wealthiest and most industrious in society amongst my confidantes. Whether with royalty or with the emerging class of capitalists, I was a man whom one needed to know to advance up the rungs of privilege."

Without looking back, Jacob reached behind himself and clapped Stanislav on the shoulder. "And I made even better friends, ones that were in tune with my way of living. They would never grow old or betray me. Today we live in a beautiful society, where everyone is cared for and appreciated—both my normal human friends and my special ones."

Craning her neck, Evelyn spat at Jacob. The move was unexpected, but she didn't come close to him, and he frowned at the spittle on the filthy floor before returning his gaze to her. A raised eyebrow told her that Jacob was impressed with her audacity, if not her aim.

Ignoring her defiance, Jacob gestured with wide arms, suggesting the whole area of the island outside the inn. "And for my normal friends, no expense or luxury is spared. I take care of everyone completely and help with their lives in any way that makes them happier. And if some tragedy should befall our domain's inhabitants, such as occurred when your husband was diagnosed with cancer, I flew in the world's best doctors and equipment for his treatment. The result was unfortunately not as we wished it to be, but the effort on my part was sincere and without holding anything back. I was your abiding benefactor, and I only had your best outcomes in my intentions. Whenever I must, I have always tried to stop the weakness that overtakes the bodies of normal humans."

Evelyn's pale face, in such a condition because her body was missing so much of its blood, sharpened into a ferocious scowl. Freed from caring about her dead family or personal well-being, she showed Jacob her clenched teeth and a disgusted grimace. "You're a fucking murderer, Jacob. No fancy words or clothes, and no fake love for your inferiors, will change that. You kill people and pat yourself on the back while you celebrate evil on your pilfered island. You are worse than a mad dog; but unlike that mindless animal, you know better and attack anyway."

Jacob, appearing amused, looked over to Stanislav, who raised his eyebrows, showing his own version of being impressed by this bound and helpless woman. Not having seen Evelyn in this light before, both men absorbed her honest appraisal of their exploits with several moments of reflective consideration.

Turning back to Evelyn, Jacob nodded and offered her a mischievous grin. "If you believe that and have convinced yourself of my evilness, Evelyn, then you also know you allowed it to happen, as did your husband and son. I suppose that, just like them, you will go to your grave with that knowledge."

Leaning down, Jacob's face drew near Evelyn. Unworried about being spat at again, he showed her a wicked expression that dripped with malevolence. "Just know that you will die a traitor's death. Your body will be mutilated and hung in the middle of the village. Everyone who is loyal and trustworthy will in turn spit on your corpse. You will reap precisely what you deserve, and not a soul will mourn you. And all through it, I will enjoy the spectacle immensely."

Taking in that reality—she knew Jacob spoke honestly—Evelyn gulped, but gone was her awed fear of him, and it was instead replaced by her grudging acceptance of what lay ahead. Speaking with a cracked voice and eyes full of hatred, her face beamed with conviction. "When you get to hell, Jacob, you will not see me there. I will be with my family in heaven."

Jacob showed some surprise at her profession of faith, as he had never known her to be a believer. Raising his tone to a cheerful inflection, he showed her an agreeable nod and made sure to focus exactly on her increasingly withdrawn eyes. "That may well be, Evelyn, but before you go, I really must ask that you tell me everything you know about your new friends, these tourists that have caused me so much trouble. Stan, with his unique set of investigatory skills, will gather all the pertinent data before seeing you on your way."

Gesturing to Stanislav, Jacob kept his smile locked in place. When Stanislav pulled a long knife from his waistband and moved toward Evelyn, assuming the look of a talented killer who was about to ply his trade, she began to shake her head and whimper.

Whatever her bravado was before, when the time came to face death, she wasn't eager to embrace it. *Nobody ever really is,* Jacob thought, and given his extensive history with violence for more than half a millennium, he was something of an expert on the subject.

Watching the torture unfold, Jacob's expression calmed, and his spirits were considerably improved from when he had first entered the inn. Smiling, he realized that he really had to learn to relax more.

As Evelyn's horrified screams echoed throughout the ruins of the motel, with pleas for mercy mixed in with excruciated and overwhelmed gasps, Jacob came to the comforting thought that happiness in life was only possible when he appreciated the small moments of cheer—whenever and wherever he could find them.

Chapter Seventeen

Creeping illumination from early daylight descended on the coastal shoreline. The gentle lapping of the lake's tides against rocky beaches occupied the crisp morning backdrop, and from emerging westerly winds, fresh air bathed the island in a pleasant sub-arctic chill. This stirring breeze, consistent and cleansing, made tree branches and scattered vegetation bend in consistent waves, helping ensure the summer day's incoming heat wouldn't be too oppressive.

The view from the tree line overlooked a meadow that stretched down to the distant waterline, and on a knoll above the lake's dark surface, a simple cottage was perched. The sighting of the building, a modest structure made of wood and painted in an off-color white, allowed it to have an expansive view of the rough coast for several miles in either direction. Below the diminutive home was a trail leading to an extended dock, but that floating pier was currently empty of any moored boats.

Karl crouched as he moved from a cluster of bushes that lay halfway towards the cottage. Moving back to the trees across the open field, he took his time, making certain his movements would not be too conspicuous on the sparsely vegetated ground.

Karl's frustrated face was just visible in the dim light, and as he moved close to the others, he frowned and shook his head. The silent group, quiet and hidden in a stand of trees and dense brush, waited for Karl's expert take on what they could expect next.

Breathing calmly, Karl squatted between Liam, Mattias, and Maria. He kept his voice low as he gestured back towards the small house. "Okay, there's some kind of farm-looking house ahead. We need to take it slow; this entire setup is sighted to act as a watch station over the coast. They do a good job of hiding its intent, but there's no reason to have a farm here. There's no animals or land to cultivate. They could also have sensors or cameras, even night-vision stuff, so we need to be careful."

Nodding, Mattias licked his cracked lips, fighting the thirst that had developed from a night of traversing the forest. "Let's wait until it gets brighter, then approach across the field. Maybe we'll get lucky, and they'll be no one home."

The companions, tired from the effort—both physically and mentally—of sneaking through the forest, nodded a silent agreement to the suggestion. Whatever their best route forward, none appeared eager to find new people to meet, especially as they knew anyone they ran into was unlikely to be friendly.

For the next half hour, the group was silent in the cover of the forest, and they took turns resting amongst the foliage while the others stood lookout. Settling into a gentle overwatch of the property, their worried eyes scanned the rural country house while they rubbed sore muscles to recuperate from their manic flight to safety.

Eventually, light from the eastern sky painted the backyard of the homestead in brighter colors, and the outlines of a boat became just visible in the gloomy area. In the midst of two serviceable pickup trucks and an all-terrain vehicle, the mid-sized boat, with a silhouetted cabin on its small deck, was evident on an attached trailer.

A feeling of optimism built up among the friends. Unfortunately, that sensation quickly dissipated when two figures emerged from the home's back door and began moving amongst the vessel and vehicles. Accompanying the relaxed male figures was the distant sound of spoken Swedish, but their exact words were muffled due to the distance.

After watching their movements for several minutes, Karl leaned close and motioned toward the scene below. "I'm gonna move down there and use the ridgeline to stay out of their view. When I get there, I'll stay behind the corner of that barn. When I wave at you, you guys come walking down, and I should have the drop on them. Walk like you're on a relaxing stroll. Don't act intimidating and maybe we'll get lucky and find someone who doesn't want to kill us. No need to go all 'black ops' just yet."

Each of the group nodded in agreement, and Karl took a deep breath to calm his nerves. He had always been told he was a cool operator, but in truth, he simply knew that to be the most effective in a precarious situation like this, a person was smart to be scared and cautious. By being guarded and prudent, acting as if every move was likely to be his last, mistakes were less common, and the consequent odds of success tended to increase. In both combat and life, Karl knew he had to make his own luck when victory seemed as much a matter of chance as due to careful planning.

Stepping from their sheltered area, Karl drew out his knife, and continuing his crouch, moved carefully through the field to the left. Descending in stooped rushes through the rolling grass, he did an admirable job of remaining hidden, and even his hyper-aware friends had a hard time discerning his hunched shape as he crept towards the back of the house.

As Karl got within twenty yards of his desired spot, his gaze, scanning around for hidden threats, stopped on a double-barreled shotgun leaning against a wall not far from the boat. Near the weapon and craft were the two men, one a grizzled man in his fifties, and the other a cocky-looking teen.

Both individuals, the oldest dressed in overalls and a straw hat and the youngest in a long T-shirt and baggy shorts, were wholly unaware of Karl. The boat absorbed the pair's attention, and they took turns shining flashlights on its large and greasy engine while tinkering with its various internal components. Relaxed and easygoing, they showed no concern with their immediate surroundings, and their voices were carefree as they chatted in the day's growing light.

"…said they weren't gonna get off the island," said Erik, the older man, who was flustered as he peered into the engine compartment. "He also said no matter what it took, they're as good as dead."

Adam, the younger person and probably the son, as Karl noticed the family resemblance, nodded enthusiastically. "Yeah, no doubt. Only time I ever saw one of the family upset. They've had poker faces my whole life, but now they look like they're going to a funeral…or at least, like they wanna make someone go to their own funeral."

Pointing to a wrench, Erik held out his hand, and Adam quickly slapped it into his waiting palm. Focusing hard, Erik fixed the tool on a bolt and broke it free from its rusty seating with a quick turn.

Satisfied for the moment, Erik spoke to Adam with a cautious voice. "Son, just make sure you do what they want. Tonight, I'll meet with 'em again, and we can hunt those fuckers down. You want to be certain you don't get the family riled up when they're serious like this. Follow orders right every time."

Chuckling, Adam shook his head. "They don't have to order me. I'll do anything to protect the island."

As their conversation droned on, Karl took three quiet steps and snatched the shotgun from its place against the house's wooden siding. Stepping around the corner of the wall, he turned the weapon over and examined it. With a wooden stock and two long silver barrels, Karl was impressed with the age and craftsmanship of the old firearm. As a 10-gauge beast-of-a-weapon, it was a sturdy and deadly tool for violence, even if aged and of an uncommon caliber. Loaded with the right shells, it could kill anything that lived.

Happy with his new toy, Karl peered up the hill and motioned to the party. Liam was first to step from the tree line, and followed by the others, they began strolling down and across the open field. Slow and steady, they were in no rush, almost like they had a calm appointment for a relaxing breakfast.

Only a few seconds passed before they were noticed, and Erik shook his son's shoulder and pointed when he detected their presence. In response, Adam's eyes went wide, and he took a fillet knife from his waistband as he met his father's concerned gaze.

Spinning around, Erik looked for his shotgun, but was surprised to see Karl already had it in his firm grip.

"Take it easy," said Karl, his voice assertive but not overly hostile. "We aren't here to harm you…unless we have to."

Adam's face became worried, and he and his dad exchanged knowing glances. The recognition passing between them was not lost on Karl, nor was it lost on Liam, who was coming closer from the field above.

"Hello folks," said Liam, trying to sound magnanimous. "Nice to meet you."

Speaking in English, Liam had surprised Erik and Adam, and they stayed quiet as they evaluated Karl and the incoming group of visitors.

Mattias, his pistol pointed at the ground, gestured with his other hand to Adam. "Please drop the knife. Nobody needs to get hurt here."

Surprisingly, Adam assumed a defiant stare, and it wasn't until his father shook his arm that the young man acquiesced and let the fishing knife fall to the ground.

Walking closer to the father and son, Karl clicked the breech open of the shotgun, checking that it was loaded. Nodding in satisfaction, he saw that two shells were inside, and he snapped it shut before cradling it in his arms.

Gulping, Erik spoke hesitantly in heavily accented English. "Who…are you people? Why have you come to my house?"

Shaking his head, Karl replied with a frown. "You know who we are…so drop the bullshit."

Interjecting his somewhat kind voice, Liam made sure to play the nice guy in the escalating exchange. "We really aren't here to hurt you or anyone else. We just want to get off your island. Are you alone? Is anyone else here?"

"It's just me and my son," said Erik, and the bashful way he said this suggested there was more to the story. Shaking his head, as if to drive away some inner torment, he went silent and peered at his unwelcome guests with ill-hidden hostility.

Pointing to the boat they were working on, Liam sounded hopeful, like he didn't want to offend them. "We just need to use your boat to get out of your hair. We won't bother you more than we have to."

Erik, evidently happy to accommodate them, walked down the side of the boat, where he pointed at a hole in the side of the craft's exterior. Putting his hand all the way through the jagged opening, he spoke in an ironic voice. "Be my guest, but it won't get ten meters in the water. And the engine is also not working. Why do you think we're out here?"

Looking first at Karl, then at Mattias and finally, Maria, who was absently rubbing the recent scar on her forehead, Liam sighed. "Well, that sucks. Guess we could try to swim, but with the water temperature, even if we became Olympic-level athletes across those currents, we might as well save time and shoot ourselves instead. Death would be quicker."

It was quiet for a time as the friends processed what this meant to their plans, or for that matter, their lack of them. Walking to a raised grassy area to the side, Liam peered over the lake's attractive surface. Staring for a considerable time, he thought about how just a few miles of water might as well be as far as Mars.

Clearing his throat, Karl spoke up, as if he could sense it was a good time to end Liam's internal deliberations. Directing his words to Erik and Adam, his voice was cold. "Well, in that case, we're going to have to ask to stay with you, probably until night. We're going to catch up on some sleep, and you're going to be our hosts until we're gone."

Motioning with the barrels of the shotgun towards the back door, Karl's voice grew even less pleasant. "If someone else is inside, now is the time to say it. You wouldn't want us to have any surprises in our fatigued state of mind. Accidents may happen."

Erik warily shook his head at the notion of anyone else being there, and he promptly steered his son in front of him as he moved toward his home. Pushing Adam ahead, he opened the door and walked inside, making sure his movements were slow and unthreatening.

Inside, the furnishings and decor of the place, in contrast to its humble exterior, were impressive. As the party filed in, Erik clicked the lights on to reveal an open main room that was filled with clean and modern furniture. The walls held bright prints of nature, as well as real paintings of oceans and mountains done by a talented artist. In the corner was a vast computer setup and desk filled with several aligned monitors and some kind of advanced radio arrangement.

On the wall near a clean and attached kitchen, one constructed for gourmet cooking with multiple stainless ovens and hanging pots, was an enormous flat-screen TV. On the display was a paused graphic of a video game where the first-person view stared into an eerie cave. In the distance of that dark cavern, it looked like several red demons had been moving in for the attack. The fact that it was all frozen in place made the view even creepier than it otherwise would have appeared, like evil was just waiting for its chance to pay a visit to the player. The pending game seemed depressingly appropriate for the entire group's island experience up to this point.

A hallway to the back of the room led to what must have been bedrooms and a toilet. Framed photos filled an entire area near the hallway's entry, and the pictures, set at proper intervals in a gridded pattern, were almost industrial in their number.

Surprised, Liam ogled the attractive interior. Looking first at the insolent teenager, then over at his worried father, he spoke with an impressed voice. "Nice place. What did you have to do to afford such a nice setup?"

Snorting, Maria broke in. Her voice was caustic as she spoke, revealing limitless hatred for this place, these people, and in fact, anything associated with this island. "I think they suck the dick of a monster and eat these crumbs he throws them. It's a lot like the Nazis, only worse, because they can leave any time they please. But they choose to stay and serve these evil fucks while they eat innocent people."

Surprised at the outburst, Liam thought for a moment before continuing. Though Maria wasn't wrong, he didn't want her longing for vengeance to interfere with their chances for escape. Pissing people off, even those whom you control and who in fact may deserve it, could be counterproductive.

"OK…thanks for that, Maria. Mattias, after they use the bathroom, let's tie up these guys," Liam said, and he then smiled at Erik and Adam, who looked less than happy with the idea of being prisoners in their own house. "We'll try to make you comfortable…because it's gonna be a long day."

#

With the raw sound of the cord being pulled tight, Mattias cinched it fully into place. Looking approvingly at his work, he ran his fingers over the bunched material, making sure that it was sufficiently firm and placed where Erik wouldn't manage to wriggle free of his bindings.

Pulling himself to his full height, Mattias peered down at Erik and Adam. Bound in separate chairs, they were tied up with taut nylon lines wrapped several times around their extremities. Scrounged from Erik's master bedroom, the material was perfect to keep the reluctant hosts securely in place. Both the newly minted captives peered back at Mattias with a mix of fear and disdain, but in Erik's case, the fright clearly pertained to the prospective fate of his son.

Shaking his head, Mattias pondered how people could display such humanity for their own family, while at the same time have no empathy for the lives of others. Working with someone who killed and ate undeserving people was not a recipe for moral clarity, and it appeared the father and son had no personal qualms about their particular roles on the island.

Mattias put on a smile and tried to sound encouraging as he further considered the situation, despite the ethical calamity which surrounded their circumstance. After all, there was really no personal need to stoop to their level of depravity, even if he found them personally detestable. "If you cooperate, you both will live through this just fine. That is, at least until I come back here with about a hundred cops—or maybe a regiment from the army. Then, your stay in prison will be long and miserable, if there's any justice to be had."

Karl snorted from a dark corner of the room, where he held his ever-present knife and was absently sharpening a piece of driftwood he had scrounged from the nearby shoreline. Unfortunately, whatever his talents were with tracking and scouting, they didn't seem to carry over to carving precise items. The elongated man-figure he was trying to create looked decidedly like a badly rendered phallus.

Frowning, Karl placed his masterpiece on the counter and slipped his knife back into his sheath. Pacing over to the now-confined family members, he leaned down and looked into each of their agitated gazes. For the moment, his stare had a bit of a predator shine to it, like he was a shark that was circling prey and gauging its nutritional value before taking a satisfying bite.

But Karl didn't say anything; instead, he took a step back and continued his steady evaluation of Erik and Adam. In response, Adam seemed to have lost his boldness, and his panicky eyes moved over to his dad.

Near the hallway, Liam had been looking at the plethora of photos that adorned the deep wood-grained wall. Staring at the host of images, he saw that Erik and Adam were posed near a host of various backdrops, from an ocean to a forest—Liam thought that must have been in Germany from its familiar look, where he had often vacationed—and even several medieval castles.

In many of the colorful and attractive environments, a weathered but attractive woman stood near them and also smiled at the camera. Given her closeness and pleasant disposition, it didn't take a genius to understand she was part of their family. This left an open question as to where she was now, and for a moment, a pang of deductive sympathy told Liam her absence from this home wasn't the preferred choice of its current residents.

Shaking away his tendencies towards mercy, Liam turned and stepped closer to his friends. He moved to stand between Mattias and Karl, where he also focused on Erik and Adam. With the three of them appearing like an impromptu version of the Holy Inquisition, Liam kept a steady tone and addressed Erik. "OK, Erik, I want you to understand where we need to go from here. We need to get off this island."

Pursing his lips, Erik nodded and showed Liam a *No Shit* expression. He may have been a grizzled country hick, but his sarcasm was well-honed and clearly expressed. "Yes, I see that."

"I'm glad you do…," continued Liam, and he motioned out the window, presumably towards the monsters that were somewhere out in the forest looking for them, "because I know you'd be happy to hand us over to that head-monster prick, just so he could buy you another entertainment center."

Karl chuckled, and for the moment, both Adam and Erik fixed their stares on the military man. Normally, Karl had a way of attracting positive attention—charisma often had that effect on people, but with his current attitude, it made everyone in the room cringe. Their wary features showed they feared Karl might do something unexpected—like ram his knife through one of the prisoners' faces.

"But that's not going to happen, gentlemen," said Karl, finally speaking to Erik in clenched and intimidating words. "Because if it does, you need to know that whatever occurs, I'm going to slit your son's throat, and you're going to watch him bleed out in front of you."

Karl drew his blade again, and rotating its sharp edge, he had an uncanny talent to make it gleam as he turned it over in front of Erik's increasingly fearful eyes. "Don't let Liam's kindness confuse you on that promise, Erik. This isn't a joke—I've never been one for humor, even when my life didn't depend on it."

Both father and son took the threat seriously, and they continued their silence as they absorbed what they were facing. The reality of the situation was not a promising one if these visitors remained at the residence, and their faces reflected a deep sense of unease, which was quickly morphing into outright terror.

Nodding to Liam and Mattias—Maria seemed to be absent entirely from both the room and discussion—Karl gestured toward the back of the house. "We can sleep in four-hour shifts to rest up. I'll take the first watch, and you guys need to eat something when it's your turn to be awake. Both our hosts and those fucking creatures want us to give up. But we aren't going to appease them—we're going to find a way to win this…and make them all pay."

Chapter Eighteen

The sharp rap on the door was jarring, and Liam's eyes popped open in response. Shaking his head, he struggled to come to the moment, letting his vision scramble across the house's interior walls in search of his forgotten purpose for being there.

Sitting fully up, Liam righted himself on the thick upholstered loveseat and blinked away his evaporating dreams. As he came awake, trying to adjust his field of view to the reality of the cottage, he briefly thought he had somehow imagined this sudden interruption to his pleasant slumber, and that he should soon be coming awake in his studio apartment back home.

But across from Liam, still bound and now gagged, Erik and Adam were also wide-eyed and had a sheen of panic over their surprised features. Looking at their scared faces evoked a feeling in Liam like he was peering at people affixed to train tracks who had no way of avoiding an oncoming locomotive.

A harsh and demanding voice, that of Sergei, shouted from the other side of the front door. "Erik, you in there? It's Sergei, open up."

From the back hallway, moving with the grace of a wary ballerina, Karl crept into the main room. His face was calm, and appearing unbothered, he held his knife up and moved next to Erik. Placing the gleaming blade at his throat, he pulled the dish towel from Erik's mouth.

As he focused into Erik's fearful eyes, Karl held a finger over his lips to suggest silence, and knowing he had his attention, he moved the blade to hover near Adam's carotid artery. The intent was clear: a simple flick of the knife would sever one of the body's essential sources for distributing blood, and his son's appointment with a lingering death would be irreversible and traumatic.

Moving cautiously but with less grace, Mattias and Maria next emerged from that same hall. Maria clutched the long shotgun in her hands, focusing intently down the barrel, while Mattias also pointed his pistol expectantly at the home's front entrance. Their vision was mottled by sleep and fatigue, but their expressions were sharp, with adrenaline and dread forcing an awareness of potential violence into their still-awakening vision.

Moving over and behind Erik, Liam began to untie the man's bindings, and from the side, Karl indicated with a nod that Erik could answer their impatient visitor outside. Erik, glancing worriedly at his son, smacked his lips together to gather sufficient spit to talk.

"Hello…Sergei…I'm um…busy," exclaimed Erik, and his voice, although impressively passive, cracked a little. "Gimme a minute."

Liam moved at a frantic pace as he sought to disentangle Erik from the thin binding. As he got close to finishing, the door shook with another heavy knock, and Sergei's voice grew less tolerant of waiting. "Hurry up."

Shaking free of the nylon cords, Erik stood and moved tentatively toward the door. Unfortunately, the circulation in his legs was reduced by his captivity, and he leaned against the door, stifling a grunt of pain as he barely kept his balance.

After fumbling to unlock it, Erik took a deep breath and cracked open the heavy door. Some light from the late afternoon blurred his vision, and he had to blink away artifacts to focus on his impatient visitor.

Sergei stood there, along with three more of the family arranged at offset intervals behind him. They were outfitted in leather shirts adorned with knives, and the obvious battle dress was not a costume he had seen them wear before. Worse, the ways they stood, with bladed postures and ready-to-fight demeanors, were completely foreign to the manner they had engaged with Erik for his entire life. To see lifetime acquaintances focus on him with aggressive intent was sobering, making the stressful moment even more awkward.

"Hey guys, what's going on?" asked Erik, and his eyes danced from one fierce man to the other. "We were out most of the night looking for those people. I'm dead tired—."

"Are you alone?" Sergei asked, and his eyes became entirely black and completely inhuman. "Where's Adam?"

Appearing uncomfortable, Erik raised his voice. "Well…Adam went to the east side of the island. Said he had to take care of something. I…got some company."

Behind Erik, Karl was quiet and unmoving. His eyes were impassive and fatalistic as he stared at Erik's back, while his knife inched closer to Adam's throat. At the back of the room, Mattias and Maria stayed focused on the door, their muscles tensing. Liam, armed only with Adam's flimsy fillet knife, was scared to death as he stood behind the now-empty kitchen chair.

Outside, Sergei and his group tilted their heads with suspicion and moved a step forward. Sergei, continuing his dark-eyed stare, peered intently into Erik's eyes, as if searching for the answer to some unknowable riddle in the uncomfortable father's bumbling behavior.

Erik blushed, avoiding Sergei's gaze with some difficulty. Frustrated, he dropped his voice to a conspiratorial whisper. "Sara is with me in the back. The widow from the village…the one with the…the big…." Erik finished the thought by moving one hand out the door to make a movement that intimated a big breast. "Please don't let her know you know—she'll die of embarrassment."

Moving his face to within a foot of Erik's, Sergei's eyes now shone with that odd yellow glow, the one that evidenced the family's intensity when they were excited or verging on changing to their more ferocious forms. Staying still, it was like Sergei gazed directly into Erik's deathly afraid soul, and Erik worried the hunter might gain access to all his secrets with his probing stare.

After a considerable time, the glow disappeared from Sergei's eyes, and he pulled back. His face was now normal, and both he and his fellow hunters relaxed into amenable postures.

Smiling, Sergei was at once calm and cheerful. "Erik, you old dog. I've been telling you for two years to move on from that old hag, and now you've finally done it. Sara is a good choice; I'm proud of you."

With his blush deepening, Erik smiled and acted even more embarrassed. Continuing the role of a reluctant and single father, he shook his head in mock modesty.

Gesturing to his comrades, Sergei turned around and pointed to the forest. Before striding away to continue their hunt, he called back over his shoulder. "Don't have too much fun. We've got to meet at the inn, or what's left of it, at eight PM. Don't be late—we'll be there every night until we get them."

Sauntering away, Sergei and the other hunters assumed a more careful and attentive manner of walking, and each of their steps was accompanied by paying particular attention to every detail in the shaded woods ahead. Looking entirely confident, like world-conquering athletes, they disappeared into the cover of the darkening trees.

Easing the door shut, Erik waited until they were far away. Afraid to breathe, as the moments passed, he expected a quick and fatal return of the creatures. Having been around them his whole life, he couldn't fathom he had actually been able to dupe people who had been alive for centuries. Everyone on the island knew they were benevolent, if you were always honest and loyal to the family, so to be deceitful seemed not only wrong but impossible for him to carry off.

But fool them he did, apparently. The problem was, despite the fact he had played the part for he and Adam to survive, he got the distinct impression this was something he couldn't easily undo later. Much like a spouse who has been unfaithful once, trust was impossible to fully regain, even if the cheater was truly forgiven. And worryingly, Jacob was not a spouse you wanted to piss off.

Sighing at his suddenly very complicated life, Erik turned around to meet the inquisitive stares of his captors.

Karl was standing close to him, and Erik was a little uncomfortable that the large man had come so close without him catching on. Karl grabbed Erik by the shoulder and escorted him back to his chair, but his grip seemed a little less tight as he returned Erik to his seat.

As Mattias worked to place him back into his bindings, Liam came over and offered Erik a slight grin. His expression was full of surprise and appeared quite genuine. "Well done, Erik. You should've been an actor—that was impressive."

Karl, looking down at him with serious features, also managed a mild nod of approval. "Yes, it would appear you get to live for a while yet."

Glancing at Karl, Liam let his gaze linger on his friend. There was something in Karl's voice and manner he didn't quite like, though he couldn't yet put a finger on what it was.

While Mattias finished re-tying the ropes, everyone gathered near their unwilling hosts, and for the present, Erik's gag wasn't replaced. As the companions took turns evaluating their captives, Erik and a petrified Adam looked back with fidgety and intimidated eyes.

Expectantly, there was an extended silence in the room.

"OK, here's the situation, then," said Liam, finally venturing to break the quiet. "Erik has to meet them in five hours at the inn. We haven't got much time to figure this out, 'cuz they're sure gonna notice him missing."

Mattias, sounding miffed, spoke up. "The only way to get to Grenna is by boat, and you may have noticed we need a working version to do that. This shit cottage was a huge mistake…they'll know we were here. We need to find another boat and get out when it's dark."

Maria, pressing her lips tight and trying to read some writing on the shotgun's barrel, spoke without raising her eyes. "Yeah, we'd be sitting ducks on the open lake if they have patrol boats.

And they're not going to let us row our way to safety—like we're on a Sunday cruise."

Walking to the large screen TV, Karl crossed his arms and stared at the image. Breathing deep, he turned and gazed at the group with a frown. Serious and dispassionate, he shook his head and peered over at Erik and Adam. "So, we go south and keep looking on the coast. Not much else to do."

Taking a step closer to his friends, Karl lowered his voice, as if announcing something only the party should hear. Gesturing to Erik, then less happily to his son, his face was solemn. "Look, I don't like it, but we can't leave them here to talk."

All together, the companions blinked, and it took a moment for them to get the gist of his meaning. Maria, after taking in his intent, smiled broadly, while Mattias appeared contemplative. Liam's expression, in direct contrast to his close friends, exploded into disbelief.

"Karl, you've got to be kidding," said Liam, and he scanned the face of Maria and Mattias, not liking what he saw.

Looking down, Karl shook his head. By way of answer, he drew out his knife and walked slowly toward the prisoners. Terrified, Erik futilely tried to hop his chair in front of his son, while Adam's panicky eyes looked for help from any of the other friends.

Distressed, Liam jumped between Karl and the captives. Holding his hands out in a calming manner, his voice rose into a whine. "Karl, you can't do this."

Looking down at Liam, Karl didn't look happy at his decided task, but neither was he dissuaded about carrying out what he saw as necessary. "Liam, I told you before, you have to choose to survive. In a struggle like this, the weak never come out alive."

Continuing his peacemaker role, Liam made sure to appear unthreatening, and his pleading tone grew even more pronounced. "That isn't survival; that's murder, and you know it."

Frowning, Karl looked impatiently at Liam. "We have four dead friends on this hellish island. And these…people…allowed it to happen."

"But they didn't do it themselves," shouted Liam, trying to show some backbone.

"They would have," grunted Karl, and now there was some emotion in his voice, like he was waking up to the enormity of their shared loss.

"But they didn't," continued Liam, and he lowered his voice, trying to maintain his composure. "And even if they would have, you can't just knife a family out of rage."

Karl shook his head, his mind sinking back into a self-protective indifference. "It's not rage, Liam. These people aren't human. They're animals, less than dogs. And even you know what's got to be done with mad dogs."

Chiding in, Maria spoke with some enthusiasm from the side. "They're less than animals."

Staring over at Maria, Liam gave her a look that said, *you're not helping*, but he moved his gaze back to Karl without replying. Concentrating, he tried a new tack. "By the time we get off the island, they'll still be tied up. It doesn't serve any purpose to kill them."

As he considered Liam's words, Karl chewed on his lip. Shaking his head, he pointed his knife at Liam, flashing it like an accusatory laser pointer. "Liam, you're acting like all the politicians that send soldiers to crazy places…to 'build a better life' for the downtrodden and the weak. And when we get there, and we have to kill all the bad people that make the place so horrible, you get cold feet. And the whole project falls apart…and good people die while they're just doing their job."

Liam, collecting himself, looked over to Mattias for support, but Mattias, clenching his jaw and furrowing his brow, seemed noncommittal at best.

Staring back at Karl, Liam lowered his voice, trying to sound understanding. "Karl, I agree. The politicians always screw over the people trying to do the right thing. Soldiers, regular people…everyone. But this is about you, not them. You're not one of them; you're my friend, and if you do this, for the first time since I've known you, I can say you'll be horribly wrong…and you'll regret killing them for the rest of your life."

The room was silent in response, and the captives, as if cheering for the home team that would keep them alive, eagerly moved their stares from one side to another.

Sighing, Karl considered Liam's words. He wasn't a man who often questioned himself, but for a long time, the room stayed quiet. Looking over to Maria and Mattias, he absently ran his callused thumb across the sharp edge of his blade.

Coming to a decision, Karl frowned and sheathed his knife. Gesturing to Erik and Adam, he sounded a bit relieved himself. "OK, Kofi Annan, you win. We leave in five minutes, then. And make sure they can't budge in those chairs. We better hope this doesn't come back to bite us in the ass."

Nodding, Liam hurried over to the father and son. With shaky hands, he hurried his preparations by checking and double-checking their bindings. As he yanked tightly on the rope, he met Erik's eyes.

"Thank you," whispered Erik, and intense appreciation filled his weathered face. "Thank you very much."

Moving quickly, Liam nodded as he prepared to leave. Not wanting a reconsideration of the planned execution by Karl, he aimed to get out of the house quickly. "I didn't do it for you. I did it for him."

"I know," responded Erik, and after some hesitation, he came to his own extended decision. Speaking calmly, he nodded his head towards the back door. "There's a dock about five kilometers south of here. It has a power boat in a locked boathouse. You'll have to pass two other houses before you get to it."

#

The remaining rays of daylight were spotty, and a series of meandering clouds partially blocked the sun as it began to dip below the western horizon. The effect of dim illumination and darkish cloud cover was eerie, with varied shades of gray making it appear like the day's end was an odious prelude to an even more wicked night ahead.

Staring into the bleak sky, Jacob smiled at the feeling of morose spookiness the view brought to his soul. He was not one to worship at the altar of evil, he even saw himself as the good guy in most of his interactions, but he nevertheless always appreciated the strange beauty of creepy skylines that often roiled above his beautiful island.

Turning to his left, Jacob took sight of the heavily damaged inn. The broken and burnt building would have to be completely rebuilt, and no doubt he would ensure the materials and details of the structure would be improved over its more than 100-year-old prior construction, but he still felt a pang of loss at having to change something he'd appreciated so much in the past.

This island, the place of his refuge and where he truly considered himself home, was supposed to be outside the realm of the worldly intrusions and everyday violence so prevalent in the rest of society. Feeling introspective, Jacob understood that recent events were all his fault, but shaking off the sense of wrongness caused by these tourist outsiders was still going to take some time.

Walking towards the inn, Jacob angled towards a group of men surrounding a large table, one that had been saved from the gutted structure and subsequently moved outside. Numerous exterior floodlights had already been arranged to bathe the area with brightness, and the men standing around the table squinted within their fierce glow as they peered down.

The mix of men included regularly dressed family, a few local police officers, and a collection of normal humans, all of whom wore severe expressions. Their faces, concentrated and worrying about the developing crisis, testified to the unusual and traumatic nature of these recent events. Though all these people were his most steadfast and dutiful followers, Jacob couldn't help but be bothered and somewhat ashamed by their apprehensive gazes.

Seeing Jacob coming toward them, the group of mismatched people quickly melted away at his approach, untangling themselves to pursue other efforts in their search for the rogue outsiders. Stanislav, now alone and staring at a map on the charred table, was the only one to remain as Jacob drew close.

"Stan," said Jacob, moving next to Stanislav and joining him in viewing a high-resolution photograph of the entire island. "What good tidings do you have for me?"

Shaking his head, Stanislav raised his gaze to meet Jacob's. "Nothing, I'm afraid. The normal men and dogs are working the east coast of the island. Our groups are working the rest, and they're being particularly thorough in their search."

Nodding, Jacob turned his attention to the specific details of the map. Placing his hands on the table, he moved his eyes over the entirety of the land mass in the middle of the vast Lake

Vettern. Using his long and whitish finger, he traced the relatively robust beaches of the west side of the island, then continued over the forested north and towards the rocky beaches of the east.

The south was near Jacob's own house and only a fool would try to flee in that direction. Whatever he felt about his confounding enemies, Jacob knew they weren't fools.

Scowling, Jacob indicated the whole map with a wave of his hand. "Have you heard anything from the watch houses on the coast? Have any boats of any type been seen at this point? Our sensors would catch any movement, correct?"

Stanislav frowned, clearly unhappy with his upcoming answer. "Our privacy and security systems are expensive and precise, but they are predicated on preventing and responding to intruders. We cannot so easily stop someone trying to get away. But…it would appear they have to still be here—neither our sensors nor the watch houses have seen any movement."

Looking up at the sky, Jacob once again appreciated the view as he mentally thumbed through his options for the ongoing search.

Growing impatient, Jacob spoke quietly while continuing his upward stare. "Call all the sentinels individually—and soon. I want confirmation we still have them trapped. I needn't tell you of the problems we could encounter if our visitors are free to spew their ridiculous stories to a public blissfully unaware of our presence."

Processing Jacob's directions, Stanislav took a moment to contemplate which location was best placed to rapidly respond to his queries for information. Each coastal house's residents were not always near their radios, and they also had different times they were supposed to report in, making instant contact with them tricky. Also, even though these series of lookouts all had their own mobile phones, the jamming equipment that was still being used by the family to prevent distress calls made their own devices useless.

Stanislav scanned the various locations circled in red across the entire exterior of the island. Nodding, he picked up his portfolio, a black binder containing the entirety of their search plans, and strode away. Moving up an embankment and to the paved road leading to the village, he walked with purpose towards a dark pickup parked under a collection of gently swaying trees.

Left alone, Jacob looked approvingly at Stanislav as he moved away, then returned his gaze to the impressively thorough map.

As Jacob examined the potential escape routes of his prey, a mischievous grin forced itself across his lips. *Ye can run, but ye cannot hide*, he thought, remembering an old maxim once taught to him by his long-dead mother. The old woman had been a horrible parent, with cruel tendencies and little empathy for others—particularly her own family.

But his dear mom also had a way of being creatively pitiless when it came to ensuring her enemies paid for their crimes against her. She had a lust for vengeance that really knew no boundaries, and anyone who crossed her was quickly eradicated. Sadly, that had only been the case for several months at the end of her life, until a cold, dark night when so many of the local peasants, having caught on to her special abilities, came and dragged her away to a fiery death.

Smiling, Jacob realized that, however brutal his mother's and his other biological family's deaths had been, at least he had inherited that entirely practical trait of ruthlessness from her. Since that distant time, Jacob's talent for inflicting woe and despair on his enemies had only grown more potent, and he had no doubt it would continue to serve him well for the rest of his living days.

Chapter Nineteen

The subdued light didn't entirely displace the darkness, but it did serve to make rolling grass and sparse shrubbery easily noticeable on the open field. Night had arrived, yet the pleasant glow of the stars and moon ensured adequate visibility to the naked eye.

A gully ran across the swaying grasslands, running at an angle toward the lake's rough coastline of rocks and broken land. Perched above the gully was one of the watch houses, and with prodigious lighting, it stood out on an elevated finger of stone and firm soil, making the area around it easy to monitor—even at this late hour.

Moving in rushes, Karl picked his way up the gully towards the taller grass farther from the house. Using his impressive ability to keep from highlighting himself on the ridgeline, he would have been difficult to follow, even if a watcher was specifically looking for him.

Dropping into a crawl, Karl emerged from the depression and scooted towards an area behind a hump in the landscape—in a place he couldn't be seen from the house. There, waiting for him with expectant stares were Liam, Mattias, and Maria. In the faint light, they looked something like hopeful children, waiting to hear some good news from their talented guide.

"Our problem is these fucking houses," whispered Karl, and even in the spotty light, the irritation in his expression was obvious. "This is just the first of 'em, according to Erik. I followed the gulch all the way down near the water, hoping we could find a way to pass by the place without being seen."

Shaking his head, Karl's tone became dour. "No luck. It opens up at the bottom and a child would be able to see us there…and that doesn't even assume they have night vision."

Peeking his head up, Karl motioned to the house, which was just visible from his viewing angle. The residence had a panoramic deck running around it, offering a gorgeous and distressingly thorough vantage point for its residents. Worse, there were currently two people, a man and a woman, who leaned against opposite railings and peered through binoculars. With an excellent view over the areas needing to be traversed, going south from the friends' current hiding spot would be a challenge.

Disappointed, Mattias nodded and gestured towards the interior tree line, towards the place they had earlier crept from to get a closer view of the coastline and house. "Then we have to work our way back inland and avoid their line of sight. This is taking too long—we aren't going to stay lucky forever."

Agreeing, Liam also motioned back toward the forest from where they emerged. "Yeah, but we really don't have a choice. I hated fucking camping my whole life, and now I gotta crawl through half of Viking land to have a chance to survive. I feel like Tom Cruise, only minus the looks and athletic ability or…um basically anything that would help us make it through this."

Liam smiled at his own joke, and his white teeth, which were really his best physical trait, appeared as if they were glowing in the dim light. Shaking their heads, none of the others took the time to laugh at his self-deprecating joke.

Instead, one-by-one they crawled back toward the collection of woods toward the inside of the island. Their progress was slow, and their untrained physiques, at least those of Liam and Mattias, were not accustomed to such fatiguing movement. Strangely, Maria and Karl were able to move without much exertion and appeared completely unbothered by their arduous efforts.

Time was running out, and they dreaded the prospect of coming late to their hoped-for departure point at the upcoming dock.

#

In the brightness of portable floodlights, a large bulletin board had been erected near the front of the inn. Serving as the gathering point for the search operations, the location was filled with various hurrying people, but standing off by himself, Jacob peered up at the exhaustive map view of the island.

The scorched smell of the nonfunctional motel had now dispersed, and only the night air, full of a clean-smelling forest aroma, remained. If not for the dire circumstances of lost friends and unobtainable food, Jacob realized his personal mood might have been considerably more pleasant.

On the enormous display board, the wide photo, detailed enough to look as if it had been taken by a low-flying satellite, held tacked notes with the disposition of the groups in each area of the island, as well as the status of each group's progress from subsequent updates. In locations that were already thoroughly swept and deemed clear of prey, the post-its were crossed off to indicate the respective grids had already been searched.

Jacob, arms crossed and with his chin held between two fingers, thought through the status and effectiveness of the operation. Slowly, his disposition grew happier, as he gradually noticed he had not been this busy and engaged for several decades.

Though clearly distressed by recent events, Jacob couldn't separate himself from the sense of feeling alive. His unique form of adrenaline, laced with chemicals unknown to normal men, sharpened his instincts and made his mind feel uncommonly perceptive. The truth of the moment was he felt invigorated and excited at the prospect of more difficulties, as well as the prospective violence that came with it.

With the death of so many of his family, it really wouldn't be appropriate to admit this feeling to Stan, but being honest with himself wouldn't cause any harm. Much like the times in his distant past, when he readied himself for battle in various parts of war-prone Europe, Jacob was giddy at the prospect of shedding blood.

Approaching quietly, Stanislav got Jacob's attention by clearing his throat. As if knowing his boss' thoughts, he frowned at the exhilaration Jacob exuded. Focusing on the losses of irreplaceable friends, Stanislav wasn't elated about the deaths of his men up to this point—or whoever else might die soon.

When Stanislav spoke, his tone was sour and irritable. "It's the northwest coast, at Erik's house. Nobody is answering the radio. He is due to rotate here soon and go out with another search group, but his son should have answered when he was absent from the residence."

Taken aback, Jacob rotated his head to peer curiously at Stanislav. "They are some of our most dependable. They must have been killed? Or perhaps, simply unavailable at the moment?"

Pressing his lips into a tight frown, Stanislav shook his head. "I don't know, Jacob. Sergei went by there earlier while doing a sweep of the area. Erik told him he had a woman with him. Sara, from the village?"

Stepping toward the map, Jacob considered that possibility. Staring at the location of Erik's house on the upper left corner of the map's image, he tapped his chin several times as he mulled over the explanation. Turning to Stanislav, he shook his head. "Erik is a martyr for his ex-wife and will never date again. I've seen such pathetic behavior many times. They must have been compromised by our tourist guests."

"I've already sent two groups to the house," Stanislav replied, and his face became troubled. "Hopefully we'll kill or catch them all, but I assume they know we're aware of their presence now. I fear for Erik and his son's safety."

Turning towards the road, Stanislav gestured towards his tinted-window pickup, with its noisy, idling diesel engine. "They should already have arrived there. Shall we follow?"

It was quiet for a moment, and Jacob ran through the possibilities of this new information. Unlike Stan, he was less worried about Erik and more concerned with what precisely had happened at the watch house. The situation as presented was not what he would have considered the likely outcome from interactions with the outsiders, and that was worrying. He would have expected a fight from his humans, not collaboration, even if it had been forced at the barrel of a gun.

Jacob had hoped the occurrence of betrayal with Evelyn was a one-off, but a more-unsettling indication was making itself known from his deepest thoughts. This place of his blackest inner self, where his paranoia had kept him alive and safe all these years, was buzzing with a sickening feeling.

Being a big enthusiast for the methods of Machiavelli, a philosopher who preached the benefits of both brutality of and tolerance for the ruled, Jacob had spent the better part of his life treating his normal human followers from the notion that they always responded better to positive reinforcement and beneficial payoffs.

But the question over time of how best to govern his people had not been without anxiety. Machiavelli had been contemporary to Jacob's formative years as a leader, and although he never had met him personally, he wondered if the tenets of rule the well-known Italian espoused were not as valid today as they once had been. *What if I have been too kind? After all these years, what if I am simply wrong? More importantly, what am I to do about it? Decisions, decisions....*

The possibility of widespread discontent was troubling in the local population—as were the solutions that such a reality would require. Such solutions were a last resort, for the degree of brutality Jacob would have to dispense to wipe out the humans wouldn't be easy to cover up, even by the family.

Nodding to Stanislav, Jacob motioned for him to lead the way to the truck. As they paced towards the vehicle, Jacob reached down to massage the dagger he had used to kill Duke Von Essen more than three hundred years prior. Its thick and weighty presence below his long coat, from where it had been drawn and used to ruthless effect many times throughout the years, was comforting.

Fighting off the temptation to grin, Jacob realized that whatever the future held, an opportunity for employing his trusty blade might soon present itself. And that was not a bad thing.

Chapter Twenty

The windows on the lakeside cottage were busted out, evidently after being used as an emergency entry point by incoming hunters from the family. Glass and the remnants of wooden frames were scattered inside the house, ruining its formerly tidy appearance. The now-tattered curtains, having been violently ripped aside in the process, twisted in a calm breeze now penetrating the home.

To add to the sour undercurrent, Erik and Adam sat expectantly in the middle of the cluttered room. They were no longer bound and gagged, but their eyes told the story of people who were uneasy and out of their element. Glancing back and forth, they peered around with disturbed gazes, unsure of what came next.

Jacob stood near the kitchen, his gaze moving across the expensive tiled floor and the collection of pricey appliances that outfitted the cooking paradise. His countenance was not overtly hostile, but neither was he contented in the role of enjoying a pleasant house-call with his followers.

"So, Erik," began Jacob, and his voice had a mocking vibe to it, like he was the Cheshire Cat from *Alice in Wonderland* fame, "how many were there?"

Erik made a show of appearing unbothered, and he even managed to look Jacob in the eye, albeit only briefly. "I already told the other guys, Jacob. There were four, and they left right after Sergei came by."

Nodding, Jacob didn't immediately respond. Stepping from the kitchen, he moved gingerly closer to the father and son. When he was within a few feet, he spoke in a calm manner, using the voice of a questioner who wanted to coax information from a reluctant target. "I know precisely what you told them, but I want to hear it again. And this time, Erik, I want to hear why you lied to Sergei when they were here."

Erik, looking over at Stanislav, who stood near the front door with an emotionless expression, gulped several times while he considered his best path forward. Glancing at his son, he wanted to show a relaxed image to their important guests, but hiding his fear at this point just made him appear more desperate.

"They had a knife to Adam's throat," Erik said, his voice quivering. "Jacob…I have always been loyal—."

"That you have, Erik," replied Jacob, coldly cutting him off. "Still, I have to ask myself an important question: when people lie to me, even when I am not present, where does it stop?"

Unimpressed with the story as it was told, Jacob crossed his arms and glared down at the family duo. At that moment, the normal-sized Jacob appeared to Erik as if he were a giant. Worse, it seemed as if he was a malevolent giant, full of stirring and righteous fury.

Continuing, Jacob motioned out the window. "And, you could have told a lie that Sergei could have easily figured out, correct? Like, 'my son is at the swimming pool,' which we do not have on the island, or some other nonsense?"

Erik, looking dejected, nodded. When he spoke, his voice took on a servile quality. "Yes, well…I could have been smarter. I do my best, but being a genius has never been my strongest quality."

Grinning, Jacob clapped Erik on the shoulder, which made both father and son recoil. Adam flinched so much that he almost hopped entirely from his chair.

Walking towards the hallway at the back of the house, Jacob stopped and raised his tone, inflecting his words with accusation. "But instead, you chose to let my enemies get away, offering them a chance to escape my wrath. Our entire island is at risk, and you focused on yourself."

Rubbing his hands over his arthritic knuckles, Erik stared at the floor. As he became increasingly nervous, he didn't respond to Jacob's unhidden incrimination. He was no psychologist, but it seemed to him that bumbling denials would just make Jacob angrier, and that man was not the type of person Erik wanted to make more upset.

The room was quiet for a moment, and Jacob let his eyes wander to the series of photos on the wall. The pictures were of widespread locations, and Jacob focused on one in particular, where Erik, Adam, and Erik's ex-wife, Astrid, stood in front of Schönbrunn Palace in Vienna, Austria. The famous location, a summer residence and seat of Hapsburg power in Central Europe for more than three hundred years, showed a long and beautiful line of gardens behind the smiling faces of the family. In the far background, the majestic outlines of a yellowish building, the central structure of the ornate grounds, were just visible.

Reaching out, Jacob touched the sturdy frame of the wide photo, and a pleasant memory briefly pushed away his agitation. "Did you know, Erik, that I traveled to this place on numerous occasions? In 1762, in October I believe, at one particularly fascinating event, I visited this palace at the behest of several royal families. They had suggested I should witness the play of a young musician who was due to visit Austria's sovereigns, Francis I and Maria Theresa."

Turning back to Erik, Jacob's changed mood continued, and he flashed Erik a genuine smile. "That young man, a prodigy by any estimation, was a certain Wolfgang Amadeus Mozart. History would come to know him well, but I was able to witness his skill in person, and I can tell you, all his written accolades were actually quite understated. His performance was marvelous, at an age when most children were still learning to use the toilet."

Turning again to the wall, absorbed in his treasured memory, Jacob spoke amicably, as if relating the touching anecdote of a dear friend. "If only you could have seen the surprised faces of all those arrogant nobles who attended the performance, you would have been witness to one of history's most precious moments. That young boy's star burned so bright that it pushed away the boundaries of class and money. Just briefly, mind you, but it was a wonder to behold. Mozart even jumped on the queen's lap in a fit of happiness. Six-year-olds can be so playful."

Lost in his thoughts, Jacob continued his walk down memory lane. For more than a minute, the silence continued, and with the home's ambiance growing more positive, Erik took the chance to look up, hoping Jacob's interrogation was coming to an end.

But it was not. Spinning away from his observation of the picture, Jacob's mood reassumed its intrusive and unforgiving direction. His mind returning to the present, Jacob stepped near Erik. "Now listen carefully, because there is a point to my story, Erik. In your small understanding of the world, do you think a man who has done such things, who has dined with long-dead and famous royalty, who has witnessed firsthand genius only now known from dusty history books, is someone that you can fool? Do you think for a moment that such a man would not see through your amateurish lies?"

Aghast and suddenly uncomprehending, Erik tried to talk but was only able to stutter a few grunts before Jacob silenced him with an extended finger.

Resuming his sharply inquisitive smile, Jacob nodded down at Erik. "Now, please pay attention to another bit of history. This story is more recent, and it revolves around your dear ex-wife. I had known for some time that she wanted to leave you, that she found you boring and her life tedious. She even came to me, hat in hand as it were, and asked my permission to depart your house and leave her husband and son. It seemed that, as her life was moving into older age, she really felt a need to explore the world and not be miserable."

Tears filled Erik's eyes, and whatever his fears for the moment, his sorrow overwhelmed him, causing him to almost burst out crying. For a disastrous few seconds, Jacob thought he would do just that, and open disgust filled Jacob's unsympathetic features.

Moving on, Jacob let his voice grow cold, as if to accentuate his next point. "And you know, Erik, in loyalty to you, I tried to talk her out of her wild urge to wander and experience life. I spent an hour or so telling her about your good side, that you were a good mate to her, blah blah blah…it was all nonsense of course, anyone with a brain could see she was right, but as a matter of course, I felt an obligation to you to fix her errors, to stop her from destroying your family."

Now overcome with emotion, Adam started to cry, and the teen, formerly a rebellious youth full of vigor, bawled like a child. Glancing over at his son, Erik put a reassuring hand on the boy's shoulder.

Sighing aloud, Jacob's tone grew lighter, and he took on a demeanor that said, *what will be, will be*. "So, she wanted to continue her life's path to freedom. But what you didn't know was this little tidbit that came next. Right there, in the reception area of my beautiful house, in an area you have worked in and done innumerable deliveries over decades, I tore her throat out. She died rather quickly, bleeding out over the white quartzite flooring that I prize so much. Cleaning the area was truly a chore for my guards."

Erik and Adam's mouths were agape, their shocked minds processing what they thought could only be a joke. They stared at each other, then at Jacob, waiting for a punchline to his horrendous bit of humor.

Unfortunately, there wasn't one coming. By way of explanation, Jacob continued. "I used my contacts in Stockholm to process the 'divorce,' but not all of this was for you, Erik. It was made necessary because Astrid could not accept her place and appreciate her family and life—or my ISLAND. Did you think I could have our local population roaming around the world on a permanent basis, revealing our manner of living to whomever they want?"

Affecting a quirky smile, one that didn't quite fit the face of a ruthless killer, Jacob shook his head. "No, of course not. So instead, she served as a plentiful source of food for the family, which of course was far more useful than anything she ever did for you or Adam. The rules for her were as they are for everyone on the island: once here, you can never leave for good. I pay for plentiful vacations and enjoyment, but that is merely to rest on occasion and enjoy your lives. The catch is that loyalty always flows both ways; your presence here lasts until we lower your casket into the ground. She knew that, as you do now, so her inauspicious end is entirely her fault."

Jacob made a movement with his hands, as if he were washing them of guilt. "My generosity and good word were, as always, fulfilled. Her actions brought about her own downfall. Not that it matters now, but I hope you see the truth in that."

Adam, hitching into crying fits, continued his blubbering exploration of grief, while Erik appeared to tense up, anger filling his face. Both Jacob and Stanislav noticed the heightening rage in Erik, and they stepped forward, as if hoping he would be foolish enough to attack them.

"Now, please do not think I tell you this to be cruel, Erik, far from it," explained Jacob, his expression slowly returning to a normal state. "I instead say this to impress upon you the need for truth in this matter of our transient tourists. It is not just your life we are discussing."

Jacob gestured with a nod of his head to Adam, who continued crying, seemingly unaware of anything except his mom's sudden status as a murder victim and the family's prior main course at a meal.

In response, Erik's mortified eyes drifted from Jacob to his son, then over to a prepared-to-fight Stanislav. Receding into despondency, he unclenched his hands and let his weight fall back into the wooden chair.

Beaten and without hope, Erik sat for some time. His eyes lost their grip on the moment, and his mind drifted into a sort of interior desolation, a place where all his fears were now fully realized. He instinctively knew this had become the endpoint in his life, both for him and his son, and somehow, he was able to accept that for it was. Sometimes the benefit of a simple life was having a simple understanding that your time was up.

Finally, as if not caring what came next, Erik spoke in a flat, detached voice. "I told them…about the boathouse south of Nils' place. The one…with the powerboat we use for running supplies."

Jacob stiffened in response, surprised at the admission, as well as the fortitude it took Erik to betray his people and then openly admit it. Such treachery was horrible, but he had to give it to Erik for having the audacity to carry through by allowing their enemies to escape. He never would have thought a weak simpleton like this coastal watchman would have had the tenacity to carry it off.

Arching an eyebrow, Jacob accepted the confession with aplomb, showing Erik a face that was rarely surprised for long. *Wonders never cease to amaze*, thought Jacob, and he exhaled a long and slow breath. Whatever his reasoning, Erik also must have known he had just signed his death warrant, so perhaps, deep inside, Erik had known what Jacob had done to his ex-wife those years before.

Erik didn't have any real knowledge of that event, of course, but human perception often performed on a higher level than even Jacob understood. It was one reason Jacob always made sure to pay off his people and treat them well, so they would have no need to resort to matters in life that left them in depression and grasping for money or other manic pursuits to make them happy. Until recently, such an approach had always worked well.

Turning to Stanislav, Jacob made eye contact, and like spouses that understood each other with only a brief glance, Jacob communicated his intent and turned away, moving back to the wall of framed photos.

Behind him, Stanislav drew his long knife and advanced on the terrified pair. As Jacob took in the sights of so many of their world-class vacations, from beautiful Rome to the stunning Acropolis of Athens, there came a surge of begging from Erik, followed by sickening sounds of blade work, then gurgling, and finally, screams.

Following that, there was pleading by Adam, which soon degenerated into helpless shrieks, then into more physical struggles and choking gasps. Soon, the bountiful splashing of liquid against the floor was matched with the wet thump of a body slopping as dead weight against the hard ground.

After that, there was nothing more. The formerly sedate residence was quiet once again.

Chapter Twenty-One

On the beach below, down and across several hundred yards of sparse shrubs and scattered stones, the mild waves of the lake's shifting tides pushed against the rocky shoreline. The water, slurping as it filled and refilled crevices in the patchy coastal gravel, created sucking sounds, which then popped in foamy discharges as the waves receded.

The entire landscape, flooded with moonlight and taking on a luminescent quality, made visibility somewhat easy in each direction. The dim beach was observable from the elevated height of a bluff above the water, and stands of trees on that ridge provided substantial cover from intruding eyes.

At the far end of the coast's open expanse, a long dock protruded into the lake, and the creaking sound of its immersed supports, moving in concert with the deep currents of the lake, made the area seem intensely lonely.

Karl crouched among some of the trees on the bluff, making certain his outline wasn't obvious to their adversaries. Focusing on the distant end of the beach, his eyes searched for potential threats to their group, as well as the easiest route to approach the apparently untended dock below.

On the far periphery of his vision, Karl's gaze lingered on a chain-locked gate straddling the dock, and the barrier looked like it prevented easy access to the boat slips beyond. The dark outline of a single boat bobbed in an open space behind the gate, showing only one vessel currently available for use. Fortunately, only one boat was necessary for the friends to escape—assuming they could find a way to get to it.

Whispering, Karl pointed at the approach to the dock. "I don't see anything, but that doesn't necessarily mean…."

Detaching from a jumble of some bushes and light trees, a lone figure stepped out and walked several steps onto the open beach. Moving carefully, the shadowy image appeared meticulously aware of its surroundings, as if it was evaluating each nook and cranny of the uneven shoreline around it.

"Well, that's not a good sign," said Liam, offering a sober assessment of the tense moment. "Think maybe we're lucky, and it's just a dude out walking his dog?"

Stooping low, Mattias tilted his head to get a better look at the unknown person through the low branches in front of him.

None of the figure's features were obvious, and with only its dark outline visible, identification was impossible. Scowling, Mattias' low voice, strained with worry, sounded less than optimistic. "It's definitely not good. Looks like we're going to have to fight our way out there. By the way, how are we going get the lock off that gate?"

Looking back, Karl patted his sheathed knife. "This should do it."

Holding her shotgun out, Maria tried sounding helpful. "Will this work?"

"I don't think so, Maria," responded Liam, his face doubtful. "That's one of those things from the movies that sounds like bullshit. I could never figure out why it always worked, and always with one shot. You'd think the bullet, just once, wouldn't precisely blow the lock off the chain…or exactly strike the door in the place it needed to. I mean, when they fire into the lock, why does it always disable and open it? Wouldn't it just bounce off the metal if the angle wasn't right?"

The companions took turns staring at Liam, like they thought he was momentarily crazy. Then, realizing he had a point, they agreed to his logic with delayed nods and tentative grins.

"Gotcha," said Maria, and with a long-absent smile, she lowered the weapon.

Karl, ever the functional pessimist, spoke carefully to Maria, his words calculated and even. "Anyway, keep your shotgun loaded and ready…you only got two shots until you need to reload, and we can't be sure we'll have the time for it. Make them count."

Maria, agreeing with a nod, gulped. Staring at the distant and unknown figure on the beach, she was at last forming her thoughts into an aggressive and focused mindset. Her intentions were beginning to crystallize into a committed and clearheaded notion of her essential part in this horrific struggle, where her crushing sorrow needed to be left behind her. The current needs of her friends were pressing now, overriding the fugue state she had been immersed in since the fight at the clinic.

This suddenly didn't seem like too difficult a task for her; Maria's mind was becoming clear, losing its kludgy and miserable obsession with the tragic moment of Johan's last time on earth. Her now-awake perception worked at full speed, and she finally understood the occasion had arrived to make these creatures pay for her husband's death. With rabid determination making her feel eager to inflict harm, she planned to make her chance for revenge count.

Johan had died for no good reason, and her man had never hurt or seriously offended anyone in his life. If it took her last breath, Maria was going to take her pound of flesh from these wicked monstrosities that had hounded and killed some of her closest friends and spouse. Conviction burned in her eyes, and at the same time, she never felt physically stronger or more capable than she did now. She supposed her changing physical state, undoubtedly attached to the infection from the orderly, had something to do with her newfound physical prowess and motivation, but that was appropriate, because it allowed her to use the monsters' own illness against them.

The others became quiet, psyching themselves up as they peered down and across the shoddy coastline. In all places where people prepare to lay their lives on the line, to face up to their destiny without faltering, there was a moment of reflection before committing themselves to a goal from which they might not return. This was that occasion and moment, and even Karl felt the urge to turn and flee, to give up on advancing toward something that could easily end in their violent deaths.

But to do so would have been a betrayal of hope itself. Throughout his military service, Karl often thought about a quote attributed to Edmund Burke, an Irish statesman from the 18th century: "The only thing necessary for the triumph of evil is for good men to do nothing." These wise words were perhaps never more relevant than now, and because of these bizarre events the group found itself in, there was also never a more appropriate circumstance for a call to arms under its terms.

Not only did the companions need to fight to survive, but they also had to do so with the full knowledge that their fight was worth having—whatever the outcome. Like steadfast gamblers that have decided to go all in on their chosen game, at a certain point it was just a matter of placing the appropriate bets—in this case, their very lives—and then throwing fate's dice as best they could, hoping for the best.

Gathering his courage, Karl gestured forward with his hand. Cautiously moving ahead, he picked his way through the bushes and tried to keep his balance over the lumpy, irregular soil. The rocks and dirt were difficult to navigate as he descended the hill and ducked through the covering brush, forcing him to be attentive with each step as he pressed his heavy boots into the squishy and sometimes craggy ground.

Mattias, Liam, and Maria followed, each trying to control their fear and keep from making a sound as they sought to match Karl's pace. The potential for a fall over the sandy rocks and dew-covered plants was high, making their wary gait particularly slow as they moved down the sloping seawall behind Karl.

Sighing, Karl mumbled to himself as he focused ahead, keeping his footfalls steady and noiseless in the night's extended silence. "Never thought I'd be doing this shit in Sweden."

#

The bright headlights probed through the misty night as the truck barreled down the twisting highway, its tires screeching to prevent a skid over the road's steep embankment. Outside, the expensive headlights of the high-end vehicle tilted automatically to illuminate the road around each of the curves, while in the interior cab, state-of-art lighting provided a robust and conspicuous glow. A high-definition map system and plush leather completed the luxurious setup, making the cab's front look like the cockpit of an exotic control room.

Stanislav sat in the driver's seat, peering intensely into the foggy night ahead. This part of the island currently held dense amounts of swirling mist, and the accumulation of haze on their path forward made his ongoing speed adventurous and incredibly nervy. Clearly unworried by the treacherous drive, he smacked his lips, almost as if bored with the effort of steering the fast-moving truck.

From the passenger's side, Jacob stared expectantly ahead, his dark eyes taking in every foot of their rapid progress toward the remote dock. Glancing backwards in the pickup, a luxury diesel version imported from America, Jacob acknowledged the dark outlines of two of the family sitting in the Crew Cab area, as well as two more crouching carefully in the truck bed all the way to the rear. There was no sound in the vehicle's interior, either from outside the sound-proofed cab compartment or from idle conversation between its anxious occupants.

After several more moments of silence, Jacob glanced inquiringly at Stanislav. "How much farther, Stan?"

Motioning down to the GPS screen, which showed a blue vehicle moving across winding roads, Stanislav responded without moving his eyes from the road. "Why not just look at the GPS?"

In answer, Jacob frowned and moved a lengthy index finger to the large and well-lit touch display on the console. After several attempts to broaden the view, then shrink it back again, then watching the truck's avatar lose its real-time orientation and needing to re-center it, he grunted in annoyance and offered Stanislav a disgusted look. "Stan, one interesting aspect of living so long is that I get to become ignorant of technology over several lifetimes, whereas others only have a few decades to be annoyed with such 'conveniences.' To think there was a time when we traveled with horses by dead reckoning and used hand-drawn maps made in a prior century."

In response, Stanislav chuckled and nodded. He remembered those times well, but his own memories recalled the aggravation of slow travel, staring at a horse's ass wherever you went, and being lost half the time with much less nostalgia.

He wasn't nearly as aged as Jacob, but Stanislav had seen many generations come and go, and the one thing that happened with each was older people thought their prior way of living was always the best way to do things. It was a bit comical, really, as all those men and women, so certain of their rightness, were now nothing but bones in forgotten graves. In fact, anyone who ever knew them, unless they were somehow connected to the family, was also completely irrelevant to history. Time made even the most important people, as well as their viewpoints, seem rather unimportant.

To Stanislav, who, even in his heightened state of living, always tried to get along well and not cause unnecessary problems, it seemed completely silly to debate who really had the better insight into how best to live. What good was it for normal people to worry themselves about trivial matters when the cold ground awaited them after their imminent and unavoidable deaths?

Biting down his desire to disagree with Jacob's love of the "old way," Stanislav pressed down on the accelerator pedal. The truck lurched faster ahead, making the trees and vegetation to either side flash by even quicker.

"Slow down, Stan," Jacob said, and he focused straight ahead, his thoughts and voice growing detached from the moment. "You'll end up losing control, and this truck was hard enough to import. You'll have me looking for six more months to find another. It is not always easy to pay off the proper customs authorities, particularly in this rules-obsessed country."

Stanislav's disappointment was palpable. Glancing at Jacob with restrained frustration, he complied by letting the truck decelerate.

Raising his tone, Jacob's voice grew commanding and grouchy. "And call those at the beach. Tell them they are not to attack until our superior numbers are assured. If needed, use our normal humans with their hunting rifles to stop them. No undue risk is to be taken."

Chapter Twenty-Two

At the bottom of the steep bluff, Karl crouched amongst some heavy bushes. In front of him was a collection of boulders, their large and bulky outlines providing substantial protection from being noticed.

Looking across the weathered beach, which contained numerous more rocks, as well as driftwood and clodded dirt, stood four dark and inquisitive figures. Repeatedly glancing around, their peculiar statures showed them to be intensely interested in protecting the approach to the dock. Though their faces and specific body outlines were not yet visible, their presence and odd bearing so near the group's goal wasn't a favorable sign.

Crouch-walking back through several trees, Karl returned to face his friends. Coming to his whole height, he frowned as he gestured back to the beach—and the site of their potential enemies. His whisper was calm, but his face filled with dread as he spoke. "It isn't good. There's now four of them, and I think they're all our ugly friends."

Liam, confused and with an incredulous expression, was first to respond. "Now four? What…does this mean? This is our only chance to get out—."

"It means they have a huge advantage," said Mattias, interrupting Liam and stating the obvious. "If we try to run by them, they can cut us off, and our chances of winning in a fight really suck against four of those ugly pricks."

Pointing his pistol at the ground, Mattias rotated the barrel and stared with some frustration at its black polymer construction. With an irritated scowl, he bizarrely wished the firearm was more formidable and could somehow launch howitzer shells, instead of the seemingly puny 165-grain bullets he carried in the gun's magazine. Most of Europe, with strict controls on private ownership of such weapons, couldn't use the firearm that he carried, but Mattias now realized with some irony that it was just his luck to face enemies whom it mostly wouldn't harm.

Pursing his lips, Karl nodded at each of the friends, then took the time to individually meet each of their anxious gazes. "Mattias is right; they have the angle and numbers on us. We have to go through them…unless…."

As he thought over their options, Karl held up a finger, an idea popping into his head. Slowly he crept back to a vantage point from where he could see their loitering adversaries. At the edge of the rock formation, he peered through the darkness, taking in the wider landscape of the beach and coastline—as well as the approximate distance to the dock from their shielded location. He squatted for several minutes, playing and replaying the scenarios and chances for success with each of his considered moves forward.

When he returned to the group, the friends gazed at him with baffled looks as they tried to figure out what he was thinking. Karl's features, depressed and noncommittal, didn't inspire their confidence.

"What is it, Karl?" asked Liam. "What is the 'unless' part? I don't like the sound of it already, and you haven't said shit."

"Unless...I attack them myself," responded Karl, continuing his earlier thought. "If I can keep them busy, and maybe take one or two out, you can run straight to the dock. You would have a chance."

Shocked, Liam took a moment to absorb the suggestion. Seeing the self-sacrifice for what it was, he shook his head. "What? You'd be killed. No fucking way...we're a team. We can't leave anyone behind. Not now...not after all our losses...."

Smiling, Karl's face showed something he hadn't yet revealed for the whole trip: thankfulness. Taking two steps toward Mattias, he held out his military knife, handle-first. "Mattias, for the lock."

His eyes panicking, Liam stepped close to Karl and Mattias, as if stopping the exchange could also stop the proposed sacrifice. His voice cracked as he continued shaking his head. "No way, Karl…we're in this together. I won't leave you behind…."

Overcome with emotion, Liam couldn't continue. Desperate, his eyes filled with tears, and he clenched his fists and put them to his face, mock-pounding them against his own forehead.

Next to Liam, Mattias' own features filled with detached horror. After several moments, he couldn't bring himself to speak, but he saw Karl's stark logic for what it was: their only hope for escape. Tentatively, he reached with a trembling hand and accepted the knife.

Addressing his friends, Karl collected himself and fought to overcome his own despair. "Look, I don't want to die here…all alone. But even if we all made it, I can't spend the rest of my life in a lab, and I'm not going to become some eternal monster that munches on dead bodies. There isn't a recipe on earth that could make that appealing."

Tears streamed down Liam's face, and though he was the only one openly weeping, the feeling of loss was overwhelming for them all. As time passed, they spent these self-reflective moments pondering how and what they would do.

A small hand, that of Maria, suddenly fell on Karl's shoulder. Spinning around, Karl peered down at his diminutive friend. She returned his gaze with a quivering jaw, but her eyes, just visible in the dim light, were determined and alive. The conviction in her attractive face was inspiring, and unusually for Karl, he felt his mood surge in appreciation of her support.

Maria brandished her shotgun, offering a hopeful grin across her sorrowful but beaming face. "You won't die alone, Karl. I've had a good life. Besides, you know how impatient Johan is when he waits for me. I could never manage to meet him on time."

To the side, Mattias choked up. Unable to speak, he held his pistol out to Karl.

Looking at the gun dangling from his extended fingers, Karl considered whether to take it. To leave Mattias unarmed was to make him an easy target for the creatures, but it was also true Karl needed a weapon to better fight their brutal enemies while Liam and Mattias made their escape.

Finally accepting the offer, Karl grabbed the weapon and expertly checked both its functionality and to see if it was loaded. There followed a pregnant silence between the two, and each considered the ramifications of transferring the pistol to the person who would soon need it in an apparently hopeless cause.

Karl gestured forward, and his voice resumed its emotionless edge. "It has to be now, so let's get on with it. Time is up, and our odds are just gonna get worse the longer we wait."

Nodding, Maria followed Karl to the edge of the jumbled rocks. Breathing heavy to prepare herself, she looked back at Mattias and Liam, then over to Karl.

Smiling, some peace came over Maria's stressed face, and she pushed away thoughts of what could have been, instead accepting reality for what it was. Panning her head to each of her treasured companions, her expression was appreciative, if somewhat sad. "Nobody has ever had better friends, guys. Some people never have a chance to properly tell their loved ones that. Wherever we're all going, I'll be a lucky girl to see you there."

Unable to stop what was happening, and somehow knowing he shouldn't, Liam watched Karl and Maria step into the open and naked view of their hyper-aware opponents. Walking towards the figures at the other end of the beach, both made their way steadily, their faces rigid and set on their task. Each clutched their firearm in their tight grips, and moving towards an uncertain outcome against undoubtedly deadly foes, they faced their end with commitment and bravery.

Shocked into action, Liam turned and screamed into Mattias' face. "Fucking run."

Pumping his arms wildly, Liam sprinted toward the waterline, stumbling and struggling as he broke free of cover and angled toward the dock. The uneven earth below him made his movements awkward, causing him to narrowly avoid falling while struggling to pick up speed.

Taller and more athletic, Mattias soon caught up with Liam, and heaving for air, the unusual pair of mismatched friends, one a slight-framed sportswriter and the other a lanky cop, ran for their lives, using all their remaining energy to flee towards the distant dock.

#

With a screech of its tires, the large pickup skidded off the pavement and stopped near the edge of the cliff. Overlooking the beach and dock, the headlights pointed at an angle over the precipice, their probing cones focused into the sky above the rugged coast and waves below.

Hopping from the passenger seat, Jacob joined Stanislav on a finger of land that jutted from the top of the ridgeline. Clusters of plants and heavier foliage lined the edge of the vista point, but easy visibility in the clear night made the view below them completely unobstructed. The entire waterline was open in both directions, and their elevated position provided a broad overview of the island's gnarled eastern coastline.

Peering down, Jacob understood the developing scene in one insightful glance. He saw Karl and Maria moving to run interference with his four men on the beach, which immediately impressed him, and farther away, he clearly made out the other two tourists running at full speed for the perceived safety of the dock. As any good leader did, Jacob readily grasped the layout, motivation, and intended disposition of his enemies.

Snapping his fingers, Jacob pointed to Karl and Maria's deliberative advance toward his hunters below. "They are undoubtedly brave, but it is a certainty their fate will not be altered by their selfless actions. Stan, change and take this group down with you. Stop this madness, and if possible, bring them to me alive. I have much to discuss with these obstinate…people."

Nodding, Stanislav immersed himself in fierce concentration, then removed and cast aside his long leather overcoat. Focusing for a moment longer, his eyes flashed with a fierce yellow illumination, and his features, like that of an image melting on a burning painting, morphed into the savage appearance of a repugnant monster.

Stanislav's pupils were now entirely black, his skin was a pale white with an oily sheen, and his mouth bulged with discolored sharp teeth. His loose clothing, outfitted with a brace of sharp daggers in a harness, was tailored to accommodate the changed physique of his enhanced condition, which allowed his now-larger frame to still comfortably fit into the apparel. In the blink of an eye, the sturdy outline and face of a normal man had changed into that of a terrifying beast.

Jumping off the sharp incline, Stanislav's elongated arms and clawed hands moved in concert with his powerful legs as he clambered down the near-vertical embankment. His muscular form made no effort to slow his frightening speed as he hurled down the rugged slope, and in only a short time he made significant progress towards their distant foes. Behind him, four more hunters followed, and with inexplicable agility and jarring speed, they bounded over and around stunted trees and dusty boulders on the way to a gully that would emerge onto the beach in a few hundred feet.

Jacob smiled as he watched his proficient fighters descend, showing an expression like a father might assume while waiting for his kids to dominate overmatched opponents in a children's sports league. He hadn't seen his people move to fight in this way for a very long time, and his pride surged from the spectacle of them rushing to engage mortal adversaries of his precious family.

Ecstatic and feeling enthralled, Jacob's own face remained normal, and with a certain joy, he fully expected his hunters would soon right all the wrongs committed by Liam and his friends.

#

The four vigilant creatures immediately noticed the emerging group, and as Karl and Maria moved directly toward the group of hunters, Sergei separated from his men and rushed to cut off Liam and Mattias from their goal of the dock. Sergei's elongated form, muscular and agile, dashed with relaxed ease as he rapidly closed the distance on the fleeing pair.

Moving with unnerving speed, Sergei's looping run was paced to quickly cut off his slower opponents. In a matter of seconds, he would be able to stop their nascent escape, ending the run of luck that had kept the friends alive for so long.

CRACKS of several gunshots suddenly filled the night air. The pops of gunfire from Mattias' weapon, now cradled in Karl's firm and experienced grip, peppered Sergei, with several of the rounds punching through the monster's shadowy form. Gore blew out from the other side of his lithe frame, and Sergei's body convulsed from each blast of the hypersonic bullets.

Spinning around, Sergei stared hatefully at Karl. As it sized him up, the calm beast tilted his head, as if gauging the mettle of this bothersome new adversary. Time moved slowly, and the enemies, separated by only a score of yards, evaluated their impending actions for the upcoming fight.

Karl focused carefully down his sight, preparing to take a killing shot at the creature's horrid face across the open beach. For a moment, the environment was surreal, with the melodious sound of the waves and the watery backdrop combining to make the tense moment appear almost peaceful.

As Karl's finger tightened on the trigger, Sergei threw himself into a frightful and unexpected move. Like a gyrating gymnast, he spun to his side and somersaulted several times, his movements fast and blurred as he closed the distance on Karl in flips and twists across the sandy ground.

Karl, not having the time to consider Sergei's bizarre movements, yanked the trigger as fast as his rapid reflexes would allow. More pops emanated from the pistol, and although several rounds tore into Sergei's form, none of the projectiles dealt a mortal blow to the creature's quickly moving head.

Landing near Karl and continuing his attack in one movement, Sergei grasped Karl's wrist and cleanly snapped the bone with a brutal twist. In a swooping movement, he pivoted and smacked the firearm from Karl's grasp. Rotating backward, Sergei then raked his claws across Karl's chest, leaving a trail of blood in a deep wound that was now enmeshed with shreds of Karl's thick sweater.

Karl, shocked by the speed and pain of the attack, was nevertheless undaunted in his effort to survive the encounter. Pulling his injured arm back, he produced a small blade in his offhand and struck out several times, stabbing Sergei deeply with the three-inch blade into his shoulder and chest.

Jumping back to create distance, Karl cradled his injured arm and held up his now-bloody blade. As he fought through his agony, he grinned at Sergei and made a movement for the creature to move forward. "Come get some, you ugly fucker."

To Karl's side, the boom of the shotgun ripped through the air. With three hunters rushing at Maria, she fired into the torso of one, with the contents of the 10-gauge shell ripping into the beast's guts. The force of the blow was overwhelming, even for such a formidable enemy, and as the shocked hunter fell backwards, half its innards were blown onto the damp rocks behind it.

Whirling and moving absurdly fast, Maria raised the barrel to within inches of the next hunter. Just as the creature was poised to deliver a lethal blow from its extended dagger, her second barrel discharged, and the flash of the blast from the dark metal barrel briefly illuminated the creature's snarling face.

Half of that hunter's head disappeared into an exploding and bloody mess. Completely blown apart, most of its face was now gone, and the creature slumped to its knees without a whimper or complaint.

From the side, Maria's third attacker, a shorter and more plump monster with maniacal eyes, was now upon her.

Throwing itself forward, it lunged out with a long knife, its sharp blade plunging into her arm. Slitting a deep gouge through her white flesh, the weapon severed tendons and sliced through her taut muscles.

Instantly unable to use her injured limb, Maria pushed away and spun to face the assault. Flipping the shotgun with her strong arm, she caught it by the barrel and held it up like a baseball bat, aggressively preparing for what came next.

As her eyes focused on the enraged and wicked face of her circling enemy, Maria tried to keep her composure. Breathing deep, she forced something like a battle growl from her dry throat. Strangely, as she faced her imminent demise, an amusing thought crossed her mind: *When you're skydiving and the parachute doesn't open, it's not the fall that kills you; instead, it's the sudden stop when you land.*

Such a ridiculous thought was unexpected, but for the time being, it somehow made Maria feel better. An impish grin crossed her face, and now it seemed to her these creatures weren't all that tough—they could be killed with the right amount of deadly force. Maybe there would be a way out of this nightmare after all. Maybe she and Karl could not just hold them back but could kill all these evil bastards. All her life she had been told revenge was the wrong thing to do, that in civilized countries people had moved beyond the need for such motivations.

But now, dealing out pain to her loathsome enemies felt perfectly acceptable. In fact, she had never felt more alive or righteous than she currently did. Maybe they could fight their way through this, and she just might have to wait a bit longer to see her precious husband in death.

With that ambivalent prospect on her mind, Stanislav and the other hunters suddenly leapt from the foliage on the raised terrain to the side. Descending on the pair with merciless eyes and ravaging intensity, both Maria and Karl were taken completely by surprise.

#

Behind Liam and Mattias, the sound of the pistol shots and shotgun blasts made clear that the battle had been joined, and although every fiber of their conscience pleaded for them to run back, to aid and support their friends in the fight of their lives, they kept their eyes focused on the floating haven to their front. At this point, whatever their feelings of guilt, they really owed it to Maria and Karl to make their sacrifice mean something.

Mattias made it first to the dock, his heavy footfalls banging against the wooden pier as he sprinted down the hardwood planks on their path toward hoped-for freedom. Slender and long, he pumped his arms like a crazed athlete, far outpacing the wheezing Liam, who chugged along some distance behind him. Whatever their training—or lack of it—in the past, adrenaline and the fear of death surged through their veins, forcing a sort of superhuman effort on them to run faster.

Hurrying up to the locked gate, which was a chain-link barrier topped by barbed wire and straddling the entirety of the dock, Mattias stopped and pulled out Karl's thick combat knife.

Struggling for breath, he squinted in the dim light as he tried to figure out how to jimmy the lock from its lightly welded connection to the sturdy fence frame.

Turning around, Liam tried guarding Mattias' back. As the taller man fiddled with the lock, Liam held out his fillet knife, but the longer he held the flimsy blade, the more he realized how pathetic his security efforts would have seemed to any observer. Liam had never been one to exude machismo in his physical endeavors, and that wouldn't change any time soon as he took in the fight of barely audible grunts and indistinguishable movements on the distant shoreline.

Yanking on the lock, Mattias pressed the blade under the hasp and heaved with all his strength and weight. Straining, he rocked back and forth, working to create leverage to break the lock free from its metal mooring. Grunting with the effort, he considered Maria's offer of her firearm to blast away the lock: *Bullshit or not, I wish I had that shotgun now.*

Behind Mattias, Liam stared into the distance at the struggling figures underneath the bluff on the beach. He was disquieted by the number of bodies that seemed to be there. Whatever the direction of the battle, it didn't bode well to see so many figures moving about where only two participants were on the side of the good guys. His heart sank as he considered what this could only mean.

"Hurry up, Mattias, we don't got any time," Liam said, his tone urgent and distressed.

Speaking through clenched teeth, Mattias maintained his ability to be sarcastic, even while their potential deaths loomed so close. "Maybe you could help, for once. This fucking thing…is tighter than a witch's ass."

Ignoring the humorous reference, Liam said nothing as he continued his powerless overwatch of the battle on the beach being fought to enable their escape. Moving his not-impressive blade from one hand to another, he finally breathed a sigh of relief when he heard the screech of the lock breaking free behind him.

Pulling the gate open, Mattias rushed farther down the dock, where a lone boat bobbed silently at the end of the otherwise-empty collection of slips. Liam followed quickly, almost overtaking his friend in a bid to see what kind of water-crossing chariot awaited them.

When they got close to the craft, Mattias and Liam saw that it appeared to be one of those boats used for smuggling something or other. The open-top vessel, outfitted with an enormous engine and a large interior area for hauling cargo, was an impressive-looking boat, one they both were happy to see up close. Of course, the cargo that it had carried in the past was not something either wanted to think too much about, but the prospect of getting away from their pursuers overrode any sense of revulsion at its prior use.

As they hurried to the vessel, Mattias hit a light switch on one of the posts near the boat. The immediate effect of lighting, from multiple buzzing and powerful lamps running the length of the extended dock, brought the entire area into bright focus. Though the influence on their vision was welcome, they couldn't avoid feeling worried about the added attention it brought to their struggle to escape the island.

Then again, it wasn't like their enemies were confused about the friends' intention to get away from this place. Shrugging, Liam wondered if there was anyone in Central Sweden who didn't know where they were at this point. With a grimace, he realized it wasn't likely they would have the ability to survive unnoticed any longer, so staying on this fucked-up piece of land was simply not an option.

Motioning with his hand to the boat's interior, Liam's voice grew panicked. "Please tell me there are keys. I don't think rowing this thing to Grenna is gonna be an option."

Nodding, Mattias used the light of the various lamps to search for the keys in the hold. Rifling through a burlap bag on the boat's floor, then opening a small container on the wheelhouse next to the steering wheel, he suddenly caught himself, interrupting his search for the key. Glancing back to the beach, he kept his tone low while his expression soured. "There're no more sounds of fighting. We have to get this thing moving."

#

Jacob hopped down from the ledge above the scene of the recent fight, landing carefully amongst the rocks and firm ground that skirted the beach area. With a steady jaw, his black eyes scoured the terrain, taking in the carnage with anger and more than a bit of personal trauma.

To the front of the recent assault was Andrey, who, sitting on his haunches, still fought to hold onto his remaining guts from the devastating blast he absorbed from Maria's double-barreled shotgun. As a qualified expert on the subject, Jacob knew they were a race of humanoids that could endure enormous amounts of damage. Accordingly, he saw that Andrey would survive his grievous wound, but the recovery process and increased feeding required for him to get better would take extensive time and resources.

On the other side of the recent combat area, Georgy was decidedly less lucky. This hunter, a long-time favorite of Jacob's with a quick wit and an expansive sense of humor, was on his knees and slumped gently forward. His skull was blown apart, and the area around him was covered by gory remnants of his brain and bones. The effect of his odd position made it almost seem like he was resting, and were it not for missing so much of his head, he might even have appeared to be sleeping. In Georgy's case, it was obvious that no amount of feeding or care would allow him to experience life again.

Jacob's eyes now flashed yellow, and he took some time to collect his disturbed thoughts. Another of his men was lost, and this disaster that seemed to never stop had him questioning his own methods and commitment to his people. It was bad enough they had taken such horrendous losses, but now, even when they were supposedly prepared for the weak and frail humans, they still took casualties. What was at one time inconceivable, being killed by ordinary people in pitched battle, was now commonplace because of these troublesome outsiders.

Sucking in his breath, Jacob controlled his desire to scream, and fortunately for his peace of mind, he got a respite from his frustration when he caught sight of Maria on the ground.

Laying in a scattered heap near the wet sand, in a place Maria had apparently retreated to protect her fleeing friends, she was torn limb from limb. Patches of her flesh and bone were barely recognizable as human, and the violence Stanislav and his men had inflicted on her made any chance of identifying her corpse unlikely. Her hand, still clenched around the barrels of her weapon, was severed from her arm, and that macabre sight showed the staunch commitment Maria held up to the very end in holding off the attacks of the creatures. In buying time for Liam and Mattias, she had given everything.

Closer to the bluff, Karl was still alive and being held down by Sergei and the last of his uninjured men. Walking up to the hunters, Jacob gave his men a disapproving stare, evidently unhappy that they seemed to be having a hard time controlling their new prisoner. Shaking his head, Jacob glowered at them, showing something like the image of a schoolteacher who was disappointed with underperforming students.

Karl, for his part unyielding, as he tried to force his way up from his knees, grunted at his condition. His arms were held by the wrist and pried up behind him, yet he still wouldn't stop struggling against the stronger creatures.

Taking his time, Jacob squatted down to get a better look at their captive. In turn, Karl flashed Jacob an agonized yet defiant scowl, but he stayed quiet, showing no indication of fear. Even a bit of mirth seemed to show itself in a glint from Karl's eyes, like he was reveling in the fact that at least one more of the family would never again see the light of day.

After a brief frown, Jacob nodded a brief show of respect at Karl's audacity and vigor. As a man that had attended a thousand battles, Jacob felt the need to honor bravery in anyone, including this particularly bothersome enemy. Granted, it wouldn't matter much in the end result, but he had to admire the man for trying.

Hurrying to Jacob's side, Stanislav cleared his throat and pointed to the dock, which was some distance away and wide open for the escape of their remaining prey. One of Stanislav's hunters was running toward it to stop Liam and Mattias' departure, but Jacob wasn't optimistic he would reach the boat before their quarry would use it to get away from his island domain.

Standing and pointing toward the dock, Jacob motioned with his head to the still-struggling Karl. "Bring him."

#

"Yes!" exclaimed Mattias, and broadly grinning, he held up a set of keys attached to a large orange floating device, the type used by boaters to ensure they were never misplaced or lost in the water. For a moment, the nature of their life-threatening danger seemed to be forgotten, and his wild grin evidenced a man overjoyed with himself.

"Well, move your ass and start it," replied Liam, and he flashed his own overly dramatic smile. One thing certain about trauma and loss was they tended to make people excessively emotional to both the up and downsides after devastating personal experiences. In their current endeavor of almost escaping, Liam and Mattias mostly dealt with the positive side of that perspective.

Coming to his senses, Mattias ran to the console and tried inserting several successive keys into the ignition slot. On the third attempt it worked, and after turning it, the deep bass of the powerful boat engine thrummed to life.

From the far entrance to the dock, the first sounds of a pursuer emerged. The patter of heavy running feet jarred Liam from his thoughts, and he looked up to see a creature bounding its way toward them down the floating pathway. It was a mid-sized monster—a fierce, ugly, and determined creature—and for a moment Liam wondered where on the scale of awfulness each new enemy they faced would fall. Strangely, it felt like they were divers stuck in a random school of ravenous sharks, and he could only hope each new predator they faced would not be the one that tore them to shreds.

"You idiot, the boat's still tied. Get us free," shouted Mattias, pointing to the back of the vessel.

Chagrined, Liam ran to disentangle the nylon rope that affixed the boat to the cleat on the dock. Unfortunately, it was tied around the metal piece several times, and Liam knew less about untying shipping knots than he did about women, which was to say, nothing whatsoever.

As Liam yanked on the line and tried to free their soon-to-be-stolen boat, he suddenly thought of all the movies where people were trying to get away but couldn't get the key in the lock, or the motor wouldn't start, or any of twenty ways film directors generated anxiety from the viewer while the main character was trying to escape a harrowing situation. In all his life of watching movies, he never saw an example where that good guy or girl was going to get eaten because they couldn't figure out how to untie a knot.

"Just cut it. Did you take stupid lessons when I wasn't watching?" screamed Mattias, who had his hand on the throttle, waiting for Liam to sever the line.

Nodding, Liam suddenly realized he had a use for the crappy fillet knife he'd been carrying around, and plucking it from his waist, he began manically sawing on the tightly woven rope. Looking up, he thought for a moment they wouldn't make it—the beast was charging fast—but the sudden release of the line's tension told him the deed was done.

"Go, hit it," yelled Liam, and when Mattias pushed the throttle forward, Liam had to regather his balance from the abrupt shift of the boat. Fortunately, he narrowly avoided pitching over the back of the surging craft.

Imagine if I'd just fallen in, and all this shit was for nothing, thought Liam, and as the boat pulled away, he watched the creature stop at the dock's end, less than forty yards from their sputtering craft.

After flipping the frustrated hunter his middle finger, Liam turned and moved forward, where he stopped next to Mattias near the wheelhouse. Focusing into the dim night ahead, his deep adrenaline surge lessened, and over the next minute, he worked to bring his harsh breathing under control. When he finally steadied himself, he was quiet as he peered at the far-away shoreline and the varied lights of the communities encircling the lake.

As the powerful craft plowed through the lake's mild current, Liam looked over at Mattias, and he realized at that moment that this dopey cop was now his only real friend left in the world. Whatever came next, he had exactly one person left besides his parents that really gave a shit about him.

Feeling reflective, Liam decided he was going to be a good friend to Mattias from here on out, which meant actually returning his calls and trying to drop an occasional Christmas card in the mail. Maybe sometimes he could actually inquire about his friend's life, instead of constantly obsessing only about his own problems and challenges? Chuckling but without any real humor, Liam realized in a morbid way that the mass murder of his friends had the side benefit of making him a better friend to the one pal who remained.

Meeting his gaze, Mattias seemed to sense his intent and musings, and offering Liam a smartass smile, he clapped the shorter man on the shoulder. Neither of them said anything more now because neither of them needed to: their world was a disaster, but they still had a companion to face it with.

Sadly, as the boat continued to gather speed, Mattias took a chance to glance back at the island, and his bulging eyes and shocked expression short-circuited their rare moment of camaraderie. Pointing to the recently departed dock, he spoke with an acute sense of dread. "They got Karl, and he's still alive."

Chapter Twenty-Three

When he turned to Mattias, Liam's face was blank and undecided. He hadn't yet had the chance to process Karl's hero-like death, and now he instead had to contend with the fact that their good friend was still among the living.

As he squinted into the distance, Liam saw that Karl was on his knees at the end of the dock. With a creature to either side of him, he was fully under their harsh control, though he was still fighting to free himself. Each of his arms was held up behind him, which looked to be both painful and out-of-character for a man Liam had openly treated like a bit of a superman for all the time he'd known him.

Farther from Karl, a pale man with a long leather coat peered out over the lake. With his hands held behind his back and looking like a school headmaster, there was little doubt he was the "Jacob" they had heard about from Evelyn. Next to him was another man, this one roughly the same height, and he evinced his right-hand status to Jacob by hovering protectively close to him.

"Yeah, he's alive…," said Liam, trying to figure out what it meant by the creatures keeping Karl alive, "but what do we do?"

His forehead furrowing, Mattias shook his head uncertainly. "I could bring the boat in slow, keeping our distance. Their king dickhead obviously wants to talk. We can't just leave Karl…."

Biting his lip, Liam nodded his agreement as Mattias trailed off. Whatever happened, they couldn't just leave him to die. In fact, it was essential they try to get him off the island—whatever the cost. It was what friends did.

Making a motion with his hands, Liam indicated caution by holding his hands down in a "take it slow" display. "Yeah, but don't get too close. With our luck, they'll be able to swim like dolphins."

Blinking, Mattias hesitantly pressed the throttle forward and aimed the boat back toward the dock. Going slow, it took several minutes to bring the vessel toward their welcoming committee, and when they were far outside the beasts' jumping range, even for these supernatural eaters of humans, Mattias let the boat idle to a wavy stop.

With the engine still burbling loudly, Mattias brought the craft around to face away from the dock to make it ready to flee at a moment's notice. When he was comfortable with the location and distance, he called out to the assembled family. "You're the asshole that caused all this…Jacob, right?"

Smiling, Jacob held off a moment before responding. The moment of silence, observed by his followers in obvious deference to his lead, dragged on, with only a few grunts from a still-struggling Karl to interrupt the quiet.

"Gentlemen, that is indeed me," said Jacob, and though his accent in English was strongly Slavic, his grammar and pronunciation were otherwise perfect. "And…I assume you are Mattias and Liam? It is interesting to me that one of our troublesome visitors is an American, which I suppose is appropriate for the situation."

Not knowing if this was a compliment or an insult, Liam made no effort to sound interested. "So, you talked to Evelyn…Jacob?"

"Yes, I have—amongst other things. She will be of no further help to you, I'm afraid."

Shaking his head, Liam tried to put every ounce of possible disrespect into his judgmental voice. "You killed her, then? One of your own 'pets'? You're quite a piece of work, and a first-class prick, as well as a murderer. And…a cannibal."

Fixing his gaze on Liam, Jacob took some time to respond. Unused to being questioned, he was surprised by Liam's open insolence. "I apologize for nothing, so it would be appreciated if you would drop your notions of being better than us. A family needs sustenance to live—that is just a matter of survival.

Anyone with loved ones will do whatever it takes for them to succeed and prosper. Your kind is no different…so with us, it's 'just business,' as they say."

Mattias scoffed, shaking his head at the cold statement but otherwise appearing uninterested in making conversation. Not one to indulge murderous psychopaths, he didn't feel the need to engage in banter simply because his enemy was a raging killer from a formerly unknown species.

Raising an eyebrow, Jacob chuckled for several moments as he took in the dynamic of open disgust from the friends. With a gleam in his eye, Jacob seemed to enjoy their comical feelings of superiority. "But aside from that, your group has done much to hurt my family—more than anyone else has ever done, in fact."

This brought a smile to both Liam's and Mattias' faces. They had to take victories where they could, so this lead asshole bemoaning his losses was something of a success. In celebration of the moment, they even chanced a smirk at each other while Jacob awaited a response.

When none came, Jacob raised his voice, sounding impatient. "Enough with the pleasantries, then. We are at a crossroads here, one that cannot be easily squared with the current state of affairs."

Taking a step to his left, Jacob indicated the tightly held Karl, who still struggled, not even able to raise his head from his restricted position. "Your remaining little group is desirous of leaving my home and rushing to tell the outside world about our little arrangement on Vising Island, I would suppose."

Appearing confident and showing a self-assurance that was as unnerving as it was irritating, Jacob waited for some time. Like an actor that sought the best time to deliver his line, he evaluated his opponents for the proper moment to fully illuminate the situation for everyone present. Now crossing his arms, he shook his head—slowly—in order that his point was made in the clearest manner possible. "And that is something I simply cannot allow."

The effect was as the arrogant monster wanted. Despite their desire to appear carefree in their dealings with Jacob, they quickly understood their choices for escape were not plentiful—and were becoming less so as time passed.

Liam was silent as he looked for a way out of their erstwhile host's trap. As he gathered his thoughts, he noticed Karl was able to raise his head slightly. Looking to give some encouragement to the man, he blithely noticed that Karl's eyes appeared much darker than before.

Moving his gaze back to Jacob, Liam sought to appear business-like. "What do you propose?"

"Propose?" asked Jacob. "There is no proposal; it is more an offer that you simply must accept. It is the only way that your friend will live to see another sun."

Liam clicked his tongue, shaking his head in mock interest. "I'm listening."

Raising his arms, Jacob gestured first to Karl, then to Liam and Mattias. "I have lost six of my valued men over the last days due to your…ingenuity."

With a quick glance, Liam now noticed Karl ever-so-gently nodding to him. His captors had released their grip a bit, and Karl's ability to move had increased.

"So, I am in need of new family," continued Jacob, oblivious to the intrigue, "men that I can be sure would be resourceful to our cause…"

Suddenly, Mattias also noticed Karl's change, and not sure if Liam was aware of it, quietly cleared his throat. In response, Liam acknowledged him with a hand motion shielded behind the wheelhouse structure.

Playing dumb, Liam otherwise kept his focused attention on Jacob.

"And that could be you," said Jacob, his voice becoming clear and positive. "Assuming you could adjust to a life of luxury, you could experience all the best the world offers. Friends in abundance, which you suddenly seem to be lacking. Women of any variety and in any number would be at your beck and call, though I can assure you this will tire you out as the decades move by. And…money, to buy what you wanted—would be yours, simply if you asked for it."

Acting interested in Jacob's words, Liam nodded ever-so-slightly to Karl.

Working himself up, Jacob flashed his white teeth, which seemed to glow as his tone assumed a successful car-salesman-like disposition. *He may never have been into marketing*, thought Liam, *but he would have been a seasoned pro in no amount of time. Why couldn't I ever sound like that when getting people to buy my sports picks? I could've purchased this island myself long ago.*

"And your life would be fruitful, without the menace of death hanging over your future. You would never grow old or infirmed," Jacob pointed out, leaving this most important explanation of benefits for last. "Many men, nearly the entirety of humanity, have wished for such a chance throughout history, but now it has fallen to you to accept such an opportunity. You have not known it up until now, but fortune has smiled on you, gentlemen."

Karl wrenched abruptly free from the captor to his right, causing the creature to cry out in alarm. Turning, he snatched a dagger from the harness of the beast to the other side, then, moving blindingly fast, push-kicked the man in the chest. That hunter, unable to stop his motion, was propelled off the dock and into the cold lake, where he splashed in unceremoniously. Judging by the panicked wallowing of the creature, swimming was not a particular strength of his race.

When Karl turned to face his remaining three enemies, they had already drawn their own knives. Jacob, appearing unperturbed, tilted his head in surprise at Karl's unexpected show of martial prowess.

Noting Karl's black eyes and obvious strength, Jacob grinned widely and spoke in glowing terms. "And one of you is already with us…that's wonderful. Your female friend was, as well? No wonder you were able to put up such a fight on the beach. And that hunger you are now feeling? I can easily help with that. In time, you will only need to feed at extended intervals."

Karl, feeling stronger by the moment, wasn't sure how to respond. Glancing over to the boat, his face was caught between a moment of exhilaration and disgust at what he was becoming.

Stepping forward, Jacob brushed back Stanislav and Sergei from advancing on the confused Karl. His face was an image of understanding and compassion, and Jacob sheathed his short-bladed dirk, then held out his hand to Karl. "Relax…Karl. You have a new home now, with people that will do anything for you. You have nowhere else to go. You are among family."

Stepping back, Karl stood at the edge of the dock. Behind him, the swimming hunter was maneuvering to extricate itself from the water, while in front, Jacob's smiling visage came closer with each careful step the leader took.

Holding his dagger in his left hand, while still cradling his fast-healing wrist close to his body, Karl didn't know what to do. On one prospective path was seemingly eternal life, while on the other his frightened friends peered from the boat. For now, their fear was not for themselves, but for their evolving friend.

Slowly raising his maimed hand to Jacob, the normally confident Karl seemed about to surrender his status as a mortal man. Licking his lips, he took a step closer to Jacob.

From the boat, Mattias shook his head and spoke under his breath, whispering *no no no* several times over, silently imploring Karl to not give up.

To his side, Liam was more forceful, shouting out, "Karl, don't do it" as the man moved closer to Jacob. Though disturbed by the prospect of his own death, the wrongness of losing Karl, the most courageous man Liam ever knew, was something far worse, and the thought made his heart ache.

Hearing Liam, Karl pivoted to look out at his friends. What was once a matter of a weekend with friends had now changed with the deaths of nearly anyone he cared about. His former life, where he followed a path of military service, and hopefully, a boring, retired life where he could escape to an occasional vacation to Thailand, had become…this.

Always the one to be quiet, to let others promote themselves in the world of rich social media personalities and empty, soulless debauchery, Karl now had to face the first choice in his life that tested his own moral code. He could face this evil down, probably losing his life for no apparent gain, or he could accept his place in this odd society, living many lifetimes in pursuit of whatever he wanted, making a place in the world that would perhaps hold no constraints on anything he ever wanted to do. Being a man of rules and discipline, he had always wondered what it would be like to live untethered to society's rules, and now he had the opportunity to discover precisely what that alien life would entail.

Now looking back at Jacob, Karl smiled, and for a moment they locked eyes in open consideration of what was at stake. After several seconds of warmness, Jacob's smile faltered—as if he could feel Karl slipping away—and a hesitant look formed over his expression.

Dropping his hand, Karl stepped back to the end of the dock, momentarily placing himself out of Jacob's reach. "No, Jacob. I have friends to meet, and they wouldn't want me to bring an asshole like you with me."

Determination filled his features, and Karl inverted the knife, took a deep breath, and plunged the shaft into his own eye socket, ramming the blade deep into his brain. Driving the weapon with such force, his body was propelled over the edge, and he splashed on his back into the gently rolling waves below. He was dead before he hit the surface, and for several moments, his body barely twitched as he floated calmly on the water, his one available eye staring up at the receding night sky.

Screaming in anguish, Mattias turned and gunned the engine. Biting down his crushing grief, he pointed the craft toward the distant lights of the awakening town of Grenna.

As the boat roared to life, Jacob cursed and fixed his eyes on Karl's corpse. To his side, Stanislav helped their waterlogged subordinate climb from the lake, and facing toward the shore, Jacob's three underlings walked calmly back to their cherished island.

The boat surged toward the far shoreline, far away from his domain, and Jacob turned to watch its steady progress. Meeting the gaze of Liam, Jacob was not hostile or bitter, only somewhat sad. As if conceding some small measure of respect for the departing friends, he nodded at the receding vessel, then turned and paced down the dock toward his well-loved home.

Watching Jacob, the distraught Liam sat himself in a seat overlooking the beautiful lake. Full of equal measures of sorrow and hopelessness, he watched the cursed landmass of Vising Island recede into the mist of the upcoming morning.

Chapter Twenty-four

Radiant sunlight from the late-morning sky illuminated the long and humble-looking police building. In common Swedish fashion, the street and calm neighborhood around the squat structure were immaculate, and due to an evidently low crime rate, were not attended by many people, either criminals or law enforcement officers.

Next to shiny double-entry doors of the staid facility, two police vehicles were parked in a well-ordered lot. The cars, painted in blue and white stripes, were of the hatchback variety, showing the uniquely Nordic manner of providing for the functionality and easy identification of emergency vehicles.

Inside, far in the interior of the calm building, Liam and Mattias sat at a long, white table. In this interview room, which was absent any furniture except for matching plastic chairs around the table, a long one-way mirror faced the pair. The space around them was blindingly bright, with the prodigious lighting turned up to ensure they couldn't relax after their long, exhausting ordeal.

Leaning back, Liam rubbed his face, seeking to bring himself awake from the fatigue clouding his brain. "Mattias, I'm getting the feeling the cops don't believe us. I gotta say I'm disappointed; I had hoped for more from your brothers in blue."

Mattias snorted, then turned to peer at an enormous clock set above the mirror. "Would you? I've been through everything in my head a hundred times, and I still get the feeling we're going to wake up from some crazy acid trip."

Nodding, Liam accepted the truth with a deep breath. It wasn't every day that people reported murderous monsters in society's midst—unless they were raving maniacs.

Some time passed in awkward silence. Sitting still, emotions of grief, loss, and anger flooded Liam's mind, as they had been doing all morning. His voice, cracked and drained of enthusiasm, took on a bit of a whine when he finally spoke. "All those good friends, our friends, gone forever. I don't see how I'll ever be able to accept it. We were just planning on our cool weekend full of steaks and wine. Now, this…."

As he gazed up at the ceiling, a mirthless smile filled Mattias' face, and he pleasantly recalled all the good times the group had shared in their past. Though equally heartbroken, his demeanor was that of a stoic and well-practiced cop, one who knew grief was a process that played out over an extended time, sometimes several years. "I've dealt with a ton of crime victims in the last ten years: murders, child abuse, and every form of debased evil people inflict on each other. With that, I can tell you, however horrible this has been, you…we…will be OK."

Looking at the mirror and realizing they were undoubtedly recorded, Mattias patted Liam on the shoulder. "Our friends are in a better place, and their happiness is eternal, Liam. Once you get that point through your head, it makes everything else we have to deal with easy in comparison. It's also the only way I can keep my sanity."

Appearing unconvinced, Liam rummaged through his memories. Speaking quietly, he repeated Karl's fateful words from their recent escape. "We have the rest of our lives to cry for them."

Sighing, Liam stretched out his legs, forcing blood into his tired extremities. Sounding ironic, he moved the conversation to his prior troubles. "Anyway, I guess Elise wouldn't find this boring. I imagine her and even her new man would be impressed we made it through this nightmare."

Mattias shook his head as he considered Liam's prior marital situation. Keeping his voice low, he offered some remarkably sage advice. "Liam, Elise is an OK person and always has been. She was just a horrible person to make a wife. Some people need to get the partying and 'explore the world' vibe out of their veins before settling down. That's the opposite of your personality, but like always, you had to ignore my advice because you finally found someone who would actually sleep with you."

Somewhat offended, Liam looked at Mattias, but the truth of his words made him grin after a moment. Never one to be dishonest, Mattias could be amazingly wise, especially when it meant destroying Liam's hopes and dreams.

Moving on from the depressing subject, Mattias snickered sarcastically. "Though, I have to be honest, the tragedy of divorce seems a bit less important when we consider cannibal monsters are roaming the world."

"Unfortunately, you're right on both accounts," said Liam, his tone resuming its depressed level.

Abruptly, the door to their otherwise-empty room swung inward. Pacing in from the dim hallway, Theodore Brosius, a pale and affable fellow of middle age, smiled down at the friends. Carrying a paper bag and an expensive-looking leather portfolio, he set the articles in front of the place next to his own intended seating spot. Huffing, the well-groomed man lowered himself and, pulling himself nearer to the table, made a show of becoming comfortable in the hard chair.

Diving into the interview, Brosius smiled openly, showing teeth that must have been bleached a thousand times over. His English was superb, even for a Swede. "So, gentlemen, you've given our small police force quite a few interesting stories."

Wrinkling his face in doubt, Liam didn't hide his displeasure with the new visitor. "I wish they were just stories. Then we wouldn't have lost all our friends, and we wouldn't be sitting in your shitty station."

Mattias crossed his arms, grunting his agreement and evaluating the new and unknown cop. "Every word we said to the other detectives is true. It sounds like the rambling of lunatics, I know, but if you get together your men, or more appropriately, a small army, you can raid the island and find out."

Brosius continued his smile as he absorbed Mattias' words. His face had a peculiar facet to it, like his pleasant expression was completely detached from his eyes. Those eyes, which were gray, clear, and insightful, made each man feel naked, like their personal thoughts were on open and obvious display.

"Well, detective," replied Brosius, sounding entirely in control of the conversation, "how would you feel if two unknown men burst into your department…and threw around stories of monsters and mayhem? Would you run around and do their bidding, calling in the army to solve such unbelievable nonsense?"

Rolling his eyes, Mattias shook his head, then stared directly at Brosius. Over several seconds they held one another's gaze, but tellingly, it was Mattias who looked away first in the mild contest of wills.

"Or you, Mr. Stone," Brosius said, moving his eager gaze to Liam. "What would you ever think if someone came to you with such preposterous tales? Would you believe such inconceivable blather?"

For a moment, Liam was taken aback. Strangely, he had never heard a Swede use the word "blather," which was interesting in itself, but further, it wasn't like Brosius was being illogical either. "I would also think they were nuts, detective. I would say, at best, that they were on drugs, or at worst, they had done something horrible, maybe even homicidal, and were possibly trying to cover it up."

Mattias gazed pointedly from the side, making an impressed expression at Liam, like for the first time in his life he thought Liam had said something intelligent. Such a look was rare from Mattias, and taking in the unspoken compliment, Liam flashed him a grin.

Brosius, ignoring their silent exchange, nodded intensely. "Then you would make an excellent detective, Mr. Stone. And you'd be right to assume that most people would think the same."

Sitting up straight, Liam, who normally avoided confrontation, particularly with people that could throw him in jail, stared into Brosius' eyes. "Listen, Mr. um...."

"Just call me Brosius."

"Brosius, the only problem with your detective's intuition and work is that you're simply wrong. What we say happened, happened, and it can be easily proved with a simple trip to the island. But, like my friend said, you better bring more than a couple of pot-bellied cops with you."

Chuckling, Brosius thought for a moment, then stood and spun toward the one-way mirror. Looking intently at his reflected image, he studied his own face, taking the time to self-consciously pick at his substantial collection of wrinkles. After frowning at the progression of his age, he eyed the companions in the reflection.

"OK, Liam and…Mattias, I understand how you feel, really I do," explained Brosius, sounding monotoned and rather bored. "I just want you both to know how these stories will always sound to a listener. Anywhere you go, people will be amazed at the lunacy you've been spouting here."

Irritated, Mattias scowled, making a show of his dislike for this new interrogator. "Well, I'm through with this, Brosius. Tell me specifically, under what law are you going to hold us? What evidence do have against us that you wouldn't check out our deadly serious report of several murders so close to your precinct? All our dead friends are well-known, and I'm sure this Jacob asshole must be famous. There's no way he could amass that fortune without being prominent—especially over hundreds of years."

Turning around, Brosius peered down at Mattias. His demeanor, formally professional and amicable, melted away, and his pretensions of kindness were replaced by…something else.

Standing, Liam joined the confrontation, and he banged both his fists on the table in protest of their unfavorable treatment by the police. Unfortunately, as there was not much weight behind the table-strike, the effect of the mild thump was somewhat pathetic.

"And I want to know exactly why I'm still here, talking to you," shouted Liam, trying to make up for his weakly assertive gesture by raising his voice. "Why haven't I been offered a lawyer, and why on fucking earth have I not been allowed to call the embassy?"

Keeping a straight face, Brosius nodded. Holding up his arms, he sought to placate the friends, and lowering his voice, his deadpan features took on a calculating manner. "Gentlemen, I'm not trying to get you upset…or have you call your embassy. I'm just trying to understand how two such worldly men could be so naive."

Perplexed, Liam and Mattias glanced at one another, then returned their inquisitive stares to Brosius.

"Because," said Brosius, a smile returning to his face, "all these events present the obvious question: why do you think these monsters, or creatures as you also call them, would only exist on Vising Island?"

Shocked, the friends' expressions, formerly apprehensive and confused, became alarmed. Rising from the table, Mattias moved protectively close to Liam.

Peering ahead, Brosius continued with his open and confident smile. Looking expectantly at Liam and Mattias, he remained calm and unruffled, even as the color of his eyes flitted to a deep and unnatural black.

<u>THE END</u>

About the Author

Tim lives in Nevada, where he makes a life enjoying all things horror and thriller-related, from films to books, and even the occasional convention. He has three children, three cats, and he enjoys providing reading entertainment for the monster and creature-loving masses.

If you like this novel, he would appreciate a review or a follow on Facebook:

https://www.facebook.com/Horrorthrillerguy

https://www.horrorthrillerguy.com

Also by Timothy Bryan:

Chindi

books2read.com/u/mlAJ7Z

The Huntsman of Corvinus

books2read.com/u/mVRyr5

Despicable

books2read.com/u/49k0ak

By Their Cold Fingers

books2read.com/u/bPgMKr

Core Ruleset

books2read.com/u/mqXyQ6